The Forgotten Promise

The Forgotten Promise

Kate Ryder

authorHOUSE®

AuthorHouse™ UK Ltd.
1663 Liberty Drive
Bloomington, IN 47403 USA
www.authorhouse.co.uk
Phone: 0800.197.4150

© 2013 by Kate Ryder. All rights reserved.

Cover Image by Chris Rankin
www.chrisrankinart.com
chrisrankinart@gmail.com

No part of this book may be reproduced, stored in a retrieval system, or transmitted by any means without the written permission of the author.

Published by AuthorHouse   12/03/2013

ISBN: 978-1-4918-8457-7 (sc)
ISBN: 978-1-4918-8458-4 (e)

Any people depicted in stock imagery provided by Thinkstock are models, and such images are being used for illustrative purposes only.
Certain stock imagery © Thinkstock.

This book is printed on acid-free paper.

Because of the dynamic nature of the Internet, any web addresses or links contained in this book may have changed since publication and may no longer be valid. The views expressed in this work are solely those of the author and do not necessarily reflect the views of the publisher, and the publisher hereby disclaims any responsibility for them.

For MJL,
With love

Acknowledgements

In the beginning, when looking for a village in which to base this book, my only criteria was that it had to have a village green. Memories of happy childhood holidays spent fossil hunting along the bay at Charmouth took me to Dorset and, by happy circumstance, I chanced upon the village of Walditch. Through my research into the village and its surrounding area I discovered historic events on which to pin my story. Most of the historical elements that I have recorded here are a true account, though I have exercised the writer's 'right' to fictionalise with, maybe, a slight tweak of location to fit the story.

Many people have played a part in getting me to the point of publication: my husband (for supplying me with copious cups of coffee throughout the whole process and never waiving in his encouragement); my family (great supporters of the writer in me); the fellow trader who initially fired my imagination with stories of a cottage she once owned with its internal stained-glass window and unaccountable cold corners; and Karen Hayes and the South Dornaford Farm Writers Group who witnessed my tentative first steps on this particular journey.

I would, however, especially like to thank Helena Ancil whose own inspirational creativity and belief in this book kept my resolve firm.

The Olde Smithy

As I looked towards the huddle of cottages nestling on the far side of the village green, I noticed how still it had become, like an expectant, held breath and somewhere deep within my soul I felt tendrils of distant memory reach out to me.

The sun was warm on that early summer's evening and yet I shivered. A thick haze hung in the air and the sounds of the pub seemed muffled, as if the world was somehow suppressed. I waited for something to happen—what, I did not know—my senses on red alert; something was coming. Suddenly, seemingly out of nowhere, I detected the slightest breeze and a wisp of air languidly encircled my body as if investigating me. I looked towards Dan to see if he had noticed the breath of wind but he seemed distant from me, as if I was cushioned and remote from the world. I didn't feel threatened. In fact, I revelled in the sensation of that warm, tender kiss of air as it gently caressed me. And, as if in some way being guided, I watched the shadows fall across the mellow coloured cottage on the far side of the village green and shivered again.

Earlier that afternoon, when one of the film crew suggested a drink after work at a local pub he'd discovered I was only too pleased to be invited. It had been a hard day's filming and a particularly trying day for me with a star whose ego was extremely large and I had already used up most of my diplomacy and patience during the previous three weeks' filming. A bit of good old R&R was in order! They were a good crowd at Hawkstone Media and I had happily worked there for the past eight years since first arriving in the UK; a fresh-faced, enthusiastic girl from Dublin full of raw ambition. Ken Hawkstone—the man behind the company—was a demanding, but fair, whirlwind of creative force and he had recognised that ambition, offering me numerous breaks along the way. I had worked my way up from continuity girl to assistant director and loved the work, albeit all-consuming and leaving little time for anything else. However, over the past couple of years I had been sleeping fitfully and often found myself awake in the small hours battling strange, disconcertingly deep thoughts about the random nature of choice, fate and destiny; thoughts that made no sense at all in the cold light of day. And as the years slipped by, however hard I tried to ignore it, I was aware of an underlying, nagging insistence for change.

As we entered the Blacksmith's Arms, the sounds of a busy pub enveloped me. A charming, two-storey, 17th Century country inn with flagstone floors and heavily beamed ceilings, the pub was obviously a popular haunt. Clusters of people sat in private alcoves enjoying an early evening's drink and through an open archway I could see tables being set for dinner. We decided to book a table for 8pm and, having ordered drinks, walked outside into that early summer's evening towards the first moment of my future.

I looked across the village green, beyond the large oak tree that stood proudly at its centre, towards the stone cottage and saw a red and yellow 'For Sale' board erected in its garden. There was the slightest breeze and, as I watched the shadows from the oak fall across the cottage, I shivered involuntarily.

"Cold, Mads?" asked Dan, one of the camera crew and my occasional lover.

He was a kindly soul and, thoughtfully, he drew me to him.

"Not really. I've just got this feeling I've been here before. Kinda spooky, in a comforting sort of way, if you know what I mean," I finished lamely.

He squeezed my shoulder. "Have you ever been to this part of Dorset?"

"No, never been to Dorset before. You know me, Dan, the bright lights, the next drink, the latest wine bar, the hippest party! I'm not a country girl, I don't know what I'd do with myself all day, and yet . . ." I swept my hand in front of me, acknowledging the village green and the cluster of cottages across the way. "This feels so familiar."

Tim, the stunt co-ordinator, had been listening to our conversation and now joined in. "Perhaps you lived here in a former life?" he said, tongue-in—cheek.

"Perhaps you were the blacksmith's wife!" contributed Emma, the newest of the make-up girls, on her first assignment. "And I bet you lived in that cottage over there."

She pointed at the 'For Sale' board and the hairs on the back of my neck stood erect.

Dan watched me intently. "Mads, you OK? You've gone really pale."

"I'm OK, really I am." I could see he wasn't convinced. "I think I'll just sit for a moment."

I joined the remainder of the crew at one of the wooden picnic benches provided by the pub.

Emma, however, was warming to the subject. "I bet you were born in this village and lived here all your life and you married the local blacksmith and brought up a batch of dark haired children who were all very practical and good with their hands."

There was a ripple of laughter around the table.

"And I bet it's called The Stables!" She pointed towards the cottage.

"No," I contradicted her quietly. "It's called The Olde Smithy."

"Let's see!" laughed Emma.

She ran across the grass, stood at the cottage's rusting gate which opened onto the village green and peered along the pathway at the property. I watched her hesitate and slowly turn; her mouth open. By now the rest of the table were listening with interest.

"Maddie, how did you know?" Emma exclaimed, as she rejoined us. "You couldn't have read the nameplate from here. It's hidden by all that foliage around the front door. I could only just make it out from the gate!"

"I don't know," I muttered. "I just knew."

Dan, standing behind me, now placed his hands on my shoulders.

"I expect Mads is just putting two and two together and coming up trumps. We all know how creative she can be!"

There was murmured acknowledgement of my story telling skills from around the table. Dan squeezed my shoulders.

"Come on you guys," he said. "Time's marching on and I'm hungry. Let's eat!"

So, we filed into the pub and became immersed in ordering food and enjoying the merriment of the evening and the déjà vu feeling subsided. I was, once again, Madeleine O'Brien, assistant director at Hawkstone Media, down from London to film a period drama at an elegant country house not far from Dorset's magnificent Jurassic coastline. But as we left the pub, much later that evening, I detected a whisper on the wind and as I climbed into Dan's car I knew that The Olde Smithy was to be mine.

It took a further three months to finish filming and by the time I arrived back in London I had bought the cottage. My colleagues were incredulous and kept reminding me of my city girl lifestyle, my cosmopolitan attitude and my need for the Underground to ferry me between watering holes. When I handed in my notice they actually pleaded with me to see sense.

"But what are you going to do there stuck out in the country all by yourself?" Dan asked. "You said it yourself, 'The bright lights, the latest wine bar, the hippest party.' If you're fed up with your job join a different production company. If you want change in your life get a dog! But don't burn your bridges, Mads. Please . . ."

We had been to the cinema to see the latest Bond movie with his sister, Caro, and her husband, John, and were now eating at our favourite Soho bistro. Dan and I were good companions. There was no great passion, but life was easy; no questions were asked and nothing ever rocked the boat.

I smiled and touched his face. He meant well.

"Dan, it's OK. I know what I'm doing. I'm going home!"

He stared at me.

"What do you mean, Maddie?" asked Caro.

"I can't explain it but when I first saw the cottage it just spoke to me." I looked at their anxious faces. "I knew I had to have it . . ."

"But Maddie, Daniel Craig speaks to me and I know I have to have him," Caro exclaimed. "But I also know it's just not going to happen," she added forlornly.

I laughed and then quickly grew serious again. "When I approached the estate agents they said that despite it having been on the market for some time there had only been two interested parties, both of which pulled out at the last minute. It hasn't been occupied since the previous owner moved out three years ago, apart from a few months when it was rented out. Basically, it's been standing empty all that time." Their worried faces made me say defiantly, "It needs to be lived in and brought back to life!"

"Sounds odd to me," Caro commented. "Well, you know if it doesn't work out you can always come and live with us, can't she John?"

She smiled at me. Like her brother, Caro was a generous soul.

"Yes, you can always stay with us in Clapham, Maddie," John echoed his wife's offer. "No loss of face there."

"Thanks you two. That's comforting to know."

"And if you ever get bored stuck out in the sticks, I'll always come down at the click of your fingers and entertain you with stories of the latest ego I have not had the pleasure to work with!" teased Dan. He squeezed my knee meaningfully under the table.

I smiled at them all. Such good friends amidst the bustle of what could, sometimes, be a lonely city and for a split-second I wondered if, in fact, I was doing the right thing. But I was on a roller-coaster now and nothing could halt me.

And so, one early October morning, I peered out from the third floor window of my rented flat at the acres of chimneys stretching as far as the eye could see, took a last look around the empty apartment and, with a deep breath, closed the door on my London life.

Dan had stayed with me since the previous weekend, following my leaving bash at the local pub. We hadn't planned it that way but I couldn't remember getting home from the party and when I did wake up the next day, sometime around mid-afternoon, he was there to ease the hangover with cups of strong coffee and soothing, cool hands and—well—sort of remained!

As I said, we were companionable together.

He had agreed to drive me to Walditch and we hired a van on the Tuesday and loaded my possessions—not that they amounted to much. We decided to leave early the following morning to miss the worst of the commuter traffic and once the outskirts of London had been left behind, a sense of well-being began to replace any slight hesitation I had experienced. By the time we joined the M3 Dan commented that the city girl had been well and truly left at the city gates and once we reached the A31 I had visibly chilled. And all the time a sense of 'coming home' grew deep within me. I couldn't understand it.

I was born in Dublin, the youngest of three girls, to Matilda and Finn O'Brien; successful, self-made business people. My sisters and I had grown up in an environment that encouraged us to follow our dreams. This had been theatre, film and TV for me, whereas Mo had pursued an interest in photography and had become a successful photojournalist, known for 'the look' of her subjects that no other photographer seemed able to capture. Martha, the eldest by ten years, had set the level by studying interior design and now had a fashionable outfit just off O'Connell Street. She was often called upon to remodel homes for titans of industry and had even been known to refit hotels for some famous musicians. They were a hard act to follow, my sisters!

Turning my back on a career in the film industry for an uncertain future was not something my family had easily understood. But, Mo—the closest in age and character to me—had said that if it was something I needed to pursue then I should follow my heart.

It was a beautiful, clear, autumnal day and an ever-increasing sense of excitement promised to engulf me. We broke the journey for breakfast and stopped in the New Forest at a charming café that Dan had discovered on a previous film shoot.

"You've certainly got some colour in your cheeks now," he said as he drew me to him. He kissed me and gently twisted a strand of my hair in his long, slender fingers. "Don't forget what we've had Mads, will you?"

I was surprised to hear the mellow tone in his voice.

"Good heavens, Daniel Carver, you're not getting all sentimental on me now are you?" I teased in the broadest of Irish accents, but was stayed by the look in his eyes.

"I've always had a soft spot for you, Mads, you know that," he said quietly. "I'd hate to think that this was it between us."

"Don't be daft!" I punched him gently on the chest. "This is a big adventure and if you think I'm not going to share it you've got another thing coming!"

He smiled but I could see he wasn't happy. Quickly I asked the waitress for the bill and busied myself in finding my purse. Dan had never hinted at any level of commitment or permanency in our relationship before and this expression of feeling was something new. Frankly, it threw me.

"I'll get this," Dan said in a flat voice as he produced his wallet.

We arrived in Walditch late morning having first visited Randall & Mather, the estate agents in Bridport, to pick up the keys for The Olde Smithy. As we pulled up alongside Walditch village green there were already a few people sitting outside the Blacksmith's Arms and, casually, I wondered whether there would be an opportunity of some work in that establishment.

I clambered down from the van, stretched and rubbed my hands together. "OK, let's get cracking!"

We spent the next couple of hours unloading and Dan only twice hit his head on the low ceiling beams to the downstairs rooms. I had no such trouble; at five feet four, I was a good nine inches shorter.

"Must have been midgets in the 17th Century!" he muttered, ferociously rubbing his skull.

According to Randall & Mather, the cottage dated back to the mid-1600s, in part. The property details had stated: *A charming, two bedroomed, period cottage situated in Walditch, a village set deep in hilly countryside yet only a mile from Bridport and West Bay. The Olde Smithy offers discerning buyers an opportunity to put their stamp on a property steeped in history but with all modern day conveniences.*

The sitting/dining room, kitchen and master bedroom were obviously in the original part of the building with heavily beamed ceilings and uneven floors, while a two-storey extension, built during the late 1980s, had created a hallway, downstairs bathroom and a first floor guest bedroom. There was a small, overgrown, cottage-style garden to the front, which opened directly onto the village green, and to the rear, immediately accessible from the kitchen, was a courtyard created by a collection of outhouses, one being an outside privy. A pathway led past the outbuildings to a further area of overgrown garden which included three gnarled and twisted fruit trees in desperate need of pruning, an outline of a long-forgotten vegetable bed and, to my delight, a small pond.

The day passed quickly and we busied ourselves unpacking furniture, stacking shelves and filling cupboards. I seemed to have energy to spare and the cottage soon began to take shape. By the time the elongating shadows of the oak tree encroached upon the front garden, the cottage felt homely and only the last remaining packing boxes stacked in the hallway and the lack of curtains at the windows declared me a new occupant. I made a mental note to buy some fabric during the next few days as I had been unable to salvage any window dressings from the flat; being a Victorian conversion, it had tall sash windows to which the landlord had fitted vertical blinds.

Dan had regained a cheerful disposition and his earlier melancholy had dissipated. He was busy cleaning the fireplace as I rummaged through a box in the kitchen, searching for elusive tea bags. I paused and looked around appreciatively, taking in the beams, the flagstone floor and the view of the courtyard through the small-paned window. I could already see next spring's hanging baskets on the walls to the outhouses and I smiled, instinctively knowing that all that had gone before had been leading to this day.

"Hey, Mads, take a look at this!" Dan called excitedly from the sitting room.

I turned and walked to the doorway. A thick haze lingered in the room and I marvelled at how much dust Dan had created. I was just about to suggest that he let in some fresh air but then noticed that the windows were all open wide. I thought it strange that the room was so full of fog; there was quite a breeze outside.

He turned and it must have been a trick of the light. His blonde hair appeared darker and longer and he seemed less tall and lean; an altogether rougher version. I blinked and shook my head as if brushing away the image and as quickly as he had appeared altered there he was, once again, the Dan I knew.

"What have you found?" I walked across the room and saw a small opening in the stonework to the side of the inglenook. "How did that happen?"

"One of the stones was loose. It came away quite easily when I investigated. I think there's something behind it."

"Clear away a bit more," I said, enthusiastically. "It might be a bread oven."

He placed his long fingers into the gap and gently worked the stones around the opening. For a while nothing happened but then one moved slightly and suddenly it came away in his hand. There was a definite finished edge to the hole. I peered inside and could just make out a hidden void.

"Wow, how exciting!"

I inserted my hand and felt around, not sure what I was expecting to find. However, apart from a thick layer of dust and some rubble, the alcove was empty.

"I'll visit a reclamation yard and find a door that fits," I said, wondering why I felt so disappointed. "I'll make a feature of it."

"This cottage will give up more of its secrets as time goes by."

As Dan spoke the words I became aware of an expectant stillness in the air. I looked at him sharply.

"Why did you say that?"

"Well, these old places always have secrets, don't they?"

At once I felt hot and short of breath.

"And this one's had over four hundred years to collect them," he continued.

Feeling dizzy I reached out to Dan, as if trying to hold onto something solid, something I could trust. He caught hold of my arm.

"Hey, steady Mads!"

Beads of perspiration pricked my forehead and I struggled to hold back the rising nausea.

"You OK?" Dan asked with concern.

"Just need to get some fresh air."

"Tell you what. Let's abandon the tea thing and go to the pub instead."

This was his answer to most things.

"Yeah, I could do with a drink," I replied and he smiled. "Oh, and dinner's on me," I said weakly, as I hurried towards the door.

"Now there's an offer I can't possibly refuse! But won't that be messy?"

Brian, the landlord of the Blacksmith's Arms, remembered us as we had visited the pub on several occasions during filming. He was a jovial, larger than life character in his mid-fifties with a wife whom we had seldom seen. Vera was kept busy behind the scenes cooking delicious homemade meals for the hordes of people who seemed to frequent the pub.

"So you bought The Olde Smithy then?" Brian placed a whisky and soda on the bar in front of me while pouring a pint of Badgers for Dan.

"Yes, I picked up the keys earlier today. We haven't stopped working since!" I replied, sipping my drink.

"It's a lovely cottage. Such a shame it's been standing empty so long. The garden was a treat when Mrs McKendrick had it. There was nothing she didn't know about plants and as for her old man's vegetables, well, he swept the board clean most years at the village show! The local horticultural society is a sorrier place without them."

"I've seen the remains of their endeavours," I said enthusiastically. "The vegetable beds are completely overgrown but I'm looking forward to clearing them and growing my own, come the spring. It will be a steep learning curve, though." I laughed, happy at the thought of those future projects.

"Mads is a city girl!" Dan explained, rather unnecessarily I thought.

"Ah, you'll have fun learning. Excuse me."

Brian winked at me as he moved away to the other end of the bar to serve a young couple that had just walked in.

I picked up a bar menu and we carried our drinks to one of the alcoves. The pub had been cleverly converted from an old coach house and private seating areas had been created out of the original stalls where horses would once have been housed. An array of old farm equipment, horse brasses, tying hooks and hay racks adorned the walls and the pub oozed a warm, welcoming ambience, helped admirably by a roaring log fire.

"I guess you'll be in here a lot," Dan said.

"Well, I had considered asking Brian if he needed any help," I responded.

"What *are* you going to do with yourself?"

"Oh, I haven't really got that far, Dan. I thought I'd spend a few months updating the cottage and in the New Year think about earning some money. Maybe I'll start writing again."

"Well, let's face it, the number of times you've kissed that Blarney Stone means you're never short of a story or two!" Dan teased.

My first assignment with Hawkstone Media had been on a period drama set in the countryside around Cork. From the first I had recognised in Dan a shared sense of humour and it had been fun spending time with him, introducing him to my country of birth. On a rare day off we had visited Blarney Castle and I had explained that I'd first kissed the Stone at the tender age of eight. I amused him with tales of visitors being held by the ankles and lowered head first over the battlements in order to kiss it. This was true, but many years before I had first encountered the Stone. On the day Dan and I visited, Health and Safety had long since come into play and, though the Stone itself was still set in the wall below the battlements, to kiss it we only had to lean backwards from the parapet walk while holding onto an iron railing. Simple—providing you didn't suffer from vertigo or lumbago.

"I might see if I can do some film reviews for a magazine or paper," I explained. "I really want to get the cottage straight first, though. I need to paint throughout and one of the window frames needs urgent attention and I'm sure I'll find some other hidden nasties."

"The inglenook would look great with a feature bread oven," Dan enthused.

But, for some reason, I was annoyed by his interest.

"I wonder why it was closed up?" he continued, unaware of my irritation.

"No idea," I said flippantly.

Why was I being so uncharacteristically defensive?

"Will you concentrate on that first?" he asked, quite reasonably.

"Haven't a clue," I answered unhelpfully. Why did I feel he was prying?

"So, you'll get a door for it?" he persevered, a questioning look on his face.

"Probably," I answered dismissively.

Not wanting to continue the conversation further, I opened a menu and started to read aloud what was on offer that evening. It was a difficult choice as it all sounded appetising but, once we'd decided, Dan went to the bar to order.

Looking around the pub, my eyes alighted on a heavily framed oil painting hanging above the fireplace. The paintwork was dark, probably not helped by the smoke from numerous fires lit beneath it over the years, but from where I sat on the far side of the pub I could just make out the figure of a man shoeing a horse in front of a timber-framed building. With a sudden rush of emotion, I felt my cheeks flush and my heart begin to race.

Rising quickly, I walked over to the fire and peered more closely at the painting. In the foreground the artist had painted a large tree and I realised that it was the view across the village green from the doorway of this pub. The building was definitely The Olde Smithy and I glanced at the artist's signature, but couldn't make it out.

If this pub had originally been a coach house, I considered, it would make sense for the blacksmith's premises to be close by. Perhaps the bread oven wasn't a bread oven after all. Maybe it was the furnace where the blacksmith had heated up the horseshoes.

Looking closely at the man in the painting I noticed the length of his hair, his build, the set of his body and shivered, even though I could feel the heat from the fire through my denim jeans. I stood staring at the strangely familiar scene for a while longer before returning to the table. I kept my observations to myself, not feeling inclined to share them with Dan.

We had a pleasant meal and during the course of the evening the pub grew steadily busier. The front of house staff seemed to consist of two waitresses, one a girl called Janet, and Brian behind the bar. I decided to give myself a week or so to settle in and then I would definitely ask if there were any vacancies.

We left the pub at around 10.30pm. I had switched on the porch light as we'd left the cottage and it now blinked in welcome at us from the far side of the village green. Lights from the neighbouring cottages also cast their beams across the grass, lighting our way. As we walked beneath the branches of the mighty oak I looked up and saw high clouds scudding across the night sky, briefly revealing a scattering of twinkling stars and a watery moon.

"Feels like rain," I commented.

"Better cosy up then."

I opened the front door and as I stepped into the hallway, detected a distinct chill in the air. "Brr . . . Even more reason to cosy up!" I teased.

"Come here you!" Dan pulled me close and kissed me. "Welcome to your new life."

Dan was a thoughtful lover and our subsequent lovemaking was gentle, comforting and familiar. Before long, exhausted from the day's exertions, we fell asleep. As I drifted off I remember thinking how easy it was with Dan, albeit uneventful, which was why I was so surprised when, in the small hours, I was awoken from a deep slumber to hot, insistent kisses all over my body.

At first I thought I must be dreaming but as I looked across to the windows and saw the inky night sky and the rain lashing against the glass, I remembered where I was. Dan's hands were greedily feeling my body as if for the very first time and when his mouth found mine, the passion took my breath away. The urgency in his caresses was like nothing I had experienced with him before and I marvelled at the way I responded. Our bodies moved in harmony and I delighted at his every touch, melting under his deep kisses.

"Damn you woman," he said, nuzzling my neck. "I am bewitched."

I thrilled at the emotion I heard in his voice but surfaced long enough to register that Dan had never before referred to me as 'woman'. Momentarily, he pulled back and I sensed him looking at me.

The moon, emerging from behind a cloud, cast an eerie green light through the window and as it alighted on my lover's face his appearance seemed altered, the Dan I had seen earlier that evening; somehow more feral. Suddenly he groaned and pulled me to him. I gasped and together we rode wave after wave of pure sensation; an insatiable rip tide of feeling. Afterwards, we held each other close and it wasn't long before I heard his deep, even, rhythmic breathing. My last conscious thought before sleep also claimed me was that this heightened passion between us had made Dan's body feel different, somehow more muscled, and that it, too, must have been the reason for his altered scent.

The next morning I rose before he awoke and made my way quietly downstairs. I wasn't sure how to handle this new dimension to our relationship and decided to let Dan take the lead. Filling the kettle, I glanced out of the window at the still, wet day. Leaves now lay scattered across the courtyard, wrenched from the trees by the terrific winds during the night. I noticed a young, black cat sitting by the outhouse door assessing me. Moving quietly to the back door, I opened the top half and called softly. The cat watched warily before turning and fleeing into the garden.

Probably lives next door, I thought.

I took the mugs of tea up to the bedroom and pushed open the door. Dan, now sitting up in bed, drew long fingers through his wayward hair and I glanced at him with an unusual shyness.

"Morning Mads."

I handed him a mug.

"Looks like one hell of a storm last night."

In more ways than one, I thought, but said nothing.

I glanced at the window overlooking the courtyard and saw that rain had seeped through a gap in the casement and formed a pool of water on the sill, which now steadily dripped onto the bare floorboards.

"Don't you remember?" I asked in an even voice.

With my back to him, I rummaged in my holdall. I found a T-shirt and mopped the sill before dropping it onto the floorboards to soak up the puddle. A movement out of the corner of my eye made me look into the garden and I saw the black cat hunting amongst the long, wet grass at the far end by the pond.

"You know me, Mads, sleep through anything. It takes more than hurricane force wind and torrential rain to wake me!"

It was true. Nothing ever disturbed Dan once his head touched the pillow. I considered this carefully. Had he been in the throes of a dream then? That would certainly explain his uncharacteristic behaviour last night, or had his subconscious taken over, like that of a sleepwalker?

"Do you not remember anything about last night?" I asked.

"I remember getting back from the pub and thinking how cold the cottage was." He arched an eyebrow and smiled suggestively. "But we didn't have much trouble finding a way to warm up, did we?"

I wondered to which round of sex he was referring.

"God, I was bushed though," he continued. "Couldn't keep awake for long."

Bewildered, I thought he must have been asleep during our later, enthusiastic lovemaking. And, yet, he had spoken to me. It didn't make sense.

"You know I've always liked this bed of yours," Dan was saying. "It's so comfortable. I could spend a lot of time in it with you."

He patted the bed beside him and I sat down where he indicated and sipped my tea, confused by this turn of events. Our passion the previous night had been so uncharacteristic that I thought he would want to acknowledge it and, perhaps, discuss where our relationship was going from here. But it seemed that Dan had no such thoughts.

"And after that?" I asked. "We can't just stay in bed. There's more to life than sex you know."

He looked at me questioningly. "You're in a funny mood this morning. You've never worried about life after sex before."

"Well maybe I should have," I replied, irritated.

"But that's why we get on so well," he said in his usual, calm, unflustered manner. "No pressure, just loads of fun."

We were silent for a while and I felt a distance between us which I had not been there before. Neither of us wanted to make the next move and it occurred to me that Dan's easygoing nature and informal way had masked a reluctance to acknowledge the passing of time and his responsibility to me as a person. I, on the other hand, had been happy to have a relationship where the boundaries were vague and non-committal and, yet, perhaps this had in no small way contributed to my growing restlessness and need for change.

So, later that morning, after I had rustled up some breakfast from amongst the few provisions I'd brought with me from London, we loaded the remaining empty packing cases into the van. Closing the rear doors, Dan turned to me and kissed me lightly on the mouth.

"Be seeing you, kiddo!" he said casually. "Don't forget you can phone me any time, day or night."

And with that he climbed into the van, turned on the engine, lowered the window and blew me a kiss. I watched the vehicle until it disappeared around the corner, heard him hoot 'goodbye' and then all was silent. In fact, it was so silent it was as if the world was holding its breath, waiting to see what I would do next.

I stood there for a while looking at the empty road, feeling numb. The previous night's passion had awakened unfamiliar feelings in me and, yet, here was Dan driving off seemingly without a care in the world, denying any subtle shift in our relationship.

Letting out a deep sigh, I turned and walked back to the cottage and, as I did so, I heard the birds begin to sing, a dog bark in the distance and Brian call from inside the pub for Janet to get the tables ready for lunch.

Early October

The weather during that first week in The Olde Smithy was changeable; high winds and lashing rain one minute, sudden stillness and stubborn drizzle the next. I tackled the kitchen, cleaning the old units as best I could and thought it would be fun to search for replacement, free-standing furniture from the numerous reclamation yards and auction houses around. What I had originally thought was a slate floor transformed into terracotta tiles and the walls and ceiling, filthy with grime, scrubbed up a treat with a good deal of elbow grease and sugar soap.

On the Saturday I caught the bus into Bridport where an obviously popular street market was in full flow and, to my joy, I found a stall selling soft furnishings. I purchased two matching pairs of dusky blue curtains patterned with lighter blue, entwining foliage which, after some nifty alterations, would prove ideal for the sitting and dining rooms. Then I visited the hardware stall where I bought two large cans of white emulsion. On my way back to the bus stop, heavily laden with my purchases, I stopped at a newsagent and bought a local paper.

By the end of the week, having given the kitchen a lick of paint, the room was bright and welcoming, even if the cabinets were not exactly my style. And all the while a pair of almond-shaped eyes watched me curiously from the safety of the outhouse, poised to flee into the garden at the first sign of any perceived threat.

I had noticed the cat drinking from the puddles that formed between the uneven stones of the courtyard floor and its forays into the garden often resulted in a triumphant return with a mouse; it was obviously an excellent hunter and wasn't going hungry. The weather was foul that week and, coupled with the fact that I was concentrating on decorating, I did not venture out into the village so was unable to make enquiries. However, I did ask the postman if he knew whose cat it was, but he simply shook his head.

"I've only just taken over the Walditch round," he said. "I'm not sure where everyone lives yet, let alone their pets!"

I explained that I didn't think it was a stray as it was in such good condition but maybe it belonged to people who had just moved into the area and was disorientated and lost, although privately I thought it looked as if it knew exactly what it was about. The postman promised he would report back if he heard anything.

During a brief respite in the weather, I put scrubbing brushes aside and sneaked out to take a look at the potting shed to investigate further. The door to the outhouse was permanently ajar, hanging off one rusty hinge. Slowly and quietly I neared the open door and peered in. It was extremely dark within, the only window filthy with years of grime and cobwebs, and it took a while for my eyes to become accustomed to the gloom. A rusting wheelbarrow stood propped against the far wall and a wooden workbench under the window housed a large selection of pots, seed trays and two watering cans which had seen better days. Stacked against the opposite wall were several old gardening tools and beside these was a pile of compost and manure bags. I scrutinised the bags closely and saw the tell-tale indentation, approximately young adult cat size.

"Aha! So this is where you sleep."

Going back into the kitchen, I grabbed a dish from the drainer and found some sliced chicken in the fridge. I returned to the outhouse and placed the dish by the side of the sacks. Before returning to the cottage, I glanced into the garden but there was no movement amongst the long grass.

I'm going to call you Storm, I thought. After all, the cat had appeared the morning after the howling gales during that first night in the cottage.

Dan phoned the following Friday to see how I was faring. It was good to hear his voice. He was light and cheerful and chatted happily about his imminent departure for deepest, darkest Wales where he was about to commence filming a documentary on the poet, Dylan Thomas. Not once did he make any reference to our night of passion and, stubbornly, I was determined it was not going to be me who would broach the subject. I was surprised at how wrong-footed I felt when he finally bade me farewell without a murmur.

My sister, Mo, texted me from Morocco where she was on a magazine shoot, something to do with the souks in Marrakech. She encouraged me to: *Go 4 it girl! Email soon. Mo xx*

And my parents rang. They were as loving as always and showed interest in my plans for the cottage. I told them I was thinking of enquiring at the local pub to see if they needed any staff and, to my irritation, noticed that I felt the need to justify my decision by saying that it would be a great way to meet people. They were warm and positive and, not for the first time, I felt fortunate that I was a part of the life of such people.

And then, just as we were saying our goodbyes, my father advised, "Enjoy the adventure, Madeleine, but don't stay in the wilderness too long."

I said goodbye and replaced the receiver, incensed. Wilderness? It wasn't some wasteland I had come to! I wasn't on some escapist trip trying to shirk the responsibilities of my life. I had come home!

I let out a groan and stared at the phone in frustration.

A vibration in the air around me made me catch my breath. Slowly and seductively, the subtlest of warm currents swirled around my body. t was as if I was being wrapped in a loving embrace and I luxuriated in the sensation. Immediately I was filled with an excited expectancy and the strongest emotion, that of pure joy.

I noticed how quiet it had become and, yet, as I looked out of the window I could see the branches of the oak tree swaying wildly in the wind, a stray plastic bag tumbling across the green on a frantic journey from dustbin to hedgerow, and the incessant rain on the window pane, but there was no sound at all. Slowly I breathed out, savouring the feeling. Suddenly, as quickly as it had happened, the world returned to normal and I heard the noise of a wet and wild afternoon.

I wasn't alarmed; I felt, somehow, blessed.

"Thank you!" I said, to whom I wasn't sure.

Maybe I was thanking the cottage for giving me such a sense of belonging.

The following lunchtime, with the Bridport & Lyme Regis News in hand, I went to the pub. Brian was emptying the glass-washer and hanging clean glasses in neat rows above the bar. He looked up as I entered.

"Hello young lady and how are you surviving over the far side of the green?"

I laughed. It was all of a hundred yards, if that.

"One room decorated, only five more to go!"

"If you need any help I know several trustworthy tradesmen. Just ask."

He closed the door of the glass-washer.

"Now, what can I get you?"

I sat at the bar and ordered a cider and a ploughman's lunch.

Opening the paper, I said, "What I do need are some trustworthy wheels. Can you recommend any garages around here?"

Brian placed a glass on the bar in front of me.

"Well, let's see. There's Masons in Bridport and Bartlett's out on the Dorchester road, though they can be a bit on the pricey side. Depends what you're looking for."

"Oh, nothing flash. Just a good, reliable run-around."

I glanced at the columns of private adverts.

"Janet's cousin has just started selling cars."

Brian called over to the waitress who had served Dan and me the previous week and she confirmed that her cousin, Bill, had recently started supplementing his job as a mechanic by trading in second-hand cars.

"He's on the industrial estate. It's easy to find. He'll do you a good deal," she volunteered. "Shall I jot his number down?"

I thanked her and said I would give him a call. I also asked if anyone had reported a missing young, black cat and explained how it was living in my outhouse.

The Forgotten Promise

"Mrs Tomkins next to you has Rex, the ginger tom," Janet said. "He's quite old now and doesn't go out much but he'll probably be in your garden once the weather's better. I've not heard she's got a new cat. And the Evans family next but one to her have dogs and rabbits."

"No, I've not heard of any new cats in the village and I hear it all in here!" Brian grinned broadly. "Sure beats watching the soaps any day."

I laughed. "Stranger than fiction."

"You can say that again! There's not much goes on that doesn't get reported within these four walls. Why don't you put a poster on the village notice board?"

A shout from the kitchen and Janet disappeared through the swing doors, reappearing a moment later with my ploughman's. She set it on the bar in front of me.

As I buttered a thick chunk of crusty bread, I looked around and noticed the pub had become progressively busier. At the far end of the bar were half-a-dozen loud businessmen ordering a mainly liquid lunch, or so it seemed to me. An elderly couple sat at one of the tables by the fire, a map spread out before them, discussing an afternoon's sightseeing, and at another table sat a young couple trying their best to deal with two noisy children who were determined to throw all their food on the floor. There were also several couples enjoying the seclusion of the private alcoves and I fancied that these were clandestine meetings snatched during lunch hours, with Brian the discreet overseer of their secrets.

The doors to the kitchen suddenly swung open and Brian's wife appeared looking harassed.

"Bri, love, can you come here a mo?"

Brian raised an eyebrow. Muttering under his breath, he followed her into the kitchen from where I could hear low voices rising rapidly. I buried my head in the paper and concentrated hard on reading the 'Cars for Sale' advertisements. A few minutes later he reappeared, red in the face, but instantly regained his bonhomie. I gave him a quizzical look.

"Don't ask," he said. "It's mayhem back there!"

It transpired that the assistant chef had done a runner a couple of days before and hadn't been seen since. They had been coping with Janet not only on waiting duties but also helping out in the kitchen as best she could, but it was not proving easy and Vera was nearing the end of her tether.

Seizing the opportunity, I told Brian how I was hoping to find part-time work and had wondered about approaching him. He looked at me in amazement. In one swift movement he was on the lounge side of the bar, embracing me in a huge bear hug.

"You excellent girl!" he exclaimed. "How soon can you start?"

And so it was agreed that I would start that week helping out behind the bar on Friday and Saturday nights with further evenings and lunchtimes as Christmas drew nearer, if I wanted them.

Feeling happy with the way things were shaping up, I finished my lunch, bade my soon-to-be colleagues goodbye and on my way back to the cottage checked out the village notice board. There were the usual posters about coffee mornings, a new pilates class starting up, mobile library and bus timetables, and a flyer announcing that Bridport Amateur Dramatics were putting on 'Puss in Boots' as their Christmas pantomime and that parts were still available for any would-be thespians. But nothing about a missing cat.

I spent the afternoon phoning the local vets and Cats Protection League to see if a black cat, approximately one-year-old, had been reported missing. Nothing. The receptionist at the veterinary surgery suggested I brought it in to see if it was micro-chipped and laughed when I said that there was no chance of that as I couldn't get within ten feet! But I agreed to do so if the cat ever decided to trust me. I then phoned a number from an advert in the paper and ordered a trailer load of logs, which a broad Dorset accent assured me would be delivered in the next couple of days and, finally, I phoned Janet's cousin who described the various cars he had for sale. I made arrangements to visit him the following day.

That night I went to bed early and decided to read for a while. It was still raining. I hadn't yet sorted out curtains for the bedroom so had improvised by pegging bath towels over the curtain rails. The towel at the window that overlooked the courtyard now billowed as gusts of wind and rain found the gap in the ill-fitting casement. Despite these improvised measures, it was a comfortable room built within the eaves of the cottage and I was just thinking how cosy it looked in the glow of the bedside lamp when I heard a thud from downstairs. Maybe a window or door had worked itself loose in a draught? I strained to listen further, but all was silent. Getting out of bed, I threw on a dressing gown, switched on the landing light and went downstairs. I checked every door and window but they were all secure. Where had the noise come from? Telling myself that these old cottages were prone to strange creaking sounds and groans—and ignoring the voice that asked, *'but a definite thud?'*—I made myself a mug of tea and was on my way up to bed when I happened to glance over at the inglenook fireplace.

Dan had swept the fireplace clean on the day I'd moved in, leaving it neat and tidy, but on the hearth there now stood a stone.

"How did you get there?" I asked out loud.

Sure, the wind was strong, but it must have been one almighty gust to dislodge that.

I placed the mug on the coffee table and walked towards the hearth. The opening to the hidden alcove appeared larger and on closer inspection I discovered that the stone had been dislodged from its entrance. I stood looking at it, trying to work out where a gust might have come from and wondered if the chimney was faulty. The wood burning stove obviously had a flue going up the stack but possibly the bread oven/furnace also had a separate flue.

As I stood there pondering, I had an overwhelming urge to put my hand inside the opening and before I knew it my fingers were, once again, searching the floor of the alcove. Each time I was in the sitting room I was drawn to the oven but, again, as on that first morning, I discovered nothing—just dust and rubble. Unsettlingly, I noticed that there wasn't the slightest suggestion of a draught coming from within the inglenook or the bread oven. Ignoring this thought, I withdrew my hand and decided that a chimney sweep or builder definitely needed to investigate further, especially if this part of Dorset was prone to the sort of weather I had experienced since first moving in.

Replacing the stone into the opening, I picked up the mug of tea and started to retreat back upstairs. I had just reached the door leading out into the hall when I heard another thud and, looking back over my shoulder, saw the stone once again on the hearth. Despite my mind telling me that there had to be a reasonable explanation, something to do with down-draughts and gusts, my skin began to crawl and goose bumps appeared on my arms.

"Oh this is ridiculous," I said more confidently than I felt. "You can jolly well stay on the floor!"

Talking to an inanimate object! Whatever next?

I marched purposefully upstairs, switched off the landing light, closed the bedroom door firmly behind me and, quickly placing the mug on the bedside cabinet, jumped into bed. I pulled the duvet covers tight up around my neck, all the while trying not to notice the tremor in my hands.

The next morning the rain had stopped. I caught the bus into Bridport and found Janet's cousin on the industrial estate. Like Janet, Bill was chatty and the morning passed quickly. I liked all the cars he showed me but the VW Golf won me over, being the newest and having the least mileage. I was assured that it was a 'one careful lady owner driver' who had brought it in for Bill to sell! Silently, I thanked my late Aunt Aileen, my mother's sister, whose generosity towards me in her will a couple of years previously had made all this possible; not just the car but the whole Dorset adventure. Once we had wrangled over the price and finally agreed upon a sum that suited us both, Bill showed me to his office and proceeded to write up the paperwork.

He filled out the relevant car details and then asked, "What's your address?"

I told him and watched as the pen stalled in mid-air. There was an odd expression on his face.

"The Olde Smithy, Walditch?" he echoed.

"Yes. Do you know it?"

"My sister's friend rented it for a few months," he said hesitantly. "She and her son." He gazed at me wide-eyed.

Disconcerted by his stare and for the want of anything better to say, I asked, "Were they happy there?"

He cleared his throat and started to write again. "Only there a few months," he said quickly. "How long have you been living there?"

"Not long." He had stirred my curiosity. "Why?"

"Oh, nothing." The look on his face changed to one of embarrassment.

I was intrigued. "What's nothing?"

He stopped writing and shifted uncomfortably in his chair. "Things happened."

I froze.

"What things, Bill?" I needed to know.

He cleared his throat again and said, "Um, said she heard noises. Felt she wasn't alone. Things like that . . ." He looked really ill at ease. "Look, it was probably just her overblown imagination. She's always been a bit of a drama queen. I shouldn't have said anything."

Suddenly the office felt hot and stifling.

"Just going to get some air." I waved towards the door and rushed outside.

The chill of the afternoon was a welcome shock to my senses. Sternly I told myself that, of course, there were noises; it was an old cottage. Everything could be explained away with a logical explanation.

"Are you OK?" Bill called from behind his desk.

"Yes, I'm fine. I'll just complete the paperwork and be on my way."

I couldn't wait to get out of there.

Nothing more was said about the cottage and we concluded the deal but as I climbed into the driver's seat and prepared to drive off, Brian knocked on the window. I lowered it.

"Don't take any notice of what I said earlier. My sister's friend is unhinged and she can make a drama out of anything."

I smiled and said, lightly, "Cheerio! See you in the Blacksmith's maybe?"

"No doubt," he replied. "That Brian serves a good pint."

Putting the car into first gear, I drove away as fast as I could.

Early November

Over the course of the next few weeks I slowly wooed Storm. At first the cat refused to respond to my attentions despite daily bribes of food but, little by little, curiosity won over his wariness. By the time November arrived he was happy to come to the back door and eat but would not come in to the cottage and continued to treat the outhouse as his home. He was a handsome cat and I couldn't understand how anyone could have mislaid him or turned him out. I asked around the village but nobody seemed to know where he'd come from.

Then, early one morning, I looked out of the kitchen window and saw him watching me from the outhouse door. There was something different about his demeanour and as soon as he saw me he got up and came to the back door. Not wanting to frighten him away, I opened the door quietly, and that was that. In he came, as if it was the most natural thing in the world and how foolish was I to think otherwise! He purred around my legs while I spooned cat food into a bowl and then head-butted my hand as I placed the bowl on the floor.

"Welcome Storm!"

And so Storm came to live with me. It was as if he had finally decided the cottage would be a far preferable place to spend the winter than the draughty old potting shed. I took him to the vets but he had not been micro-chipped and, so, his future with me was assured.

The Forgotten Promise

I enjoyed working at the Blacksmith's Arms and was comfortable working the bar, pouring drinks and chatting to the locals. Some of the regulars were true characters and I felt dormant creativity begin to stir; soon I was itching to start writing again. I also continued to work on the cottage. The previous owners had wallpapered throughout, as was probably the fashion during their time there. Slowly and painstakingly I worked my way through the layers, making discoveries on a daily basis—like the imprint of another staircase in the dining room. It was an exciting time and energy coursed through my veins. Storm had taken over the cottage completely and was often found lying on my bed when I had forgotten to shut the bedroom door. He was charming and cheeky, and liked to be involved in everything; he would amuse me for hours jumping at the strips of wallpaper hanging from the walls. I was busy and happy and not at all lonely, even when Dan phoned me and excitedly announced that he'd met someone whilst filming in Wales.

"She's a freelance props dresser and has worked on loads of historical pieces. You'd really like her, Mads. She's such fun!"

I declined to comment.

"Where does she live?" I asked, keeping my voice light.

"She's been living in Bristol for the past four years but says it's too parochial for her. She's wanted to move to London for ages to further her career."

I snorted. So, she was already moving in on him and they'd only known each other five weeks. How naive men could be!

"Careful, Dan." I said. "What baggage does she come with?"

He laughed. "Very little. Usually just an overnighter!"

"You know what I mean."

"I think there's an 'ex' lurking somewhere, but she hasn't got any kids. Oh Mads, she's great!"

I raised an eyebrow at Storm who was sitting in the chair by the wood burner watching me.

Trying to steer the conversation to another subject I asked whether he knew if any of his contacts needed a freelance writer. He had always been supportive of my creative side.

He thought for a while and then said, "Do you remember Richard, my old university pal? He's just started publishing an 'eco' magazine. I bet he wants 'green' articles. I'll give you his number."

I found a pad of paper and jotted down the details as Dan gave them to me. I could tell he still wanted to talk about the girlfriend and, sure enough, before long the conversation came back to her.

"I've got to tell you, Mads, life's pretty good at present. She's so vibrant and full on. It's sugar for the soul! She's making an old man very happy."

"Old man? What are you talking about?" I exclaimed. Dan was a mere six years older than me. "How old is she for God's sake? You haven't gone and got yourself involved with some Lolita have you?"

"She's thirty three, same age as you."

At least I hadn't been thrown over for someone older.

"I just know you two will hit it off," he continued enthusiastically. "I really want you to meet her and I was wondering if we could come down next weekend?"

The bombshell. Hell! How was I going to get out of that?

"I don't know, Dan. You see, I work Friday and Saturday nights now," I said lamely, feeling guilty that I was looking for excuses.

"We'd be no trouble, Mads. We'd do our own thing and meet up with you when you were free. I really want you to meet—the two most important women in my life!"

And so I met Lucy.

The following Friday night I was behind the bar, pouring a pint of bitter for one of the regulars, when the door to the Blacksmith's Arms opened and in walked Dan looking slightly flustered, I thought, with a tall, leggy blonde in tow. He smiled at me sheepishly as he quickly covered the distance from door to bar. Introductions followed and I noticed how Lucy stood very close to him, possessively touching him at every opportunity. She was slim and attractive with a wide, generous mouth and wore jeans and a short white T-shirt which exposed several inches of toned, tanned stomach. Her tousled blonde hair looked as if she'd only just got out of bed. I was surprised at how easily the thought popped into my head; it was unlike me to be quite so catty! She possessed a winsome appeal but, instinctively, I felt this was carefully manufactured. She laughed easily—and a lot—and appeared to hang onto Dan's every word. At every given opportunity she touched his arm, his face, his hand, or fiddled with his hair. She never left him alone!

I was relieved the pub was so busy and I had an excuse to escape. I suggested they had something to eat in the restaurant and if I hadn't finished my shift by the time they wanted to leave, they could go back to the cottage and make themselves comfortable. This seemed to please Lucy well.

Throughout the evening I found myself stealing glances at them seated at their table. Lucy's laugh rippled across the restaurant and they seemed to have no end of things to talk about. Dan appeared enchanted.

It was an unusual situation for me. Dan and I had always had such a casual, companionable friendship and even though there had been other people for both of us during the time we had known each other, there had never been a 'significant other'. I felt Lucy's eyes on me a couple of times during the evening but refused to meet her gaze and on the occasion that she did catch my eye, her eyes quickly slid away from mine.

At 11pm they left.

Brian, working the bar beside me, commented, "She's quite something, isn't she?"

I gritted my teeth, shoving back the fingers of jealousy that threatened to strangle me.

"Where did he find her?" he asked.

"In Wales."

I concentrated hard on stacking dirty glasses in the washer.

"What, up a mountain?" Brian laughed.

"While filming a documentary. She was on the props team, or something," I said dismissively, not looking at Brian.

"Do I detect a slight green note, Madeleine?"

The grin in his voice did not go undetected.

"No chance!" I answered, slightly too swiftly.

He laughed out loud and I looked up sharply, feeling uncharacteristically vulnerable.

"Never a more interesting development in a relationship than when a bit of competition comes along," he said. He walked from behind the bar to collect more empty glasses but looked back at me and winked.

It wasn't as if I hadn't had my chance with Dan. We'd known each other for eight years and our relationship had never cemented into anything approaching solid. Surely, if it was going to, it would have done so by now?

I felt unsettled and finished cleaning the counter with extra gusto, trying to rid myself of the uncomfortable feeling. I groaned inwardly. Ahead of me stretched two whole days with them but, thankfully, I was working the following night.

By the time I finished at the pub it was past midnight. Walking slowly back to the cottage, I noticed the light on in the guest bedroom and paused at the front door. I knew Lucy's type and I was sure she would be in a hurry to let me hear how well she and Dan were getting on. Quietly I let myself in. Dan was sitting on the sofa, idly flicking through a magazine. He looked up and smiled at me; a warm, open smile.

"How you doin' kiddo? You must be exhausted!"

"Oh, I'm quickly getting used to the pressures of being a barmaid," I answered flippantly. "As long as I keep moving, my feet don't hurt too much. It's very sociable."

"Yeah, I could see that. Everyone seems to want only you to serve them!" he replied easily. "You've obviously made your mark." There followed an awkward pause before he continued, "Your hair's grown."

During the time Dan had known me I had always kept my hair at shoulder length, spending many a minute studiously straightening out its natural curl, but since moving to Dorset I had let it do its own thing. It was now longer and a mass of loose curls.

"It suits you," he commented. "You look softer. A true Irish country lass."

I didn't know what to say. Commenting on my appearance had never been something Dan had indulged in and I wasn't a 'country lass'. I was Dublin born and bred.

"Do you want a nightcap?" I asked.

Dan and I seemed to be out of synch.

"No thanks. I'm bushed. I think I'll turn in. It's been quite a week, what with one thing and another."

He rose, stretched and crossed the few yards between us.

"'Night Mads." He kissed me lightly on the cheek.

"'Night," I responded, thinking how only two months ago that kiss would have been directed at my mouth.

With a sinking feeling, I knew sleep was not going to come easily to me that night. And so it was. I tossed and turned and kept checking the time which, irritatingly, seemed to only progress in ten-minute segments. I was hot and restless and the brief moments of sleep that I did manage to snatch were littered with strange images and shadowy figures and somewhere a child was crying. At around 5am I gave up.

Without putting the landing light on, I tiptoed downstairs to the bathroom. As I reached the bottom step I had the strongest feeling that there was someone else downstairs. Looking towards the kitchen door I saw Lucy standing naked at the sink, a glass of water in her hand, her body silhouetted in the pale moonlight. She was oblivious to my presence and stood staring out of the window, a contented smile on her face, humming to herself. I couldn't help but notice the long shapely legs and the lithe feminine curve of her body and a sickening knot settled in the pit of my stomach. Very carefully I opened the bathroom door and quietly slipped in.

Argh! Two whole days!

By the time I emerged, Lucy had gone and as I passed the spare bedroom door I heard low murmuring coming from within. I climbed back into bed and lay there, my mind racing, getting progressively more hot and bothered. Eventually, I could stand it no longer. I got up and showered.

The day passed by in a blur. Dan and Lucy appeared mid-morning, glowing in mutual contentment, and I busied myself making breakfast and fussing over their needs. Dan immediately made himself comfortable on the sofa while Lucy joined me in the kitchen. She talked in a light, carefree banter but occasionally the mask slipped.

"Dan tells me you were the assistant director at Hawkstone."

"Yes, that's right."

I placed bowls and a selection of cereal packets on the kitchen counter and rummaged in the drawer for spoons. She moved out of the way for me but watched me like a hawk.

"Don't you find it very quiet down here?" she asked in an innocent voice. "I mean, when you've been used to London and a life in the media circus the charms of the countryside must surely wane after a while."

"Not at all, Lucy," I replied evenly. "I can go to London any time but, to date, I haven't felt the need."

I indicated to her to help herself to cereal and, through the open doorway, held up a box of cornflakes at Dan, knowing that this would be his choice. He nodded, Lucy all the while carefully watching the two of us. I poured milk onto the cereal and carried the bowls through to the sitting room.

"But what on earth do you find to do?" she continued her interrogation as she followed me into the room.

I handed Dan a bowl and sat down next to him.

"There's so much going on in the country," I said, carefully masking my rising defensiveness.

The look on her face was one of complicity; it suggested that she knew I was lying but was prepared to go along with the lie.

Irritated by her, supposed, superiority, I said, "And people make time for each other, which isn't always the case in a city."

"But surely being a barmaid must be so dreary after being in the centre of all the action on a film set?" she persisted.

She sat in the chair opposite us and elegantly arranged her legs in a manner which suggested to me that she knew exactly the pretty picture she presented.

I sensed Dan's eyes travelling up her long shapely limbs, following the toned curve of her belly and savouring her firm, pert breasts before finally resting upon her face. I glanced at him and was taken aback by the lust and adulation I saw in his eyes. But there was something else, too. Something unsettling. A madness, which reminded me of the addict desperate for the next fix; only Dan's 'fix' was Lucy.

Glancing over at Lucy I saw that she was fully aware of the power she had over Dan. Panicked by what was occurring, I spoke to her as if speaking to a rather dense child who was having trouble understanding a simple truth.

"No, I assure you Lucy, I haven't found it to be so. There are so many characters in the pub it's giving me plenty of material."

Hearing the tone in my voice, Dan shifted uneasily.

"Mads is going to start writing again, Luce," he interjected.

Lucy studied me a while longer, a fixed smile on her face, her eyes cold and calculating, before deciding it was better to abandon her cross-examination for the time-being.

"Well, I just know I couldn't survive down here in the sticks."

She beamed across the coffee table at Dan.

"I just have to be in London with my Danny."

Dan smiled back adoringly and I wondered if I had time to get to the bathroom before I threw up.

Feeling the need for wide open spaces, I suggested we went to Chesil Beach. Dan was instantly up for it. Enthusiastically he informed us that it stretched for more than ten miles from the Isle of Portland to Abbotsbury and, in places, stood as high as forty feet. Lucy looked dubiously out of the window at the grey, overcast sky and opened her mouth to say something. I watched dispassionately as she glanced at Dan's face and quickly swallowed her words. With feigned excitement she agreed.

The curve of the beach was magical and awe-inspiring. We walked a good way along the shingle bank separated from the mainland by a lagoon, and Dan continued to bombard us with facts about the area. Lucy appeared to lap up his every word. Skittishly she ran around him, goading him to chase her across the pebbles and Dan obliged by dashing after her, his arms encircling her waist and several times lifting her high into the air, swirling her around and around. Her laughter was light and flirty above the sound of the sea and the gulls and he glowed in the attention she bestowed upon him, but it didn't ring true with me.

We stood for a while watching a man and boy line-fishing from the shore and soon became mesmerised by the crashing waves. The rain kept away until mid-afternoon by which time we had returned to the car, driven past the famous Abbotsbury Swannery and had found a teashop in the village in which to while away a couple more hours. It was hard-going and I felt sickened by what was unfolding between the two of them.

That evening I left Dan and Lucy at the cottage and walked over to the pub for my evening shift. I was happy to escape for a few hours and felt comforted by the warm and hearty atmosphere of the Blacksmith's Arms.

"How are the two love birds?" asked Brian as I entered the pub. He was not at all gentle with my sensitive soul!

"Cooing nicely," I replied.

He laughed and then informed me that a table of twenty had booked in the restaurant that evening.

"Vera's enlisted Janet's help in the kitchen so you and Gayle will waitress," he explained. "I'll look after the bar."

Slight problem; he didn't know what he'd asked of me. I was certainly no waitress. However, I soon became immersed in the job as the restaurant began to fill.

The group of twenty turned out to be members of Bridport Arts & Crafts, out for an early pre-Christmas gathering as their tutor, a great looking guy called Nick, would be in Australia over the festive period. They were a lively, cheerful crowd and they teased me mercilessly for my non-waiting skills.

I did my best but had to laugh when Nick asked, "What do you actually do, Maddie, 'cos waitressing certainly ain't your bag?"

I was attempting to balance precariously stacked plates while trying to prevent a wayward piece of cutlery from falling into his lap for the second time that evening. Deftly, he caught the fork and handed it back to me with a smile.

The Forgotten Promise

I muttered something about painting and decorating and that I could pull a mean pint.

"Ah, a girl after my own heart!" he said, looking very directly at me.

I felt myself blush.

"Oh leave the poor girl alone, Nick," laughed one of the other men. "She'll drop the lot if you're not careful."

I excused myself and hurried towards the kitchen. As I went through the swing doors Brian caught my eye.

"Remind me not to employ you as a waitress next time!" he teased.

At 11.15pm the art group began to depart amidst much noise and with great hugs and kisses all round. I was sitting at the bar, perched on a stool and chatting to Brian who had poured me, what he called, 'a well-earned drink' when Nick approached to settle his party's bill.

As Brian processed his credit card Nick turned to me and said, "I hope I didn't offend you earlier?"

"Not at all," I replied lightly. "You're lucky to be leaving unscathed!"

Was it my imagination or did the sounds of the pub diminish and become suddenly muffled, as if coming from a great distance? And where had all the people gone? It seemed to me there were only the two of us in the room.

"You did a great job," he continued graciously, his clear blue-grey eyes meeting mine. There was an amused glint in those eyes as he added, " . . . for a painter and decorator!"

I laughed good-naturedly.

There was something distinctly familiar about Nick. Perhaps he'd been in the pub on one of my previous visits when I'd been drinking there with the film crew. The room beyond appeared undefined and out of focus but there was nothing whatsoever blurred about the man that stood before me.

He hesitated . . . and I waited.

I noticed it all. The fall of his hair; the sharp cheekbones; the shape of his nose; the sensual lips; the set of his chin. And those eyes! I was mesmerised.

He reached into an inner jacket pocket and pulled out a card. "If you ever need a carpenter just give me a ring." He handed me the business card.

Instantly I thought of a hundred and one carpentry jobs that needed urgent and immediate attention. Aware that Nick's eyes were on me, I quickly thanked him and mumbled something about it always being useful to have a list of good tradesmen. He smiled.

Turning to Brian, he said, "Great evening, Brian. Thank Vera for me. She did us proud."

He looked back at me, smiled, and then followed the last of his group out of the pub. I peered at the card.

Nick Corbin
Carpenter & Joiner
Bespoke service offered
Awkward corners a speciality
No job too small!
Mob: 07890 538264

I stared at the closed door, deep in thought. Becoming aware of someone's close scrutiny, I glanced out of the corner of my eye and saw Brian leaning on the bar watching me, a huge grin on his face.

"What?" I asked, indignantly.

"I don't know!" he teased. "You've got one bloke holed up at your place—admittedly with a new girlfriend, though it looks to me she might wear him out before too long—and here you are but a hundred yards away and you're already reeling in another!" He laughed.

"I'm not reeling anyone in!" I exclaimed. "But I *do* need a carpenter."

Despite blushing furiously I smiled at Brian, attempting to keep some control of the situation.

"Young lady, you have no idea what you're doing and you've certainly no idea the effect you have on my customers."

"I do know what I'm doing," I countered in mock outrage.

He arched an eyebrow.

"And the effect I'm having on your customers is hopefully encouraging them to come back!"

"Well, that's for sure. Takings were never so good when Bev worked the bar." He winked at me.

I finished my drink, said good night to them all and walked slowly back to the cottage. Dan's car was parked at the edge of the village green and the cottage was in darkness apart from the outside light, which meant that he and Lucy had either gone for a midnight walk or had retired to bed. I knew which option they would have chosen.

Slowly I climbed the stairs. As I passed the door to the spare bedroom, I heard deep, guttural moans coming from within. Sighing deeply, I opened the door to my room and lay there wondering how I was going to get any sleep with all the noisy activity occurring just a few feet away in the adjacent room, let alone survive another day without losing my composure. I thought of the evening and couldn't help but smile as I recalled my performance as a waitress, and then I thought of Nick Corbin. Who was he? Why did he seem familiar? The bubbling excitement coursing through my body took me by surprise as I recalled his face and, particularly, those blue-grey eyes. I wondered if there was a Mrs Corbin and any little Corbins and I berated myself for not checking to see if he wore a ring. It was something I never remembered to do, but plenty of my girl friends did and it always seemed a very wise thing to do. I sighed again, turned over, closed my eyes and put a pillow over my head trying to block out the noise, resigned to the fact that sleep would not come easily. But the evening's stresses had exhausted me more than I realised and I was asleep in an instant.

It was some time later that I came to, disorientated, as I felt the covers move and a body cuddle up to me. From the glow of the digital clock I could just make out Dan.

"What?" I exclaimed.

"Shhh! You'll wake her."

He kissed my mouth hard and I felt the longing in his kiss. Despite my confusion, my body rose to meet his and before long we were entwined as one.

"My love," he whispered in my ear.

I remember thinking that Dan was behaving uncharacteristically fast and loose and then my next thought was that this was so unlike the Dan I knew. He nuzzled my neck, which drove me wild, and a deep voice filled with emotion called out, "Come to me, my love! Come to me!"

I experienced the same thrill at hearing the intensity in his voice as I had that first night we had stayed at the cottage. But the words were not Dan-speak.

I tried to focus on him, which proved near impossible as he had me pinned to the bed, and now that I came to think of it, his body felt more muscular and there was that altered scent again.

Above our passion we heard a sound from the next room and Dan instantly rolled away from me.

In muffled tones he said, "I'll go to her."

Yes, indeed, I thought, you go to her. It will be interesting to hear how you explain away your presence in my room!

He headed towards the door.

I lay back in bed, considering what had just happened, when suddenly there was an insistent cry from the corner of the room. Thinking it must be Storm, I switched on the bedside lamp and couldn't believe what I saw.

In the corner of the room stood a large, rustic wooden cot, the crying emanating from within. Vaguely, it occurred to me that I might be in the middle of a very strange dream. Getting out of bed, I walked cautiously towards the cot and peered in. A very red-faced, hot and sweating child—a boy, aged about three—looked up at me. He stretched his arms towards me, crying and whimpering all the time and I was immediately overcome with a deep sense of sadness. I found it difficult to breathe and my vision blurred, a black tunnel threatening to engulf me. I called out, struggling to stay upright, but my legs gave way beneath me and I fainted to the floor.

The next thing I remember was Dan lifting me onto the bed. Lucy, dressed in only a T-shirt, which I noticed showed off her long, shapely legs to perfection, stood behind him watching carefully.

"Mads. What is it?" His voice was full of concern.

"The boy, Dan. He's ill!"

"What boy? What are you talking about?"

I didn't know what to think. I was so distressed. I struggled to sit up and looked towards the cot but the corner of the room was empty.

I burst into tears and sobbed, "He's ill! He needs me."

Dan sat on the bed beside me and gently stroked my hair, making soothing noises. Through my tears I saw Lucy frown.

Without looking at her, Dan said, "Luce, go and make Mads a cup of tea."

She didn't look too happy at being given orders but obediently left the room.

"Hush Mads, everything's OK."

His hands were cool and soothing and I clung to him for comfort.

"Dan, what's going on?" I asked.

"I think you must have had a bad dream," he replied.

"But earlier . . ." I sobbed.

"What do you mean earlier?"

"Earlier tonight," I cried. "You and me!"

Dan frowned. "What do you mean 'you and me'?"

"You came to me!"

"No, Mads," he said slowly. "I've been with Luce all night."

I felt as if I was going out of my mind. Had he been sleepwalking again? My body told me that we had made love and, yet, here he was denying it. And what of that child? My heart was breaking; the boy needed me.

"Dan, we had sex," I said.

He stopped stroking my hair.

"Mads, I've been next door all night. I think you have been in the throes of a very unusual dream."

The Forgotten Promise

A sound at the door made him look up and Lucy walked in with three mugs of tea. "I thought we all needed one," she said flatly.

I was exhausted and felt so sad, as if I had lost something very dear to me. I started to weep again.

"Don't cry!" Dan placed a cool hand on my forehead. "God, Mads, you're burning up!"

"Maybe she's caught a fever and is delusional," Lucy added, unhelpfully.

Dan frowned at her.

"It was only a suggestion," she said, answering his look.

His attention, once more on me, he said gently, "I want you to stay in bed today. We'll stay as long as we can."

Lucy started to say that she needed to get back to London in good time but Dan silenced her with another look. At least Lucy hadn't taken over Dan completely . . . yet.

"If you're not feeling better by the evening I want you to book an appointment with the doctor first thing on Monday morning. Promise?"

I nodded weakly. It was so like Dan to take control of a situation and ease things over. This was the Dan I knew so well.

"Now, do you think you can get some sleep?" he asked kindly.

I nodded again and he helped me into bed, tucking me in like a child. I noticed with some satisfaction that Lucy was not at all happy.

I drifted off into a fitful sleep and found myself in a dark, claustrophobic tunnel, desperately searching for something very important. But, try as I might, I couldn't remember what it was. Each time I came close to its discovery it turned to dust and I was left worrying, knowing that it was imperative that I remembered what it was I was looking for.

I awoke some time around mid-afternoon to find Dan at the bedroom door with bread and soup. Setting the tray on the bedside table, he sat on the edge of the bed and felt my forehead again, telling me that he believed the worst of the fever had passed. He encouraged me to have some food and watched attentively as I slowly dunked the roll into the tomato soup and tried a few mouthfuls. I lay back exhausted.

"Mads, what you said earlier," Dan said. "About us having sex . . ." He seemed truly uncomfortable. "We didn't."

"I can't explain it then," I sighed.

"I mean," Dan continued falteringly. "We couldn't have. You see, Luce won't let me out of her sight."

I gave him a long look.

"You're not complaining are you, Dan?"

"Hell, no! I mean she's great and we get on really well."

I ignored the voice inside my head saying that we, too, had got on really well.

"It's just, sometimes, well, she's . . ."

He hesitated, looking for the right words.

"She won't leave you alone?" I volunteered, surprised that she hadn't already appeared at the doorway.

"Well yes, that. But, no, that's not all of it! Oh, this is kind of awkward." He looked embarrassed and took a deep breath before continuing. "Luce is extremely fit. I don't have the energy for anyone else."

Dear exhausted Dan!

"Well at least you won't have to renew your gym membership," I said.

He laughed. "That sounds more like my Mads. Are you OK now? We need to be on the road soon. Shall I let Brian know you're feeling unwell and ask him to keep an eye on you?"

I shook my head.

Although I was still reeling from the sadness I had felt earlier I put on a brave face and said, "Don't worry about me. I'll survive."

He leant towards me and kissed me tenderly on the forehead. "My sweet Mads." His long fingers tenderly stroked my hair.

A clearing of the throat just outside the door announced that Lucy had been eavesdropping. "Are you ready, Dan?" she called brightly.

"Coming!"

He smiled down at me as Lucy stuck her head around the door. In a sickeningly patronising tone she said, "It was nice meeting you, Mads, and staying in your sweet little cottage."

I cringed.

"But, darling," she paused dramatically. "*Do* take it easy!"

I was instantly incensed. I hated anyone calling me 'darling'—unless, of course, I was their darling—especially by someone of my own age. She smiled at me, a false, sickly sweet smile, before turning and heading downstairs.

"Bye kiddo, I'll be in touch."

Dan was trying hard not to laugh.

"Glad you're so entertained," I muttered through gritted teeth.

He burst out laughing and followed Lucy downstairs.

Early December

Christmas drew ever nearer and Brian asked me to increase my hours and work a couple of mid-week lunchtime sessions in addition to covering Sunday lunches. I was pleased to have the extra work as the recent experience at the cottage had left me feeling unaccountably bereft and unsettled. I phoned my parents and arranged to visit them in Dublin for a week over Christmas. It would be a sociable family event. Our family extended the length and breadth of Southern Ireland and the O'Briens knew how to celebrate. Mo, though, would not be there as she was spending the Christmas period with a boyfriend in New York. I was sad to hear this as I wanted to see her again, but I phoned her and she promised to visit between assignments early in the new year.

"Are you OK sis?" she asked just before we said goodbye. "You sound kind of flat."

"I'm fine!" I said, brightly. "It's just . . ." I hesitated, took a deep breath and soldiered on. "There are some things happening here in the cottage. They're not freaking me out but I need to speak to you about them. Not over the phone, though."

Mo fell silent at the other end. She was a very sensitive soul, which explained why her photography had a different, ethereal quality to it; when comparing her photographs to those of other photographers, her images often captured a unique vision. Being a true Irish family,

The Forgotten Promise

we children had been brought up on Ireland's various myths and legends and these had always resonated very deeply, particularly with Mo. We naturally accepted the fact that it was she who was the member of our family who could tap into abilities that the rest of us did not possess. I wouldn't actually use the word 'psychic' but Mo saw the world we inhabited on a different level.

"If these things don't worry you then you're meant to be there," she said carefully.

"They don't worry me, as such, but they are emotionally draining."

"Has anyone else experienced anything?" she asked.

"Well, I've heard rumours," I said, thinking of Bill's sister's friend. "But Dan's stayed over and he's never picked up on anything."

I had told her about Dan and Lucy descending upon me.

"Probably because his mind's on other things!" she said in a gently sarcastic tone.

I snorted.

"Can you speak to anyone about this?" she continued.

"I don't know." I thought of all the people I had met since coming to Walditch and, surprisingly, Nick Corbin sprang to mind. But I didn't know him. "I don't think so."

"Oh why am I going away for Christmas?" Mo exclaimed. "Such bad timing!"

"Because you really fancy Jeff?" I suggested.

"Well, yes, there's that!" she laughed.

"Don't worry about me, I'll be all right."

"Look, Mads, if things get too much then move into a B&B or go stay with friends. I promise I'll come to Dorset as soon as I can."

"OK Mo. Thanks. Oh, and don't do anything I wouldn't do in New York!"

"Well, that leaves me with huge scope then," she laughed and we wished each other a Happy Christmas.

Later, I drove into Dorchester and had an enjoyable afternoon rummaging through several antique shops. I didn't find what I was looking for but I did find something I wasn't expecting. As I walked back to the car park, I passed a passageway leading to a cobbled courtyard. A board listed a selection of shops not immediately obvious from the high street. Always curious, I walked down the alleyway and discovered a collection of interesting craftspeople; a glass designer, a potter, an art gallery, a fabric studio and, in the far corner, a shop selling pine furniture.

I gazed through the window of the art gallery and decided that a picture on display would be a fitting Christmas present for my sister, Martha. I entered the shop and a bell hanging above the door announced my arrival. It was bright in the gallery. All the walls and shelf units had been painted white and the various pictures on display were carefully lit by rows of mini spotlights. Occasional, strategically placed, large-leafed plants cleverly broke up the white canvas.

A smartly dressed young girl appeared from the depths of the shop and I asked to see the painting. As she lifted it out of the window display she explained that the artist lived locally and was well-known for her oil paintings of Dorset landscapes but was now experimenting with abstracts such as this one using an acrylic medium. I could already see the picture hanging in my sister's living room and so, without further ado, I said I would buy it. While she wrapped the picture, I perused the other paintings and various objet d'art displayed around the gallery and purchased a small, bronze, moon-gazing hare for my mother. I paid for my purchases, thanked the girl and stepped out into the courtyard with my packages.

"Hello," a voice with a soft Dorset accent said to my right. "I thought it was you. What brings you to town?"

I turned and there was Nick Corbin leaning against the door of the furniture store. My eyes took in the scene in an instant. Casually dressed in jeans and sweatshirt, I noticed he was covered in a light dusting of wood shavings.

"Hi!" I responded, flustered.

He smiled.

"Well? So what *does* bring you to town?" he repeated the question, eyes twinkling.

"I—I was looking for something," I spluttered.

I felt my cheeks burn and, frantically, hoped he didn't think I had come into town to check him out.

He raised an eyebrow. "And what something was that?" he teased, amusement creasing the corners of his mouth.

"Oh . . ." I took a deep breath and gained some composure. "I'm looking for a door for a bread oven but none of the shops I've visited have had anything suitable."

"You need to visit Jamie's reclamation yard."

In the quiet of the courtyard I was again struck by a familiarity, but still couldn't quite place it.

"It's just out of town. He always has a number of interesting objects," Nick continued. "Come in and I'll find his card for you."

He turned and disappeared through the open doorway. Obediently, I followed.

The shop consisted of two rooms leading off each other. The smaller, front room had been laid out as a showroom with select items on display, while the second, larger room was stacked with various pieces of furniture in differing stages of completion. An intense smell of pine pervaded the air mingled with a vanilla scent, which I discovered emanated from half-a-dozen candles arranged on a large Welsh dresser. The space was light and airy due to the full width window to the front of the shop. The back room had French doors that opened onto a small paved courtyard in the centre of which stood a smooth, wooden sculpture standing about four feet tall—an impression of a woman and two children holding hands and dancing in a circle. Beyond this, on the far side of the courtyard I noticed a further building.

Noticing my line of vision, Nick said, "That's the workshop where all the sweaty stuff takes place. It keeps these rooms dust-free . . . well, relatively!"

He glanced at the shavings on his arms and laughed, and suddenly I was filled with an unaccountable happiness at the sound.

Rifling through a drawer of papers he announced, "Ah, here it is."

With my cheeks burning ever more fiercely he handed me his friend's business card.

"Are you in a hurry or have you time for coffee?" he asked.

"Coffee would be great."

I carefully placed my precious packages on the floor and concentrated hard on the business card. It was unlike me to be so 'at sea'. Nick smiled and his gaze lingered on me for a moment before he turned and walked through an open doorway into a small, side kitchen. He either hadn't noticed the colour of my cheeks or had kindly chosen not to comment. I watched as he switched on a kettle, spooned coffee into a couple of mugs and produced a carton of milk from the fridge. It was so easy to watch him; he was so easy on the eye. I hoped I wasn't staring.

"That's lucky," he said. "Just enough milk for two. Must have known I was going to have company!"

I removed my jacket and, dragging my eyes away from him, looked out of the French doors at the sculpture.

"That's beautiful!"

"Thanks. Glad you like it."

"What wood is it?"

It had a wonderful mellow quality.

"Yew. From the grounds of The Hyde, the care home in Walditch," he explained.

I wondered if it had been modelled on anyone in particular and remembered that I needed to check out the ring situation. He came into the room with two mugs of coffee and, as he handed me one, I surreptitiously glanced at his left hand. Instantly—and ridiculously—I was relieved to see that there was neither a ring nor an impression of one. He pulled up a couple of chairs and invited me to sit.

"The home had a few trees come down in high winds a couple of years back," he explained. "They offered me the yew as they know I like to work with different wood."

"Is it one piece?" I asked.

He nodded. Indicating to the furniture in the room, he said, "I do this to pay the bills but my first love is sculpture."

I was feeling ludicrously shy. Me, an Irish girl who had kissed the Blarney Stone several times during her life!

Frantically, I searched my mind for something intelligent to say, but I was falling into a paralysing mental fog.

Thankfully he broke the silence. "So, how's the waitressing coming along?"

I looked up and saw the merriment in his eyes.

"They've put me back behind the bar. Much safer!"

He laughed and asked, "It's obvious from your lilt that you don't come from this neck of the woods. What's blown you our way?"

"A feeling," I said, surprised at my honesty.

He looked at me curiously. "A feeling? That sounds interesting."

I found myself telling him about the months I'd spent filming in Dorset and how The Olde Smithy had spoken to me. "It just seemed meant to be," I explained. "The whole process was so easy that before I knew it I was its new owner"

"Time to put down roots, maybe?"

"Yes, I think so."

I looked at the small amount of coffee left in my mug and wondered how long I could string out this serendipitous meeting.

"I've always lived around here," he said, without any regret in his voice. And then in an exaggerated Dorset accent, he added, "Us Corbins go back centuries in these 'ere parts."

"That's so nice not having to wander the world looking for work but making it happen in your own county of birth," I responded.

He looked at me thoughtfully before asking, "And where were you born?"

I told him about being brought up in Dublin and how I'd followed my dream into film and TV and how this had

The Forgotten Promise

eventually brought me to London. And, as the minutes ticked by, I became aware of a deep sense of well-being and a delicious peace settling upon my soul.

The mug of coffee was long since empty when the phone rang. Nick glanced at his watch and quickly rose to answer it.

"Didn't notice the time," he said into the mouthpiece. "See you in twenty."

He replaced the receiver and, turning to me, said, "I'm late and will have some explaining to do!"

Ludicrously, my heart sank.

He held out his hand for my mug. I handed it to him and rose to my feet, hoping that my face wouldn't betray me and give away my heightened emotions.

I recalled that the Bridport Arts & Crafts group had arranged their Christmas gathering early because he wouldn't be around over Christmas. To mask my disappointment I asked, "When are you off to Australia?"

"The nineteenth."

Ten days, I thought.

"Can't wait. Visiting my brother," he explained as he put the empty mugs in the sink. "Now there's a guy who couldn't settle locally. Moved to the Gold Coast as soon as he'd scraped enough money together and been there ever since."

As he switched off the lights, I put on my jacket and picked up the packages. He shrugged on a refer jacket before following me out into the main courtyard and locked the door. It was past 6pm and the other shops were in darkness but an old-fashioned lamp post cast its yellow light across the cobbled yard. There was a brisk chill to the early evening air and I hunched deeply into my jacket, zipping it up to the neck. In companionable silence we walked up the alleyway and emerged out onto the high street where a passing couple stopped and greeted him. They chatted briefly, the girl coolly looking me up and down, and as the couple walked away she linked arms with the man and looked back over her shoulder.

"Don't forget Greg's on Friday, Nick," she called out brightly.

"I haven't Becky. See you there."

Turning to me, he motioned to his right. "My car's this way."

"Oh, I'm in the car park," I said, looking in the opposite direction. "Thanks for the coffee."

Suddenly I felt very awkward and before I knew what I was doing, offered him my hand to shake. He didn't accept it but simply smiled.

Walking backwards away from me down the street, he said, "Don't forget to give Jamie a ring."

I worked the following lunchtime shift. It was busy and by the time I finished it was mid-afternoon. I walked back to the cottage and stood by the phone, breathing deeply; trying to calm my nerves. Twice I picked up the phone and punched in part of the number before chickening out. Ridiculous! Quickly—before I had a chance to change my mind—I phoned the number printed on the business card, half-hoping there would be no reply.

"Nick Corbin."

His lovely soft voice resonated deep within me and I tried to catch the thought frustratingly teasing my subconscious.

"Hello Nick. Maddie O'Brien here."

"Hi Maddie. You got back OK?"

"Oh yes, thanks. No problem."

I had expected hesitation while he tried to remember who I was. He had wrong-footed me again!

"What can I do for you?"

"I need a carpenter," I said, and was immediately devastated at how upfront that sounded.

"Well, you've phoned the right number!" Once again I heard the amusement in his voice.

My cheeks began to burn.

"I've got a faulty window which lets in the weather and I'm also looking for a small dining table and chairs," I explained in a rush. "I was hoping to sort it before you depart for sunnier climes."

"Four or six seater?" he asked.

"A small six if possible. If not, a largish four would do."

"No trouble. I've got a couple tucked away out back. Good weight chairs too. I'll have to come out and measure up for the window, though. I could bring the table and chairs with me then. When's a good time for you?"

I paused, trying not to sound too eager and pretending to work out when would be the best time.

"Well, let me see. I'm working tomorrow lunchtime but any time after that would be fine."

He said he'd visit the following day as soon as he'd closed up shop and I explained where the cottage was. After he'd rung off I stood in the courtyard outside the back door to cool down.

I had been standing there for about three minutes, deep in thought, when I heard Storm hissing and growling a warning. He had been happily eating from his bowl in the corner of the kitchen but now stood with tail erect, hackles raised, staring through the doorway into the sitting room.

"Storm," I said soothingly. "What is it?"

The growling turned more insistent. I walked towards the doorway and looked through. The room was empty. The cat continued to stare intently towards the corner of the room by the bread oven, growling softly.

"Storm. What do you see?"

I moved through the doorway into the sitting room and was immediately struck by the silence.

Who are you? I silently asked of the empty room.

The room appeared to be shrouded in a fine fog and to my heightened senses there seemed to be a slight vibration in the air. Once again, I found myself drawn to the hidden alcove and I put my hand inside, my fingers searching. I felt the floor of the oven and around the walls as far as my arm could reach but, as before, there was nothing there.

"What are you trying to show me?" I said out loud.

As soon as I spoke the words, the sounds of the world returned and the room cleared of mist. Looking back through the kitchen door I saw that Storm had returned to his bowl, his coat, once more, sleek against his body.

I perched on the arm of the chair. I definitely needed to find out more about the history of The Olde Smithy. I shivered as I remembered Dan saying the cottage would give up more of its secrets as time went by, and then I thought of Dan and sadly realised that I missed him.

The following morning I awoke in high excitement. I worked the lunchtime shift at the pub merely going through the motions and with a sense of increasing anxiety. By the time the afternoon drew to a close I was feeling decidedly agitated. At around 5pm I heard a van pull up on the green and, looking out of the window, saw

Nick striding towards the cottage. My heart raced. Taking a deep breath, I opened the front door and forced a smile.

"Hi," he greeted me casually.

"Come in."

I moved back from the door so that he could enter and there he stood; Nick Corbin in *my* hallway. I turned and he followed me into the dining room.

"I love these old cottages," he said, looking around appreciatively. "They're so solidly built and honest."

I agreed, noticing that he wasn't as tall as Dan and didn't have the same trouble with the beams.

"This is where I want the table to go," I explained.

He nodded.

"I hope the one you've brought will fit." What a stupid thing to say!

"It will," he replied, a wry smile on his face. "But if you're not happy with it I'll make you another. After all, the customer is always right." He looked across at the glass room divide. "That's fantastic."

Partly separating the dining and sitting rooms was a large internal window made up of small-paned, leaded stained-glass, the different colours creating a subtle mood in each room.

He walked towards it and touched it lightly. "This is very old glass."

"I don't know much about it but the estate agents played heavily on it in their sales particulars."

"If you want to know more about its origins the glass maker next door to me would be able to help. Pru has a wealth of knowledge."

He ran his hand gently over the glass and I shivered involuntarily, imagining what it would be like to feel that touch. He glanced at me and, quickly, I suggested we brought in the table and chairs from his van. True to his word, the table fitted just fine and the solid pine chairs had smartly upholstered seats in a blue and cream striped fabric. I was pleased with the over-all effect.

"Would you like a cup of tea, or something stronger perhaps?"

Nick was carrying the last chair in from the van, a writing pad, steel tape and pen balanced on its seat. He set the chair down and glanced at his watch.

"Better not. I'm pushed for time tonight. I'll just measure up the window and see what I can do for you."

I masked my disappointment. He followed me upstairs and, shyly, I pushed open the door to the bedroom. Almost mockingly, the bed seemed to loom hugely and fill the room. Once again, I felt the start of a blush.

"Great use of space," he commented as he looked around the room which had been created within the roof space.

"It is good, isn't it? I'm short of storage space though."

Stacked against one wall were packing cases filled with clothes still looking for a home.

"You could easily fit a wardrobe in under the eaves," he suggested, indicating the far wall under the sloping ceiling. "That would work. Now, which window is the problem?"

I pointed to the one overlooking the courtyard and Nick started to measure up, opening the offending casement and jotting down a series of calculations on his pad.

"It's great to see you've still got wooden windows. So many of these cottages have had the life modernised out of them."

The Forgotten Promise

He leant out of the window and strained, peering up towards the roof. "This cottage was probably thatched at one point."

"Do you think so?" I asked, savouring the fit, muscular outline of his body.

"You can tell from the height and pitch of the roof." He came back inside and closed the window. Glancing at his calculations he said, "I can do one of two things. I can either shave off the inner edge of this window, the two openers will sit snugly together then and keep out the worst of the weather for the time being—I'll pack out the hinges to compensate. Or I can make you a new window but I won't be able to do that until after Christmas."

My thought processes were lightning-quick. Realising that if I asked him to 'make good' and then think about having a new window on his return from Australia, I would at least have the excuse of seeing him again before he departed as well as on his return. I was just about to ask him to do that when his mobile rang. Fishing it out of his back pocket, he glanced at the screen and, turning his back to me, looked out of the window.

"Hi."

Inexplicably, I felt agitated.

"No, I'm in Walditch. Shouldn't be too long, I'm almost done here." He looked back at me and smiled.

That smile!

"Yeah, OK. I'll pick up a bottle." He put the phone back in his pocket. "Sorry about that."

Casually, I gestured that it was nothing but my mind raced with a thousand questions, desperate to know who would be sharing that bottle.

"So, if I come over Monday after work I can get you weather-tight?" he questioned.

"That would be great, Nick. Thanks."

He followed me downstairs and I thanked him again for delivering the table and chairs.

"No trouble." He handed me his invoice and I noticed the stylised writing. There was something about Nick which reminded me of an older, more chivalrous era and it came as no surprise that the letters were carefully formed, resonating of a time when these things mattered.

I wrote out a cheque and handed it to him.

I said goodbye and stood at the door, watching as he walked across the village green. He climbed into his van and, as he drove away from the curb, Nick looked back at me and smiled.

Second week in December

Monday seemed an age away and so I decided to busy myself in the cottage and further expose the inglenook oven. I searched the outhouse for a bucket in which to collect the stone and noticed Storm busy devouring a mouse at the back of the potting shed.

"And you always make out you're so hungry!"

I started working away at the stones around the already exposed entrance. The stonework was tight and I used a wallpaper scraper and screwdriver to dislodge the render, these being the only implements to hand. As the minutes passed by, the stones began to work loose and by early afternoon there was a definite opening measuring approximately twelve inches square. And all the time I was aware of a curious, rising excitement.

I stopped work to make a drink and heard Storm scratching at the back door. As I opened the door, he rushed in and dropped the remains of the mouse at my feet just as the phone started to ring. I was thanking Storm for my gift as I answered it.

"Hi Maddie. Has someone brought you a present?" It was Dan's sister.

"Caro! So good to hear from you." I reached across the room and deposited the remains of the mouse in the swing bin. "Oh, just the cat bringing me an extremely mauled mouse."

"Very thoughtful! Is that a delicacy in your part of the world?" She laughed.

"I'm not that desperate yet!" I replied. "The pub feeds me quite well, you know."

We chatted for a while and she asked what I was doing for Christmas and seemed relieved when I said I was visiting family in Dublin.

"I'll be back for New Year's Eve, though. Brian's asked me to work that evening. Double pay, which will be useful."

Apologetically, she informed me that Dan and Lucy were spending Christmas with her and I experienced a sharp twinge of regret.

"How is Dan?" I asked. "I hardly ever get a phone call from him now."

"That doesn't surprise me, Maddie. We don't see much of him anymore but when we do I'm always shocked at how shattered he looks."

I remembered what Dan had said. Poor, dear exhausted Dan!

"Hope he's getting what he wants out of that relationship," I said.

"So far he hasn't complained, at least not to me," Caro replied. "And John and he talk quite openly and nothing's been mentioned. But I do worry about the swiftness of it all, Maddie. It seems that as soon as Lucy arrived in London she moved in with him, though Dan says otherwise."

I groaned inwardly. Dan had always been so protective of his space. This sounded permanent.

We changed the subject and she promised to come and visit me in the spring. We chatted a while longer before she wished me a Happy Christmas and said farewell, promising to be in touch early in the New Year.

Sadly, I thought of Dan and realised how fortunate I had been to have him as a friend and lover for all those years. Lucy would ensure that the distance between us now grew. How mockingly cruel hindsight can be; I had not fully appreciated how lucky I had been.

To rid me of these thoughts I returned to the bread oven and, with mounting feverishness, started to remove the debris from its base into the bucket. I swept the oven clean and stood back to admire my handiwork. I had discovered precisely nothing and felt an unaccountable overwhelming despair and anti-climax. Sternly telling myself that I should not be prey to these unchecked emotions, I found the business card Nick had given me and, picking up the phone, punched in the number.

"Strippers," announced a heavy smoker's voice.

I laughed. "Hi, is that Jamie?"

"Jamie Langdon. How can I help?"

I explained that Nick had suggested I phone him and asked if he had any bread oven doors amongst his stock.

"Got a few. Just done a reclamation over Bockhampton way. Different sizes too."

"That sounds promising. Where exactly is your yard?"

He gave me directions and I arranged to go over the following day.

It had started raining again and the wind had picked up. With nothing better to do, I whiled away a couple of hours in the bath and later, with hair dried and lounging around in my dressing gown, I made supper and watched television with Storm on my lap. There was little of interest and at around 9pm, having flicked through the channels several times, I decided to go to bed and read. Storm immediately jumped off my lap and rushed upstairs. And so we settled in my cosy bedroom, the cat curled up contentedly on the bed, the bedside lamp casting a warm glow across the room and the towel at the window billowing as ferocious gusts of wind found their way through the gap in the casement. It was shortly after 9.30pm when Storm suddenly looked up and stared intently at the bedroom door, his ears pricked and alert; his fur beginning to bristle.

I laid the book face down, splayed open on the bed, and stroked him soothingly but he shook off my caress, listening keenly, a low growl resonating from deep within his throat. The bedside light flickered and suddenly dimmed and I noticed the luminous green numbers of the digital clock displaying 21:33. I could still hear the rain hammering on the windows but an impenetrable stillness seemed to linger thick in the air. Curiously, even though the wind still gusted furiously outside, the towel now hung motionless on its pole.

And then I heard them—footsteps on the stairs.

My senses heightened and I sat very still, every fibre in my body straining; my hearing acute. Who, or what, was in the cottage coming up the stairs?

A sudden chill in the air and I felt the hairs prick on the back of my neck. I shivered and broke out into a cold, clammy sweat, my heart racing and the blood coursing through my veins. But, underlying my fear, I was aware of a sense of ever-increasing anticipation.

I held my breath, counting each footstep—six, seven, eight and nine. The tension in the room was palpable. Who was out there? As if in slow motion I turned towards the door, bracing myself and waited for it to open. But it remained firmly closed.

The Forgotten Promise

Storm was still staring at the door, growling quietly. Slipping out of bed, I stood at the door undecided as to what to do next. Holding my breath, I strained to hear any noise from the other side of the door but there was no sound. Slowly and quietly I lifted the latch and opened the door half-an-inch. I couldn't see anyone through the crack so, tentatively, I opened the door a fraction wider. There was no-one there. I walked out onto the landing and switched on the light before opening the door to the spare bedroom. The room was empty. I went downstairs and searched every room—nothing!

I stood in the centre of the sitting room and, looking in the direction of the bread oven, whispered, "Who are you? What do you want with me?"

The silence was deafening. Whoever, or whatever, had gone.

I stood there a while longer, the cold air nipping at my heels, and slowly made my way upstairs again. I had been downstairs maybe ten minutes but as I climbed into bed I noticed the clock—21:35.

"That can't be!" I said out loud.

Perhaps the bedside light had dimmed because of an interruption to the electricity supply, I thought. Maybe this had stopped the clock, but then the digital reading would have re-set to zero.

Suddenly the display changed to 21:36.

Storm was still on the bed, relaxed once again; his coat lying smooth and sleek against his body. I stroked him and he stretched, stood up, circled once and then immediately settled again, curling up with one paw over his face.

Wondering why this latest twist had filled me with such anticipation, over-riding my fear, I burrowed deep within the duvet and tried to concentrate on reading. It was still blowing a gale and I noticed how the towel had resumed its billowing at the window.

I must have fallen asleep as I awoke sometime around 3am to find the lamp still on, the book open on the pillow. I closed the book, placed it on the bedside cabinet and switched off the light. Turning onto my side, I moved Storm slightly with my feet, to which he grunted his disapproval, and a dream-filled sleep soon came to me. Something to do with Lucy, Dan and me. By the time the alarm went off at 7.30am I awoke exhausted and unable to recall the dream.

Couldn't have been important, I thought dismissively.

After breakfast I drove to Winterborne Monkton under a grey, overcast sky which threatened rain. The journey took me through stunning, hilly countryside between Bridport and Dorchester, past the old fort at Chilcombe Hill. On reaching Winterbourne Abbas I turned off towards Winterborne Monkton, following Jamie's directions. I took the road that skirted the hill with Maiden Castle at its summit—the largest fortified Iron Age Hill Fort in Britain dating back more than two thousand years—and turned right down a farm lane. After approximately five hundred yards the lane rounded a bend and emerged into a yard surrounded by a magnificent range of stone barns nestling in a fold of the hills. Above a doorway hung a sign. '*STRIPPERS Salvage & Reclamation*'. I parked next to the only other vehicle in the car park, a battered yellow van that had definitely seen better days.

The yard was littered with objects—a statue here, a bedstead there—and as I picked my way towards the doorway an Alsatian appeared in the entrance, watching my approach. I hesitated.

"Satan, come here!" growled a deep voice from within.

Satan. Great!

The dog turned and retreated and I gingerly peered through the doorway. The barn was enormous. Open to the rafters two floors above, it was crammed full of a vast array of salvage. Through the gloom, I saw a man sitting at a desk against the far wall with the dog at his feet.

"Hi. Jamie?" I called.

The man looked up. "That's me."

Aged about sixty, he wore his silver hair tied in a pony tail and I thought he wouldn't have looked out of place hanging out with the Rolling Stones. Dressed in denim jeans, a black fleece jacket, woollen fingerless gloves and a bohemian-style scarf casually slung around his neck, he was well wrapped up against the cold of the barn. As I walked towards him I noticed the twinkle in the beady blue eyes that surveyed me from his lived-in, weather-beaten face. What was it about these Dorset guys? It seemed as if they all shared a secret joke.

I explained that I'd phoned yesterday and was looking for a bread oven door. He motioned me to follow him through a doorway into another vast barn, again stacked high with reclaimed material, and told me not to worry about Satan.

"He's a pussy cat!" he explained.

I stared at the dog. It stared back.

"I only named him that to deter any overly interested visitors," Jamie continued. "It seems to work."

And Satan did prove to be a real softy. He stayed close, accompanying us through the barns, his wet nose occasionally nudging me for attention.

I followed Jamie past neat rows of architectural salvage—paving stones, cast iron baths, ancient wooden doors, old fireplaces—and then he stopped at a stack of slates and scratched his head. "They're round here somewhere."

We turned down a narrow pathway between the slates and, propped on low beams, a collection of stone gargoyles followed us with their cold, unseeing eyes. On reaching the rear alleyway he pointed to a row of old oven doors neatly stacked against the back wall.

"There's fancy ones and plain ones, little ones and large," the man explained in his gravelly voice. "What size are you after?"

I explained it was an approximate twelve-inch opening and he pointed to a few that might fit. Leaving me to examine them, he called to his dog and walked back to the main barn.

One door immediately caught my eye. Adorned with a shield depicting three horseshoes and three nails, I thought it very suitable for The Olde Smithy. Picking it up, I turned it over in my hands. It was heavy and in good condition, the black-coloured lead hardly marked. I checked out the other doors on display but there were no others as befitting. I had found what I was looking for. I checked out the remaining salvage in that barn and knew that this was not a one-off visit; Satan and I were to become well-acquainted.

Walking back into the main barn, Jamie was once again sitting at his desk with the dog at his feet. He was rolling a cigarette but stopped to clear some space on his desk so that I could write out a cheque for my purchase.

"So you know Nick Corbin then?" He studied me curiously as he ran his tongue in one smooth lick down the length of the paper.

The Forgotten Promise

I felt a warm glow that the man had suggested I knew Nick, as if I somehow belonged to his inner circle. "Yes. He recommended you."

"Good bloke that Nick. Salt of the earth."

I was ridiculously happy that this man should think so and agreed enthusiastically, even though I didn't have a clue whether Nick was a *'good bloke'* or not.

The sound of a car pulling up in the yard and then voices, as doors opened and slammed shut, prompted Satan to get up from where he lay. Walking to the open doorway the dog stood and looked out into the yard; this was obviously a favourite pastime. I thanked Jamie for the oven door and said I would be back. He nodded and watched me as I walked towards the door while calling Satan to come away from the door.

The weekend dragged by, even though I worked at the pub on both evenings plus the Sunday lunchtime shift. I was jittery and on edge and knew it was because I wanted Monday evening to arrive. Brian asked me if everything was all right as I seemed distracted and I attempted to pull myself together and concentrate on the job in hand, but it was hard-going. Janet's cousin, Bill, came in with his girlfriend on the Sunday and was embarrassed to see me behind the bar, so I made it easy for him. I assured him that the car was running well and that I was happy with my purchase. Not once did he refer to our conversation about the cottage though I knew it was on the tip of his tongue. At one point he took Janet aside and whispered something to her. She looked across at me with a quizzical look, but nothing was said.

That evening, still in an unsettled mood and wanting the next day to arrive quickly, I had a light supper and went early to bed. But sleep evaded me and I lay there, my mind racing. I tried to steer my thoughts away from Nick. I told myself that I didn't know anything about him and even though he seemed a really nice guy I should try and subdue my feelings until I found out more—easier said than done! My thoughts then, sadly, turned to Dan and I resolved to phone him. Even if he didn't think about me anymore, Lucy couldn't stop me from contacting him. This, in turn, brought me around to thinking about Dan's friend, the eco publisher, and I made a resolution to contact him in early January to discuss the possibility of submitting 'green' articles with a Dorset bias.

And then I heard them again. Footsteps on the stairs.

I glanced at the flickering numbers of the bedside clock—21.33—and, holding my breath, counted six, seven, eight and nine. I looked towards the door, half-expecting it to open but, of course, it didn't. I switched on the light, checked the spare room and then went downstairs and checked all the other rooms. Again, nothing.

Frantic scratching at the back door made me jump but it was merely Storm announcing his return. He marched in, prickly with indignation.

"Sorry boy. Didn't hear you out there."

He ignored me and immediately went to investigate his bowl. I switched off the lights and mounted the stairs, subconsciously counting the treads as I went. I stopped on step nine and stood there for an age, the hairs pricking the back of my neck. There was still one more step to go.

Tentatively, I asked, "Who are you?"

But there was no reply, not even a whisper.

Next morning it was raining again. Storm had forgiven me for locking him out the previous evening and enthusiastically joined in with the decorating, chasing strips of wallpaper around the room. I was working on the last papered wall in the dining room when the phone rang. Breathlessly, I answered it.

"Hi Maddie, it's Nick," said that lovely soft voice. "Hope I'm not interrupting anything?"

"Oh," I was taken aback.

"Hoped you'd be home," he continued. "I've finished early tonight and wondered if I could come over now?"

"Oh!" I said again, and glanced at my watch.

"If it's not convenient I can come another time?"

"Oh!"

This was getting ridiculous. Get a grip!

"No. I mean, yes, it's fine!"

He laughed and, maddeningly, I started to colour up.

I heard the amusement in his voice as he said, "I'll see you in half-an-hour then."

I replaced the receiver and thought he must think me a gibbering fool. To try and calm my nerves, I returned to stripping wallpaper and it was some minutes later that it occurred to me I was probably looking a mess. I downed tools and ran to the bathroom and looked in the mirror. Oh great! I was wearing a paint-splattered work shirt and there were scrapings of wallpaper stuck to my face and bits trapped in my hair. I washed my face and was trying to remove the paper from my hair when there was a knock at the door. Noticing the heightened colour in my cheeks, I pulled a face at my reflection before walking to the front door. With a deep breath I opened it, as nonchalantly as I could.

There he stood, mobile phone in hand, all bunched up in his jacket against the weather, trying to shelter from the rain under the small canopy above the front door.

"Hi," I said, standing back to let him in.

"What weather!" he exclaimed as he crossed the threshold. "Can't wait to get to the other side of the world."

I took his jacket, shook the worst of the rain from it and hung it on a hook in the hall.

Looking at me closely, he said, "You've obviously been busy!"

"Yes, nearly finished. Come and see."

Feeling the beginnings of a blush brought on by his scrutiny, I quickly turned and walked through to the dining room. He followed and placed his mobile phone on the pine table.

"Looks like you're winning," he said.

He glanced around and, seeing the impression of the other staircase clearly outlined on the wall, moved closer to investigate. Turning, he walked to the window which overlooked the village green and looked back at the opposite wall.

"You know, the original doorway was probably here," he indicated the window. "There was probably a narrow passageway running from front to back with these stairs leading up to an upper room."

"Do you think this is the original staircase then?" I asked quietly.

"Could be. They were much steeper in earlier centuries. It's only current building regs that demand a shallower tread. The original was probably little more than a glorified ladder."

I stared at the nine risers clearly marked on the wall. The air about me seemed suddenly thick and still and Nick said something but I didn't respond. I couldn't hear a sound. The world seemed to be holding its breath; full of expectation.

He turned and looked at me and in the deepening afternoon gloom it appeared to me that he was that other man, the one I had seen when I first moved into the cottage. But, as swiftly as it happened, the moment passed. It must have been the light playing tricks again.

"What are you going to do with the walls?" Nick was asking.

I regained my composure and answered, "If they're good enough I'll simply paint them. If not I'll plaster them. By the way, I saw your friend Jamie last week."

"Did he have anything of interest?"

"Yes. Look."

He followed me through to the sitting room.

Storm was curled up asleep in the chair by the wood burner, as yet unlit, and I watched as Nick gently stroked him. The cat sleepily opened one eye and coolly surveyed him.

"Cracking cat!" he commented.

I showed him the bread oven door, which I had propped against the wall beneath the opening. He picked it up and carefully turned it over in his strong, capable craftsman's hands, examining it with an appreciate eye.

"It's in good condition. I think this shield is part of the Worshipful Company of Farriers Coat of Arms."

"Perfect for The Olde Smithy then!"

He agreed and held the door up to the opening. It was a good fit. "How are you going to secure it?" he asked.

"Not sure. I can turn my hand to most things but I don't think my skills extend that far."

I looked through the window towards the pub on the other side of the green.

"Brian said he could point me in the direction of several tradesmen so I'll probably ask him."

Replacing the door on the hearth, Nick turned to me and announced that he had better get on with the job he had come to do. I suggested I made tea while he did so and he agreed, saying that he took his tea white with one sugar. I busied myself in the kitchen and he disappeared upstairs. I heard him switch on the light in the bedroom and then curse under his breath. The next minute he reappeared in the hallway.

"Everything OK?" I asked.

Looking sheepish, he raised his eyebrows and said, "Left my tool bag in the van!"

Searching through the pockets of his jacket hanging in the hall, he fished out a set of keys, opened the front door and sprinted across the green through the rain. I was waiting for the kettle to boil when his mobile rang. Glancing out of the front window, I couldn't see Nick anywhere, so I walked through to the dining room and picked it up.

"Hello. Nick's phone."

Silence.

"Hello?" I repeated.

"Where's Nick?" asked a female voice with a strong, local accent.

I looked through the window again but still couldn't see him.

"In his van, I think."

"Tell him the travel agent's just phoned, will you? The flight's been brought forward two hours and we need to be at Heathrow by six."

My heart pounding, I said I would pass the message on. There followed a long pause.

"What did you say your name was?" she asked.

I hadn't.

"Maddie. Nick's doing a job for me."

There was another long hesitation. "Bye then," she said.

I replaced the phone on the table and walked back to the kitchen, desperate to know who the caller was. Distractedly, I noticed that it had at last stopped raining. Was she his sister? It was feasible that he was going to visit his brother in Australia with family—I hoped—or was she his girlfriend? A guy like Nick couldn't be single. Frustrated, I cursed myself for being a slave to these unguarded emotions.

A blast of cold air and Nick came through the front door carrying his tool bag, followed by a flurry of leaves. He looked windswept and I had an overwhelming urge to gather him up in my arms.

"Sometimes I think I could lose my head!" he exclaimed, taking the stairs two treads at a time.

I finished making the tea, walked slowly upstairs and opened the bedroom door. He stood on the far side of the room, having unscrewed the ill-fitting casement and was now bending over it, the window secured between his legs. Slowly and rhythmically he was shaving off the offending edge with a plane. I stood and stared. The scene seemed strangely familiar. I noticed the length of his hair, his build, the set of his body, and shivered with a strong sense of déjà vu.

He was absorbed in his work and so I set the mugs of tea on the bedside cabinet. My conversation with the mystery female caller had taken the wind out of my sails and I felt deflated and resigned. I sat on the bed and watched him as he worked. He looked up and smiled as he saw me closely observing him. That smile!

"Maddie," he said, looking down at the window again and concentrating on his rhythm. "Do you have kids?"

"No, why do you ask?"

"I thought I heard a child crying."

I froze.

"Must have been next door," he said.

"Don't think so," I said slowly. "Mrs Tomkins is over seventy."

He laughed and then glanced at me, a puzzled look on his face. "I could have sworn . . ." The sentence petered out.

"Must have been the wind."

Straightening up, he tried the window in the frame. "That should do the trick," he said. "For a while, at least."

He packed out the hinges and while he screwed them in place I mentioned the phone call.

"Your mobile went off earlier. Hope you don't mind, I answered it."

"Who was it?" he asked, without pausing in his work.

"A girl. She didn't give her name."

She had asked for mine, though.

"Apparently your flight's been brought forward two hours."

"Great!" he exclaimed. "That means getting up at some ungodly hour!"

I desperately wanted to ask who she was, but how could I?

"There, how's that?" He stood back and surveyed his work.

I got off the bed and tried the catch. The window opened smoothly and, when closed, sat snugly alongside the other opening casement.

"Looks great to me. Thanks. Now I won't freeze all night."

He smiled and I held out the mug of tea to him. He reached towards it and as he closed his hand around the mug, inadvertently he trapped my fingers beneath his. The bolt of electricity between us was astounding.

"Ouch!"

Jumping back, tea slopped over the edge of the mug onto the floorboards. I looked at him in astonishment and started to laugh nervously.

"Wow!"

Had he felt it too—or was it just me, the gibbering wreck? I tried hard to stop the hysterical laughter.

Shyly, I glanced at him and saw a look in his eyes that I had seen before, here in this very bedroom. He wasn't laughing, just looking at me in that way.

Awkwardly I said, "Harness that if you will!"

I handed him the mug again and, this time, he took it without touching me. We drank the tea in silence, Nick quickly finishing his. Swiftly he put away his tools.

"If you've got a brush I'll sweep up," he offered.

"Don't worry about that. I'll do it later."

The afternoon had long since turned to evening and it was now dark outside.

Looking at his watch he announced, "Guess I'd better be going."

"How much do I owe you?" I asked.

"Nothing. It's a favour." He looked at me with an inscrutable look on his face.

Suddenly I felt very sober, realising that he would now be out of the country for at least a month and then who knows when I would see him again.

I turned towards the door, walked out to the landing and started to descend the stairs. I heard him pick up his tool bag, switch off the light and follow me down. It was cramped in the hallway for two people to stand side by side and, as I took his jacket from the hook by the front door, I was very aware of his presence. He took the jacket from me and appeared to be about to say something but then obviously thought better of it.

"Happy Christmas, Maddie," he said eventually.

"And you too, Nick."

Smiling, he indicated to the bits of wallpaper still caught in my hair.

"By the way, I like the look!"

Reluctantly I opened the front door and let him go out into the cold, wintry night.

Third week in December

I didn't see or speak to Nick again before he left for Australia. I was due to work the evening shift on the day of his departure but asked if I could do the lunchtime shift as well as I was so restless and wanted to be distracted. I couldn't forget that shock of electricity between us. Brian was pleased to have the extra help and was more than happy to oblige. I was still feeling deflated, imagining Nick flying off to the wide open beaches of Australia with a devastatingly beautiful girlfriend and enjoying sun, sea and . . .

I knew I was beating myself up but I couldn't do anything to stop the thoughts. And to make matters worse, the day dawned bright and clear, as if to mock my melancholy humour.

I was busy laying tables when Brian called me over to the bar. "See that family sitting over there by the fire?"

I nodded.

"The old lady's Mrs McKendrick. Used to own your cottage."

I looked across to the people sitting at the table and noticed a petite, smartly dressed, grey-haired lady. She had delicate features and must have been very pretty in her youth. She was flanked by a younger woman who looked remarkably like her and whom I assumed must be her daughter, and a man of a similar age to the woman.

Opposite them sat three cheeky looking boys ranging in ages, the eldest about twelve. They looked a decent family.

"Does she live around here now?" I asked.

"No. Lives with them."

I studied Mrs McKendrick. The estate agent had told me that she had owned the cottage for over thirty years and I wondered if she had ever experienced any unusual happenings there.

"Bet she misses her independence," said Brian.

As we were discussing her, Mrs McKendrick suddenly put down the menu she had been studying and looked over in our direction. Brian immediately started to furiously polish a glass and I busied myself repositioning beer mats on the counter. The man sitting next to her said something to her and then called over, saying that they were ready to place an order.

"Maddie will be with you in a minute," Brian replied.

"Do you think she heard what we were saying?" I asked Brian quietly.

"Doubt it. At her age her hearing's probably shot."

I picked up a pen and notepad from under the bar and dutifully walked over to the group. As I grew closer I realised that Mrs McKendrick's prettiness masked her true age. She was older than she had appeared from a distance and she also seemed fairly frail; a walking stick hung over the back of her chair.

I took their order and all the while she watched me like a hawk, her pale blue eyes never once leaving my face. When I turned to go, she put her hand on my arm and stopped me.

"You live at the cottage don't you, dear?"

Surprised, but assuming that Brian must have said something to her, I replied that if she meant The Olde

The Forgotten Promise

Smithy then, yes, I did and that I'd been there for just under three months.

"Mum and dad used to live there," explained the woman at her side.

I smiled and turned to Mrs McKendrick. "Where do you live now?" I asked the elderly lady.

"With my daughter and her family in Winchester."

"That's nice," I said.

"The stairs got too much for her," said the daughter. "And the boys love having their grandma around."

I looked at the three young lads. They were at an age when they still had time for the older generation.

"Grandma's wick-ed!" said the eldest boy, pronouncing the latter word as two definite syllables.

And not to be outdone, the youngest, aged about five, enthusiastically agreed. "Grandma tells wicked stories."

"How lucky you are!"

I glanced at Mrs McKendrick and wondered what she thought of being described as 'wick-ed'.

Excusing myself from their table, I took the order through to the kitchen before returning to the bar. I served a couple of walkers who had hiked over from Shipton Gorge. They told me that were keen tennis players and had been advised by the owners of the B&B where they were staying that Walditch had a real tennis court. They had come to investigate. While I poured their drinks I gave them directions to the court and explained that I had read that Henry VII had played at the site during his visits to the area.

Sensing someone's eyes on me, I glanced across at the family and saw that Mrs McKendrick was still watching me. I felt uncomfortable under her scrutinising gaze but thought she was probably just curious to see who was now living in her cottage. After all, it had been her home for nearly as long as I'd been alive.

Presently Vera shouted from the kitchen that the McKendricks' order was ready. I took their meals over and the boys started squabbling over which plate had the more chips.

As I took my leave, I said, "Just catch my attention if you want anything."

"Thank you, Mary," replied Mrs McKendrick.

"Maddie," I corrected.

She looked at me, her pale blue eyes seemingly piercing my very soul. "Yes dear. Whatever you say."

I frowned and her son-in-law smiled at me apologetically. I moved away from the group telling myself that she must be a little senile and that was probably the reason why she had gone to live with her daughter and son-in-law. Nevertheless, I felt curiously unsettled.

The pub was getting busier and I served drinks to several customers and took more food orders before returning to the group by the fire. I cleared away the empty plates while the boys studied the menus and decided which desserts they wanted.

"Are you happy at the cottage, dear?" Mrs McKendrick asked.

I felt the question was loaded but didn't want to go into it, especially in front of her grandsons.

"Oh yes," I said lightly. "It immediately felt like home. But you lived there for so long you must have felt that too?"

"Oh no, Mary, it was always your home. We just looked after it."

I was really confused and glanced at her daughter.

"Don't worry about mum, she's a bit, um, unclear these days," she explained, choosing her words with care.

The old lady clicked her tongue but said nothing. She looked up at the painting hanging above the fire.

"You know that's your cottage, don't you?" she said.

I answered that I had guessed it was.

"It's always been a smithy," she continued. "This is it in the 17th Century."

"Not the *actual* smithy, Joyce," interjected the man. "An artist's impression of what it might have looked like at that time!"

I was instantly incensed by his patronising tone but wondered why I felt it was such a personal affront. Mrs McKendrick tutted again. Ignoring her son-in-law's comment, she pointed to the man in the painting.

"And that's the blacksmith."

Looking directly at me, her intense gaze bored right through me. Contrary to what her daughter thought, I realised there was very little about Mrs McKendrick that was 'unclear'.

The oldest boy, following his father's lead, said, "Grandma, of course he's a blacksmith! He's shoeing a horse!"

His brothers giggled.

"James! Don't be rude," scolded Mrs McKendrick's daughter.

"Come on boys," said the man. "Make up your minds what you want for pudding. Maddie hasn't got all day to wait on you!"

I took their orders and made a note that the adults only wanted coffee. I passed the order for desserts through to the kitchen and went back to the bar to prepare the coffees. My mind was working overtime and I didn't hear Brian when he asked, "Penny for them?"

Eventually, he prodded me. "Maddie?"

"Oh, sorry Brian. I was miles away."

On a flight to Brisbane—amongst other things . . .

"Yes. I can see that! Hope they're nice thoughts."

I smiled grimly but said nothing.

The McKendrick party left at around 2.30pm. As they prepared to leave the man approached the bar to pay.

"Thanks for being so understanding," he said in a low voice. He jerked his head in his mother-in-law's direction. "Joyce is a bit gaga these days. She can't walk very well but was determined to come back to Walditch before she becomes totally housebound. We thought it would be fun to have a family trip out."

I glanced across at the group and noticed his wife helping Mrs McKendrick to her feet.

"I hope she enjoyed her visit," I said.

He assured me that she had and, with a wink, pressed a tip into my hand. I thanked him and watched as he returned to his family. The eldest grandson held out the walking stick to his grandmother and, linking arms with her, together they walked slowly towards the exit. As she reached the door, Mrs McKendrick stopped, looked back and stared at the painting and then slowly turned to look at me with those far-seeing, pale blue eyes.

"Don't stop looking, Mary," she called out across the room.

Her daughter, standing behind her, mouthed 'sorry' and the younger boys giggled. I watched as the family departed through the doorway. What did she mean? Suddenly I felt very cold despite the warmth of the pub.

"What was all that about, Mary?" teased Brian.

"I have no idea!" I said in a far stronger voice than I felt.

I phoned Dan later that afternoon, thinking it would be a good time to catch him. Lucy answered in a ridiculously sophisticated voice, announcing, "The Carver residence."

I tried not to choke. Who did she think she was? She was sitting in Dan's flat in Islington for God's sake, not some country pile! I was incensed before I even opened my mouth to speak.

"Hi Lucy," I said, as calmly as I could.

"Who's speaking?" she asked in that false voice.

"Maddie."

"Oh hiya Maddie." The sophistication slipped. "And how's life in the sticks?"

My blood boiled but I refused to rise to her bait.

"Great! How's life in the big bad city."

"Fabulous. I couldn't have made a better move."

I had already run out of things to say so decided to cut to the chase.

"Is Dan there? I'd like to speak to him before I leave for Dublin."

"'Fraid not, darling. He's away filming until Christmas eve. We're spending the festivities with his sis. She's such a hun."

I seethed.

"Well, perhaps you'd let him know I rang to wish him happy times," I said.

"Will do. Bye!"

Before I could say another word, the receiver at the other end was abruptly replaced and I was left hanging on the line. No love lost there, then.

New Year's Eve

The following Tuesday, having arranged with Janet that she would feed Storm while I was away, I drove to Exeter Airport and boarded a flight for Dublin. My suitcase was filled with Christmas presents and a few clothes and I was feeling happy and excited at the prospect of spending time with my family. I spent the next week luxuriating in being back in the fold and spent a couple of evenings drinking in and around Temple Bar, catching up with old friends. My family, being typically Irish, knew how to party and it was great craic. By the time I returned to Dorset I was exhausted, but refreshed.

I had a day to myself before going back to work at the pub on New Year's Eve and I spent it trying to ingratiate myself with Storm who was most put out that I had gone away. He had been asleep on his favourite chair when I first arrived home and although he looked up when I came in, he had studiously ignored any attempt on my part to make a fuss of him. I carefully unpacked my Christmas presents and set the fabulous, peacock-blue, glass mosaic fruit bowl that Martha and her husband had given me on the coffee table. Then I sorted out my clothes, putting the first load of dirty washing into the washing machine. As I stood in the kitchen I saw there was a message on the answer phone and half-expected it would be from Dan. It wasn't. It was Janet informing me that Storm had been a breeze to look after and very friendly. I glanced through into the sitting room and saw that Storm had now turned his back on me. I sorted through the post, which Janet had stacked on the dining room table. Dan's Christmas card would be amongst the pile of post, I thought. But there wasn't a card from him. Irritated that he had forgotten me, I noticed with dismay that the feeling was also tinged with sadness.

The day passed quickly and that evening I decided there was no time like the present to start making a list of contacts I intended to approach for freelance writing jobs. My generous parents had given me a laptop and I now placed it on the dining room table, made a cup of coffee and set to work. Storm had come around to me slightly during the afternoon and was playing with a catnip mouse I'd given him as a Christmas gift. He was busy flinging it around, noisily racing up and down the stairs.

I had closed the curtains and was searching the internet for Dorset-based magazines and newspapers when, out of the corner of my eye, I thought I saw a movement through the leaded glass divide between the rooms. I peered through the curtains of the window overlooking the village green to see if an outside light could have cast a shadow into the room, but the night was calm, the boughs of the ancient oak still. How odd, I thought, and then put it out of my mind as I, once again, became engrossed in my research.

A while later I heard Storm growl. He was standing on the stairs, looking intently through the archway into the sitting room, his hackles raised. As I followed his gaze, again I saw a shadow move across the internal window. Instantly, there was a stillness in the room and a chill that made the hairs on the back of my neck stand erect. I strained to hear the slightest sound and, holding my breath, silently got up, walked towards the archway and cautiously peered around the divide. The room was empty.

"This is a new one," I said to the cat, with more confidence than I felt.

He blinked at me. The growling ceased and he started to play with the mouse once again.

Immediately I texted Mo, knowing that she probably wouldn't respond until after the New Year seeing as she was busy partying in New York, but I felt the need to make contact.

Hi Mo. Wot u doing?

Surprisingly, within five minutes she texted back: *Following yr advice—enjoying myself! Wots up sis?*

I texted a brief outline of the latest twist to the unusual happenings at the cottage. I needed to talk to her face-to-face and, hoping that I didn't sound too unhinged, asked when she could visit.

About fifteen minutes later she texted: *Sorry 4 delay, had 2 find diary among mess in Jeff's flat. He says, Greetings lil sis!*

Hmm, very familiar! I thought. I had yet to meet Jeff.

Can visit UK 15-18 Jan b4 trip 2 Geneva. Happy New Year! Mo xx

I wrote the dates on the calendar that my young nephew, Sean, had given me—sweeping vistas of the West Coast of Ireland—*'to remind ye of yer true home'* he had cheekily explained before ducking out of the way as I attempted to cuff him.

Feeling lazy, I put a ready-made meal into the Rayburn, lit the wood burner and settled down to watch TV. Once Storm had tired of torturing the catnip toy, he joined me in the sitting room and stretched out in front of the fire. Nothing else happened to disturb the peace that night.

The following day was New Year's Eve and I worked the evening shift. The pub was packed. Brian had booked a local band and it promised to be a great night for all, even me, although I couldn't help but wonder how a certain person was celebrating on the other side of the world. But I was stoic and every time my thoughts turned in that direction I firmly told myself to focus on the moment.

"Nice to see you're back with us!" Brian grinned.

Attempting to fulfil drinks orders at both ends of the bar, he held several bottles of mixers aloft as he squeezed behind me.

"I was getting worried about you. Dublin's done you a world of good!"

I grudgingly acknowledged that I might not have been completely present during my recent shifts but decided not to offer an explanation. It was fun behind the bar with Brian. He was always so jolly, even when Vera gave him a hard time because she was stressed and run off her feet in the kitchen. They had hired a new assistant chef, Kevin, who seemed a nice enough lad but he had been thrown in at the deep end over the Christmas period and was still finding his feet. I often caught him muttering to himself and stealing copious cigarette breaks out back and, privately, I wondered whether he would survive the baptism of fire and how long he would stay.

At around 10pm a group of rowdy revellers entered the pub and amongst them I recognised the couple I'd seen in Dorchester the day I had bumped into Nick. While the girls made their way through the crowd to find tables with a good view of the band, the guys approached the bar and ordered drinks. They were friendly and in high spirits and flirted outrageously while I poured their drinks.

The girl I had recognised, and now remembered was called Becky, unsteadily approached the men.

Loudly she said, "Come on. We're dying of thirst over here!" She looked at me and I could see that she vaguely recognised me. "They're not causing you trouble, are they?" she shouted above the noise of the pub.

I laughed and said no and that if they were Brian would soon kick them into touch!

She picked up the glass of gin and tonic I had just placed on the bar in front of her and sipped it, looking slyly over the rim at me. I could see the cogs furiously turning.

"I know where I've seen you before!" she suddenly exclaimed. "You were with Nick the other week, weren't you?"

"Err, yes," I said vaguely.

"Have you heard from him?" she asked, her eyes narrowing to slits.

Instinctively, I felt she was being devious and wondered where this was heading. "No."

I moved away to serve another group at the other end of the bar, but when I had finished the girl was still there. It was obvious she had been drinking all evening and she must have thought I looked fair sport. I was trapped behind the bar and couldn't escape.

"I had a text from Sarah the other day," she said casually. "She said the weather's amazing and they're having a fab time."

She paused, letting me absorb this information, not once taking those calculating eyes off my face.

"Nick's brother's place is to die for, apparently," she continued. "Right on the beach."

"That's nice," I said, politely.

The Forgotten Promise

"Sarah says they're both coming back with an all-over tan, dirty cow!"

I swallowed hard, acutely aware that the girl was watching my every reaction.

"She's so lucky being taken to Oz," she said jealously. She waved vaguely in the direction of the man I had seen her with in Dorchester. "Mark wouldn't dream of spending that sort of money on me!"

I mumbled something about fortunate people and she took one last punch at me. "I think this is it, don't you? I mean . . ." she paused dramatically. "They've been together soooo long! I bet she comes back wearing a sparkler."

She waggled her wedding finger in my face, took one last look at me, laughed, and swayed her way through the throng towards her friends. So there it was. The female I had spoken to on his mobile wasn't his sister. I felt numb.

The rest of the evening passed in an unhappy daze. I smiled when people spoke to me and allowed myself to be kissed by a couple of the regulars when we counted down the seconds to midnight, but the girl's comments rang in my ears. When midnight eventually arrived I had trouble fighting back tears thinking that it would already be New Year's Day in Australia and that, no doubt, Nick had romantically got down on one knee at the stroke of midnight, their time, and proposed to his girlfriend.

I didn't even feel any sense of smugness when towards the end of the evening Becky was dragged out of the pub by her boyfriend and I saw her throwing up outside. I went through the motions of bidding customers farewell and wishing them a "Happy New Year" and then Janet and I methodically cleared away empty glasses from the tables and cleaned the ashtrays.

A while later Brian said, "Go on you two, go home to your beds. I'll divvy out the tips tomorrow. You've earned every penny tonight. Thanks a million."

Kissing us both dramatically on both cheeks, he waved us off the premises before locking the door. I turned to Janet and hugged her.

"I'm shattered," she said. "Not sure I can make it home." She lived all of five doors down from the pub.

I smiled and pushed her gently in the direction of her house. "Happy New Year, Janet."

Walking across the village green towards The Olde Smithy, I felt the loneliest person on the planet.

The next day I awoke sometime around 11am. I had forgotten to shut the bedroom door the night before and came to with Storm rubbing his face against mine, insisting that he needed food *now*. I rolled over and groaned as the events of the previous evening came flooding back to me. But, surprisingly, instead of feeling desperate I became angry and wondered why I had let the bitchy girl get to me so much. And as for Nick, well, damn him! I didn't even know him. I was irritated that he'd got under my skin so deeply without me being aware of it. And then I thought of Dan. Damn him too! I'd expected him to at least phone me in Dublin after I'd rung him, but he hadn't. No doubt too tired keeping Lucy satisfied, I thought bitchily. And so I decided there and then that I had two options; either wallow in self-pity or get on with my life.

"Come on, Storm," I said, as I threw back the duvet and jumped out of bed. "Let's have breakfast!"

I didn't have to report for work until the evening and wondered how to spend the afternoon. For some reason I decided to walk over to Shipton Gorge. It was a grey, still day, as if the first day of the new year was nursing a hangover, and there was a chill in the air. I threw on my waterproof jacket and scarf and walked across the village green, turning right towards The Hyde Real Tennis Court. Storm thought it great sport and came with me part of the way.

I turned left before the court and took the footpath that follows the valley around the curve of the hill encompassing the village. About fifty yards further along the path, I passed a couple of horse riders coming in the opposite direction and Storm decided that this was far enough for him; a steady rustling in the long grass was just too exciting to ignore and he left me to continue on my own.

It was a pleasant walk and I carried on climbing ever upwards. I hadn't walked in the area before but had often overheard pub customers discussing the various walks and bridlepaths in the neighbourhood. The track, however, seemed familiar to me and when I evenutally came to a fork in the path I instinctively knew that the right fork led through a farm and on towards Burton Bradstock and that I needed the left path for Shipton Gorge. I carried on walking, enjoying being out in the open air and started to hum a pleasant, rhythmic melody with a distinctly old-fashioned lilt. Where had that come from? It wasn't a tune I recognised. The tune persisted and finished in a flourish.

It wasn't far to Shipton Gorge, possibly two miles, but the path traversed Walditch Knapp and was steep in places. By the time I reached level ground I was hot and short of breath. I removed my scarf and tied it around my waist before continuing my journey. On reaching the crossroads in the middle of the village I continued straight ahead without hesitation. Where was I going with such determination? It was as if my feet were no longer mine to control.

Presently, I came to the 14th Century church of St. Martin's. I paused at the lych gate and looked up at the tower with its elaborate doorway and smiled up at the gargoyles as if they were old friends. I had the strangest sense of having been there before, though I had never visited Shipton Gorge. As I walked through the gate, the size of the church confused me, though I wasn't sure why.

"No, this is all wrong. It's too large!" I said out loud.

Why had I said that? Self-consciously I looked around and breathed a sigh of relief when I realised there was nobody else about. I walked all the way around the outside of the church with a sense of disquiet and only when I came back to the West Tower did the feeling leave me. I tried the door; it was open. Silently, I entered.

The church had a wonderfully peaceful atmosphere and I slipped into one of the pews and immediately started to pray. I hadn't prayed for years, in fact since attending the local Catholic school for girls in Dublin, and it took me by surprise that I should automatically want to do so.

I glanced around and looked up at the ceiling, noticing the carved stone corbels that supported the main timbers in the aisle and the open framework of the interior. I walked up the aisle, amazed by the size of the church, and walked past the stone pulpit with its handsomely carved panels. As I approached the font I knew that it would have seven sides. How did I know that? Distractedly, I looked at the open benches and wondered where the box pews and galleries had gone. An intense disorientation overwhelmed me.

What was I thinking?

The Forgotten Promise

Feeling foolish, and not without a certain amount of rising panic, I walked back up the aisle in a purposeful manner towards the entrance. On a table by the door lay several neatly stacked piles of literature about the church and the parish and I picked up a pamphlet entitled *'A Guide to St Martin's'*. Dropping some coins into the box provided, I walked back outside into the cold afternoon air and meandered amongst the gravestones, idly read the epitaphs and noticing how ancient some of them where. On rounding the corner at the far end of the church I stopped abruptly. A man was carefully placing flowers at the foot of a gravestone, a wirehaired terrier sitting patiently at his feet.

I kept a discreet distance, respecting his privacy, but something about him drew me and I couldn't help but watch. He was aged about forty and wore his dark blonde hair tied back in a ponytail. It occurred to me that he might be one of the actors in the local pantomime as he was dressed so unusually; loose cotton breeches, long leather boots turned over at the top, a leather jerkin with large white scalloped collar and a short cloak slung casually over one shoulder. In his left hand he held a soft, felt, broad-brimmed hat. The terrier remained seated but moved position constantly in that busy way that terriers have, not once taking its eyes off the man's face. There was something about the man's stance that I recognised and I wondered if he was one of the regulars in the pub.

Suddenly an overpowering wave of despair swept over me and I gasped. The man turned towards me and I stood rooted to the spot, embarrassment overwhelming me as I saw the utter retchedness and helplessness shrouding him. And then I noticed his face, wet with tears, and gasped again. He appeared not to see me, his eyes scanning the graveyard, a frown forming on his forehead. My legs buckled from under me. On seeing me fall to the ground, the terrier immediately stood up, stared intently in my direction and started yapping wildly, though I heard not a sound. I sat there in the grass trying to catch my breath. That face! That dear, sweet face! A face so familiar to me it was as if it were part of my very soul. And yet, try as I might, I could not name him.

After a while, breathing more easily, I looked up. Both man and dog had gone. Unsteadily I got to my feet and looked around. There was no-one about. I walked towards the gravestone where he'd been standing and saw that it was a very old gravestone, the lichen spreading across the stonework. I tried to read the inscription but it was difficult to make out the words. Ravaged by time, the elements had all but destroyed the letters carved into the stone.

I could just read a date. Was it 1844 or 1644? I frowned in puzzlement. Why would anyone be so affected by such an ancient grave? And I could just make out some letters: e m y. There were more words underneath, but I couldn't decipher them.

Looking down at the base of the gravestone, I was surprised not to see the flowers the man had placed so carefully and then I noticed there were no impressions in the grass from where the man and the dog had been standing. Immediately I realised my mistake. I must have the wrong grave. I looked around for a newer headstone but couldn't find one.

Feeling a few spots of rain, I looked skywards to see dark clouds gathering and shivered. Perhaps it was time to head back to Walditch.

As I stood there wondering about the man, a great sense of peace and tranquility settled upon my soul.

The Forgotten Promise

I was exhausted by the bewildering emotions I had experienced that afternoon and yet, now, I felt a deep sense of . . . What? What did I feel? Belonging? Release? I wasn't sure. I couldn't explain it but for some reason I was at peace with the world. All the irritation and sadness I felt over Dan and the intense feelings and irrational despair concerning Nick didn't seem to matter a jot.

I whispered into the wind, "God bless you, whoever you are."

Mid January

The next couple of weeks flew by and I was pleased with all that I managed to accomplish. I made phonecalls to various magazine editors and was encouraged by the number who asked me to send in freelance material, and I spoke to Dan's eco friend who was keen for me to search out projects in and around Dorset and we negotiated a favourable deal. I visited Bridport Street Market again and discovered a fabulous stall selling country-style items and purchased curtains for both bedrooms and having finally finished stripping wallpaper from the downstairs rooms, I started to paint the walls. I thought about phoning Dan, but I still felt piqued that he hadn't bothered to contact me at all over the Christmas period and decided that I would leave it up to him to make contact, should he ever find the time.

Mo arrived on the evening of the 15th January. I picked her up from Exeter airport along with several bags of camera equipment; she was visiting me en route to a photoshoot in Switzerland. Since she had embarked on her chosen career in photojournalism there were very few countries she had not visited. It was so good to see her again and she hugged me warmly.

"Wow, just look at you!" She tweaked my long curly hair. "Haven't seen you looking so soft and . . ." she searched for the right description. "Irish, for how long? Years!"

I laughed. "Well, hair does have a tendency to grow over the course of eight months."

"No!" she exclaimed. "Is that the last time we saw each other?"

I took her suitcase and started walking towards the car park.

"Must be. You visited me in London just before I started shooting that drama in Dorset and that was last May."

She strode confidently beside me and I noticed several people turn to watch us.

"You looked very much the assistant director then," she said. "Wouldn't take any nonsense from anyone, let alone a star!"

I laughed again and wondered if I was still that person underneath or whether Dorset had softened me out of all recognition.

Mo was just two years older and we had always been close, sharing similar attitudes and possessing the same sense of adventure. We also bore a striking resemblance to each other, though she was a couple of inches taller than me, and people often mistook us for twins. We had inherited our father's hazel green eyes and curly auburn hair, which Mo wore cut short as she said it was easier to cope with on assignment. Martha, ten years my senior, was out of a different mould entirely what with her sophisticated attitude, sleek black hair and piercing blue 'Paul Newman' eyes.

I had lit the wood burner before leaving for the airport and by the time we arrived back the cottage was warm and welcoming against the bitter night air. Storm thought it was great fun checking out Mo's bags and had to jump on each one in turn, sniffing furiously.

"This is so homely, Maddie!" exclaimed Mo, as I showed her around the cottage. "I can see why you fell in love with it."

We carried her bags up to the spare bedroom and she sat on the bed looking appreciatively around the room. The guest room had been designed to match the original bedroom and it, too, was in the eaves with some cleverly newly-aged, exposed beams. It had a charming country feel and the new curtains added to the cosy ambience. I left her to settle in and went downstairs to the kitchen. I put the chilli con carne I had made earlier into the Rayburn together with some crusty rolls, started to prepare a salad and poured a couple of glasses of red wine. Presently, Mo joined me with Storm purring contentedly in her arms.

"Look who came and made himself comfortable on my bed," she said.

I smiled.

"Well, you realise that The Olde Smithy really belongs to him. I'm just here to feed him!" I tickled him under the chin and handed Mo a glass of wine. "How was New York?"

"W-o-n-d-e-r-f-u-l!" She strung out the word, pronouncing each syllable. "Jeff took me to loads of parties and I made some really good contacts. We had a ball."

Being an O'Brien, Mo could party like the rest of us. She knew how to have a good time.

I chopped tomatoes and added them to the salad bowl. "So, this Jeff, he's cool is he?"

"Well, his Manhattan apartment is pretty cool," she grinned at me. "But he's red hot!"

I laughed and drank some wine.

"In fact, he's so damn hot we had to spend hours in his jacuzzi! And the view from that jacuzzi, well I could have stayed there all the time and not seen any more of New York than its skyline!"

We had a great evening, chatting amiably and catching up. I told Mo about the unusual happenings at The Olde Smithy and how meeting Mrs McKendrick had completely thrown me.

"Even though her family thinks she's going senile, I disagree. I believe she's far-seeing and knows something about the cottage—or me . . ." I left the sentence unfinished.

Mo frowned. Eventually she said, "If this cottage has anything to tell you, Maddie, it will. It'll give up more of its secrets as time goes by."

A shiver ran down the full length of my spine. "That's exactly what Dan said."

"It's true," she said simply. "These old buildings have been witness to a lot of life and if momentous things have taken place, well, the memories linger. Sometimes we who follow are privileged to learn of them."

"But," and I wasn't really sure what I was saying. "It's more than memories."

"What do you mean?"

"I don't know," I said in exasperation. I knew that my next sentence would sound truly off the wall. "Mo, I think I'm somehow linked to The Olde Smithy."

Glancing at me, she frowned again. "Did Dan say that too?"

"No."

She looked at me a while longer. She was about to say something but hesitated and changed the subject. "How is 'Dan the man'?" she asked lightly.

"Who knows? The rotten sod hasn't bothered to contact me for weeks. Obviously too knackered to pick up the phone or a pen."

It still smarted that he hadn't sent a Christmas card.

"Must be quite a girl, this Lucy!"

I had kept her up-to-date with the Dan/Lucy 'thing'. I refused to sanction it with the term 'relationship'.

"According to Caro, the minute Lucy arrived in London she moved in with him. She's certainly wasted no time in getting her feet under his table."

"Or into his bed!" Mo laughed.

But I didn't join in. I was still unsure how I felt at no longer having Dan in my life.

At around 1.30am, having polished off a couple of bottles of wine, we retired to bed. I noticed Storm sneaking into Mo's room and just knew that she wouldn't throw him out.

The next morning I was awake before my sister and made my way quietly downstairs to make tea. It was a beautiful morning; the sky was clear and blue and it promised to be a good day. I was pleased the weather was fair as it would allow me to show Mo the area I had chosen for my home. Or had it chosen me? Brian had generously given me time off knowing that I had family visiting and I didn't have to work at all that weekend. The area offered many things for us to do, but I decided to ask Mo how she would like to spend the time.

I heard floorboards creak upstairs and then the spare bedroom door open.

"Mornin' sis!" Mo called down. "One hungry cat coming your way."

Storm appeared at the kitchen door and immediately went to his empty bowl. He looked at me indignantly.

"No point you looking at me like that!" I scolded. "Traitor!"

He came over and walked around my legs, rubbing against me as I opened a tin of cat food, trying to curry favour with me. A short while later, I heard Mo come downstairs to the bathroom. I started to lay the table for breakfast and about five minutes later, the bathroom door opened again.

"What do you want for breakfast?" I called.

"Cereal and toast will be fine," she answered. "I'll just go and throw some clothes on."

I heard her climbing the stairs as I walked back to the kitchen. I poured orange juice into a couple of glasses and was bringing them through to the dining room when she appeared in the open doorway leading into the hallway. I thought she looked pale as she stared back up the stairs. There was a look on her face that I couldn't quite place.

"Is there something you're not telling me Maddie?" she asked slowly.

"Don't think so," I replied, placing the glasses on the table.

"Well, who was that hunk I just passed on the stairs?"

The hairs on the back of my neck pricked and I noticed that Mo was shaking.

"You saw someone?"

"Well, yes!"

"What did he look like?"

She looked at me strangely. "Are you telling me, Maddie, you haven't got some dishy man stowed away in this cottage?"

I shook my head.

"Well . . ." she paused, searching for the right words. Eventually she said, "Country."

For some reason I instantly thought of the man I had seen at the graveyard.

"What do you mean 'country'?"

"He was wearing rough clothes, now that I come to think of it. Like work clothes."

"But what did he look like? How old was he?" I asked, the urgency in my voice taking us both by surprise.

"It was so quick, Maddie, I can't recall exactly," she said apologetically. "He had good aura though." She said it as if, somehow, that made everything all right.

I smiled weakly. Aura was important to Mo. I started to climb the stairs and she followed. I knew there wouldn't be anyone there but I had to look. Of course, both bedrooms were empty.

I slumped down on my bed and looked at my sister. "Why do you think you saw something?" I asked.

"No idea. But the figure was as solid as you and me."

"I've started to keep a diary of all the things that have been happening," I said. "There seems to be a pattern."

She sat down next to me. "That's a good idea, Maddie." She put her arm around my shoulder. "But do you think you should try and find out about the history of this place?"

I nodded. "But where to start?"

"How about breakfast?" she suggested, the colour returning to her cheeks.

We spent the day driving around the countryside visiting several places of interest. We parked at West Bay and walked along West Cliff to Eype, stopping for a light lunch at the hotel there. Mo took lots of photos and with her photographer's eye captured some amazing views along the way. I found myself looking anew at the

The Forgotten Promise

vistas before me. We carried on down the coast by car and eventually arrived at Lyme Regis. There were very few people about and we wandered around without the crush of holidaymakers that I had been told often made visiting the town a trial.

And then Mo said she wanted to take some photos of me on the Cobb, saying that my long curly hair reminded her of Meryl Streep in the French Lieutenant's Woman. As she directed me in various poses at the end of the Cobb, the professional photojournalist came to the fore. She had me looking wistfully out to sea or furtively glancing back over my shoulder, at one point draping me in her black scarf and ordering me to look into the camera with a haunted look. She said all that was missing was Jeremy Irons. A man walking his dog asked if I was a professional model to which Mo replied that we were doing a shoot for Vogue. I thought for one moment she was going to ask him to join in but, thankfully, she didn't. I couldn't stop laughing.

Later, we browsed the various shops and Mo said she wanted to buy me something as a late Christmas present. At the back of an Aladdin's Cave we found a large mirror set in a beautifully crafted driftwood frame.

As we deposited the mirror in the car, she said, "This will look very well in your charming cottage. Now, what shall we do for supper? I'm paying and it's not up for discussion."

We decided to stay in Lyme and found a little bistro in the town, run by a couple of gays who had moved down from London the previous year. They were great company and we had a delicious meal with plenty of laughter thrown in. It was an easy, unhurried day, spent in good company.

Driving back to The Olde Smithy, Mo said, "It's been really good spending time with you again, Mads. My work schedule over the next few months is chaotic, to say the least, and I'm so pleased we've been able to get together before it gets fully under way."

"Will you fly back to New York at all?" I asked.

"Probably for my birthday, but not before. Jeff's said he'll travel out to wherever I'm based. One of the perks of being a high-flier in the airline industry; nowhere in the world is inaccessible."

She smiled at me.

"Is it serious, Mo?"

"Not at the moment. It's party, party all the way. But who knows what the future may bring."

She laughed.

"But what about you Maddie? We all thought you and Dan would eventually get it together. God knows he's been a part of your life forever!"

"Oh, you know us. We were so comfortable together there was never any urgency to do anything differently. It was only when Lucy showed up that I wondered if we hadn't been quite as clever as we thought."

She nodded and gently asked, "So have you discovered any new talent in Dorset?"

I instantly coloured, thankful that it was dark. "Well, yes and no," I mumbled.

"Good God Maddie, what does that mean?" She turned to look at me, laughing.

And so I told her about Nick and my instant feelings for him although they were going nowhere fast due to a long-standing girlfriend being on the scene.

"Nothing like a challenge to make one inventive in pursuit," said my wiser, older sister.

The Forgotten Promise

I shook my head. "Not this time, Mo. No pursuit."

"That doesn't sound like the sister I know."

I sighed, the weight of the world pressing heavily upon my shoulders. Life shouldn't be this complicated.

"He took his girlfriend to Australia for Christmas and New Year and his friends think he will have proposed to her out there."

Even to my ears I sounded morbidly dejected.

Taking control, my sister said in a brisk, no-nonsense voice, "Well, don't forget it's a big pond out there Mads and there's plenty more fish."

Trouble was I only wanted that particular 'fish'.

Sunday dawned, another beautiful day. We woke late and decided upon a leisurely day. We tried the mirror in several locations, eventually choosing the hallway at the bottom of the stairs. As I stood back to admire it I noticed the internal stained-glass window beautifully reflected in it; the different colours of the leaded panes made it a work of art in its own right.

I started to cook brunch while Mo walked around the cottage taking photographs. She took several from the village green and also in the back garden and Storm, her constant companion, managed to put in an appearance in most.

As I made coffee and toasted bread on the Rayburn, Mo lay on the sofa with Storm stretched out on top of her and flicked through the pamphlet I had brought back from the church in Shipton Gorge. "This looks interesting," she said.

I explained how I'd visited it the other day and seen the mystery man at the graveside.

"Maybe we could visit it today?" she suggested.

I agreed and said that the walk over Walditch Knapp would do us good after such a calorie-laden brunch. She gently moved Storm who was trying to lick her chin.

"It says here," she said as I checked the sizzling bacon, "'. . . *Visible from almost everywhere in the village, the 14th Century church of St. Martin's stands on a small plateau on the south side of Brook Street. It retains its original 14th Century tower with an elaborate doorway but the remainder of the church was rebuilt in 1862, which more than doubled the seating of the old building'.*"

I stopped stirring the baked beans, a distant memory surfacing as I remembered how I had expected the church to be smaller. I tried to catch the thought but it eluded me.

She continued reading aloud, "'*The architect was John Hicks of Dorchester for whom Thomas Hardy was then working and the contractor, from a village of masons, was one of the Swaffield family. There has certainly been a church here for a very long time and the 13th Century font is unusual in that it has seven sides. There was likely to have been a partial rebuild in the 17th Century which added box pews and galleries. However, apart from the tower, the church was completely rebuilt in the 19th Century'.*"

I stood looking at the saucepan of simmering beans, my senses sharp. I had instinctively known the font would be seven-sided and I had also wondered where the box pews and galleries had gone. But what did it all mean?

"Storm, you're really cute but I've already washed!" Mo exclaimed. I heard her getting up from the sofa. "That smells good! How's it coming along?"

Shaken from my reverie I called out, "Two minutes."

After brunch, we walked across the village green and turned right towards The Hyde Real Tennis Court. Mo thought the chapel-like building built of Dorset ham stone was beautiful and took several photographs.

"Apparently, the court was built in 1885 to entertain the, then, Prince of Wales who was a real tennis fanatic," I said.

"Has it always been used for that purpose?"

"No. It was a real tennis court up until the First World War and during the Second World War it was used as an army facility. Since then it's been a vehicle repair shed and agricultural building, or so Brian informs me!"

"Am I going to meet this Brian?"

"We could go to the pub for supper tonight," I suggested.

She put her hands on my hips and spun me around. "Well then, we'd better build up an appetite," she said. "Come on, race you up the hill!" Laughing, she set off up the footpath at a fast jog, the camera bouncing on its strap around her neck.

I followed in hot pursuit and was immediately transported back to our wild, carefree, childhood days in Ireland. The younger O'Brien girls, 'peas in a pod' we were told; the world our oyster and the future stretching tantalisingly before us.

We stopped to catch our breath at the top of Walditch Knapp and to admire the view. It was a fine afternoon and high cirrus clouds scudded in from the west. I played the historian, authoritatively telling Mo that there was supposed to be a Roman fort above the village and we scanned the landscape looking for tell-tale signs but without success. I also explained that the series of terraces along the hillside were known as lynchets and that these were the first signs of arable farming from prehistoric times. My sister was very impressed but, eventually, I had to admit that a local historian had been in the pub the previous week.

Presently, we arrived at Shipton Gorge. When we finally reached St Martin's Church I, again, experienced the same sense of bewilderment at how altered the building appeared to me, even though I now knew that it had been rebuilt in 1862. As we entered the church a couple of ladies looked up from their flower arranging and welcomed us in. The older of the two asked if I was the bride for the forthcoming wedding for which they were dressing the church. I smiled and said no but what a wonderful church to get married in and complimented them on their beautiful floral displays. We walked around quietly reading from the booklet I'd picked up on my previous visit. It was very peaceful.

Once outside, Mo took some photos of the lych gate and the 14th Century tower in the winter sunshine while I walked amongst the gravestones towards the area where I had seen the man. I clearly remembered that he had set flowers at the foot of a shiny new headstone, yet the graves at this end of the church were ancient. It didn't make sense.

I looked over at Mo working her way down the rows, reading the epitaphs.

"Some of these are so sad," she said. "Listen to this, Maddie. *In Loving Memory of Miriam Bowden, born 21st January 1860, died 21st January 1884 and of her beloved husband William Bowden born 18th October 1856, died 8th September 1888'.* She died on her birthday and was only 24!"

"Better for him to have passed on only four years later than to have survived another twenty without her," I commented.

Suddenly, I felt very cold; as if someone had just walked over my grave. Briskly, I walked to the spot where

The Forgotten Promise

I had seen the man and his dog and looked at the angle it made with the church.

"I don't understand it, Mo," I said, as she joined me. "I'm sure this is the grave where I saw the man but there are no new stones here."

The headstone was leaning at a precarious angle, giving the impression that with one push it would topple over. The grass grew long at its base. Together we tried to decipher the words carved into the stone.

"There are a couple of names here. I can't make out the first one but I think this one says Elisa. There are some more letters so it's probably Elisabeth," Mo said, pointing to the lower lettering.

I shivered as she spoke the name.

"And the date is either 1844 or 1644. Are you sure this is the one Maddie?"

I nodded.

She took a photo of the headstone and we stood in silence, trying to make sense of it all. At the sound of the church door creaking open, I looked up and saw the younger of the two flower arrangers emerging, a posy in her hand. She turned and headed away from us, down the path leading to the lych gate. Quickly I followed her.

"Excuse me. Do you know if there are any recent burials in this part of the graveyard?"

She turned and I indicated to where Mo was standing.

"No. They're all on the other side. I'm going there now. My grandmother," she said, raising the posy she was carrying.

I thanked her and walked back to Mo. "I really don't understand it. There are no recent burials on this side of the church but this is definitely where I saw him."

I paused as a thought came to me. "I wonder . . ." I looked back at the headstone. "Mo!"

The urgent tone of my voice made her look up sharply. "What?"

"When the man looked in my direction he didn't see me and yet I was only twenty yards away. I assumed it was because he was so distraught, but . . ." I faltered, not sure whether I dare speak the thought.

"Go on."

"What if he couldn't see me because I wasn't there?" I said slowly.

She looked at me, a puzzled look on her face and then understanding dawned. We both gazed at the gravestone.

"And where are his flowers?" I asked.

Slowly she nodded her head. "This is important, Maddie. You've got to find out what it all means. I have a friend who specialises in film enhancement. I'll see if he can clean up the photo and decipher the wording."

The last of the daylight was fast disappearing and suddenly floodlights came on, bathing the church in glorious light. We walked back to Walditch in the gathering dusk and by the time we reached The Olde Smithy it was nearly dark.

Later that evening I took Mo to the Blacksmith's Arms for supper. Brian was charm personified and the perfect host.

"I had no idea there was another stunner in the O'Brien household," he exclaimed, as I introduced my sister.

Mo laughed and graciously accepted the compliment.

"Now, what can I get you two lovely ladies?"

We ordered drinks and I asked what Vera had prepared for the special that night.

"Not Vera, it's a Kevin 'special' tonight. I've given Vera the evening off to visit her sister in Salisbury. Now there's a family lacking in the looks department, I can tell you!"

"Brian! That poor woman," I scolded. "You work her to the bone and in return she looks after you magnificently. She's given you the best years of her life. The least you can do is support her!"

"That's true, she certainly looks after me," he patted his belly. "Can't complain about that, but you must agree she's no oil painting."

"You're a shocker and you don't deserve her!"

"I know," he laughed. "She's too good for me."

We sat at the bar chatting easily with Brian and, not for the first time, I thought how lucky I was to have found this job only yards from my home. Being a Sunday evening, the pub was not particularly busy but a few people had ventured out and I was vaguely aware of a group entering the pub and moving towards one of the private alcoves by the restaurant entrance.

We decided to risk the 'special', placed our order and debated whether to eat at the bar or move to one of the tables nearer the fire. Suddenly, Mo leant forward with a conspiratorial look on her face.

"Don't turn around, Maddie," she whispered. "A guy over there keeps looking your way."

I was itching to turn around. "What does he look like?"

"Nice. Oh! You'll find out in a minute. He's heading over."

She leant back and I watched her smile at the approaching man. The next minute I was aware of a presence next to me and heard a voice that was as music to my ears.

"Hi Maddie. Thought it was you."

I turned my head and there stood Nick, tanned and gorgeous. My heart skipped a beat. "Hello Nick. You look well."

He looked happy and carefree, his blue-grey eyes seemingly all the more intense within his lovely, open, tanned face. He smiled and immediately butterflies took flight in the pit of my stomach. Suppressing them and, without missing a beat, I made the introductions.

"This is my sister, Mo. Mo meet Nick Corbin."

He shook her offered hand. "I thought you must be family. The resemblance is very strong."

I was ridiculously jealous that my sister had actually touched him.

"How was Australia?" I asked, trying to keep rising emotions under control.

"Good. Very hot and over in a flash! It was great to see Chris again." Turning to Mo he enlightened her, "My brother."

She smiled and agreed that it was good to spend Christmas with family, although she had missed out this year.

"We've been catching up over the last couple of days instead," I explained. "Quality sister time. It's gone by so quickly though and, sadly, Mo leaves tomorrow."

I noticed his hair was longer and his fringe flopped over his eyes, making him look like a romantic smuggler. It suited him.

"So how do you like our neck of the woods?" he asked Mo in that lovely, soft, Dorset lilt of his.

"I like it very much and I can see why Maddie has fallen in love with the area and wants to make a life here."

Had I imagined it or did this news cause him to smile? I was on edge and stole her a quick glance to see if there was any hidden meaning to her comment, but she was being sincere. It was just paranoia and my heightened nerves playing tricks on me.

"Then we are very fortunate indeed!"

He looked from Mo to me, the merriment dancing in his eyes. Infuriatingly, a blush started to creep up my neck. He seemed so at ease and I felt so out of control.

"And how's the window holding up?" he asked.

"Great! No draughts. I've been very snug."

Damn! I shouldn't have said that. Now I would have to find some other job for him to do if I wanted to see him again. But in the next sentence he paved the way for more meetings.

"Glad to hear that. It is only a temporary measure though, Maddie." He seemed to be about to say something else but then looked over in the direction of his friends. "I'd better return to my table. Nice to have met you Mo. Hope you visit your sister again soon. Enjoy the evening."

He walked away and I instantly felt the chill. Mo sat looking at me thoughtfully.

"Who's he with?" I demanded.

She didn't answer immediately so I repeated the question. "Mo! Who's he with?"

"Can't see who's sitting opposite him but there's a girl there."

She wasn't giving much away.

Brian came through the kitchen swing doors with our order and we decided to sit more comfortably by the fire.

As we changed areas I took the opportunity to look over at Nick's table and instantly wished I hadn't. The girl sitting next to him was as equally tanned and he sat with his arm casually draped over her shoulder, chatting to whoever sat opposite. They looked comfortable and relaxed together. I sat down at the table and looked across at Mo who was watching me carefully.

"Oh this is hopeless!" I said in an anguished voice.

"I don't see why."

"How can you say that? He's with her!"

"Yes, and he needn't have come over to say hello but he did!"

She had a point.

"Tuck in Maddie and as Nick said, 'enjoy the evening'."

I tried to swallow my disappointment. I so wanted to enjoy my last evening with Mo.

"Have you noticed that painting?" I pointed to the picture hanging above the fireplace.

Mo studied it, an expression of surprise settling upon her face. Without taking her eyes from the painting she said, "Maddie, that man . . ."

I looked up at the figure shoeing the horse.

"I swear he's the one I saw on your stairs!" She turned and looked at me, wide-eyed but, on seeing my expression, said, "You're not surprised are you?"

I shook my head. "It's obviously The Olde Smithy. Every time I look at the painting I feel as if I know the scene. I mean . . ." I paused, searching for the right words. "Somehow I think I'm connected with the scene."

Her eyes were large and round.

I pointed to the blacksmith. "This man is very familiar to me and yet I can't place him."

The Forgotten Promise

"Mads, you've got to discover the history of your cottage."

I agreed.

We finished our meal, decided against dessert and ordered two Irish coffees. Brian brought them over announcing they were 'on the house' and as the two best looking girls in the pub that night we had earned the right to have a double whisky in each plus an extra dollop of cream. We laughed.

Presently, I became aware of Nick's table preparing to leave. Surreptitiously I watched as the other couple emerged from the alcove. It was Becky, the bitchy girl who had warned me off Nick on New Year's Eve and her partner, Mark. I watched as the two girls chatted happily together as they put on their jackets. The tanned girl, who I assumed was Sarah, looked to be in her late twenties. Of medium height and build, she wore her long blonde hair tied back in a loose ponytail and, although not overtly pretty, she had a healthy, wholesome, girl-next-door appeal. I was consumed with envy for her relationship with Nick and the legitimate time she could spend with him.

I dragged my eyes away from her and met Mo's unwavering gaze. I groaned and pulled a face at her and watched as Mo looked up at the approaching party. Mark passed by and continued on towards the door but Nick stopped at our table and wished Mo a safe onward journey.

Then he looked me straight in the eye. "Bye Maddie. I'll give you a ring in the week and arrange a time for delivering the window."

What window? I hadn't asked him to make a new one. We had only discussed the eventual inevitability of replacing the temporary, patched-up one.

"Great!" I said, wondering if I had lost the plot.

Sarah, standing behind Nick, met my glance with a quizzical look. Turning to his girlfriend, Nick placed his arm around her waist and ushered her towards the door. As Becky passed by she glared at me, which caused Mo to laugh out loud. The girl, momentarily thrown, faltered but quickly regained her composure, glaring furiously at my sister before hurrying after her friends.

I sat there, a jumble of emotions, trying to work out what had just happened. Mo slowly sipped her coffee.

"Well, this certainly has been a most entertaining evening!" she announced.

"I'm glad you think so! I'm an emotional wreck."

"Why?" she laughed.

"Because Sarah's got Nick and no doubt they're about to get married and have loads of kids. In fact, they were probably discussing wedding plans tonight and that couple with them are to be their Best Man and Chief Bridesmaid."

"Oh Maddie! Your imagination! You are your own worst enemy."

Mo set her glass down on the table.

"But it's probably true," I wailed.

"Did you see a ring glinting on her finger?" she asked.

Damn, I had forgotten to look. I was so hopeless at this and Mo was so together.

"No," she answered her own question. "The only thing I saw her wearing was one pretty fine tan."

"All over," I said dryly, remembering what Becky had been so eager to tell me. "No white bits."

Mo laughed again but I couldn't see the funny side.

"And what's all this about a window?" she enquired.

"Not sure."

"Well, case closed!" Mo declared. Leaning back in her chair, she smiled broadly at me. "Be a good little Catholic girl, Maddie, and have faith."

The following morning I drove my sister to Exeter Airport to catch her flight to Geneva where she was to join the rest of her team. Once she had checked in I found myself strangely tearful. Mo hugged me hard.

"Look after yourself little sis" she said. "That cottage of yours has an unsolved mystery and it wants you to unravel it."

I nodded, unable to speak.

"And as for that gorgeous man . . ." She squeezed me tighter. "What will be, will be, Maddie, but if I can give you a little advice based on my seniority . . ." She arched an eyebrow and pulled a mock-superior face. "Have a little faith!"

She picked up her hand luggage and joined the back of the queue working its way towards security. When she had checked through she turned, smiled and waved. And then she was gone.

The day had not dawned clear and as I walked back to the car park I noticed the dark grey clouds threatening rain. It suited my sombre mood.

On the drive back to Walditch I cajoled myself into forming a plan. I made a decision to visit the museums at Bridport and Dorchester as soon as possible to find out as much as I could about Walditch and the surrounding area and I also set myself a daily schedule during which time I would carry out research, both locally and on the internet. Soon, my simplistic diary of unusual happenings at The Olde Smithy would grow to become a journal with more meat on the bone but, as I became engrossed in Dorset's history, frustratingly little information came to light about The Olde Smithy itself.

The following Friday was a particularly cold day. I had just lit the wood burner, made myself a mug of coffee and was planning on an afternoon of research on the internet when the phone rang. Storm, lying in his favourite chair by the fire, stretched as the shrill ringing disturbed him from his slumbers. I walked to the kitchen and lifted the handset from its cradle.

"Hi Maddie, hope I'm not disturbing anything?"

A swarm of butterflies took to the wing.

"Nick!" I swallowed hard. "Nothing that can't wait."

"Just wondered if you'd got around to fitting that bread oven door?"

I looked through the open doorway into the sitting room and laughed. "Nope, it's still where it was before Christmas!"

"Would you like me to come round and fit it for you? I could check the repairs on your window at the same time."

"That's very chivalrous of you. Yes please!"

"How are you fixed next week then?" he asked.

I explained that I had started writing on a freelance basis so would be at the cottage most days. He sounded interested and asked me what sort of writing I was doing.

"General interest pieces with a Dorset flavour and also eco projects within the county. I don't suppose you know anyone who's doing their bit for the planet?"

There was a pause on the other end. "Yes, as it happens. Me."

"In what way?"

He described how he was in the process of renovating his barn, the goal being to create a low carbon footprint home that was as self-sustaining as possible.

"That's exactly the sort of thing Richard's after," I said. "I don't suppose I could do a piece on it?"

"Sure. How soon do you need it?"

"Sooner rather than later." The little white lie tripped off my tongue.

"How about this weekend?" he suggested.

I smiled. "You'd better give me an address and directions then."

And so it was agreed that I would go over late morning on the Sunday.

"Look forward to seeing you then," he said.

Did he truly mean that?

I said goodbye and stood for a while, taking it all in.

Returning once more to research, I became so engrossed that I didn't notice the diminishing light as the afternoon faded to early evening. Storm came through the open archway between the two rooms reminding me that he needed to be fed.

"Sorry boy, you're being rather neglected at the moment."

I made to rise from my chair but stopped as I noticed a movement on the other side of the stained-glass room divide. To my amazement, a figure appeared in the archway moving from the front to the rear of the cottage. I froze, aware that Storm mirrored my stance. Slowly I rose and walked to the archway and cautiously peered towards the kitchen. There was no-one there. Storm made me jump as he brushed past me on his way to his bowl and, deep in thought, I followed him into the kitchen.

Was this the figure that Mo had seen on the stairs?

It amazed me how easily I accepted this latest turn of events. Apart from the initial shock, I was not at all fazed by what had just happened; it seemed perfectly natural. I spooned cat food into Storm's bowl and returned to the computer, opened the file entitled 'Happenings' and noted the time. There was a definite pattern emerging. I described everything I had just witnessed. The figure was a man aged approximately mid-forties with a weathered face and shoulder length, dark blonde hair. His clothes were grubby; a shirt, possibly made of linen, and loose trousers, which were equally in need of a wash, and he wore a pair of well-worn, leather boots.

As I typed my observations I realised that this was the man I had seen at the graveside. It seemed impossible to my rational mind and yet these things were happening to me. The figure was no fleeting suggestion or spectre on the edge of my vision. And I remembered Mo's words following her visitation on the stairs, *'As solid as you and me'.*

Ashton Chase Barn

I turned off the road, as directed, drove past the main house, on towards the farm and, just before reaching the farm buildings, turned right onto a stone track. After another three hundred yards or so, the track rounded a corner and came to an end in a roughly circular parking area to one side of Ashton Chase Barn; a stone and green oak barn nestling in a fold of the Black Down Hills.

I parked next to a silver Nissan pick-up, switched off the engine and sat looking at the view. It was simply stunning. The land fell away from the barn in a series of terraces, still under construction, each enjoying uninterrupted views of the magnificent vista stretching as far as the eye could see to the coast and beyond. On an area of lawn immediately in front of the barn, three dogs romped together in the morning sunshine.

I sat a moment longer, savouring the sights, before reaching over to the passenger seat and picking up my bag and camera. On hearing the car door open, one of the dogs looked up and started to approach. I hesitated and, sensing someone watching me, gazed up at the barn.

Nick stood at the open door, dressed casually in jeans and sweatshirt, a mug in one hand. He looked happy and relaxed. The Weimeraner crossed the stone parking area towards me.

"Don't worry about Baron," he said. "He likes the fairer sex."

"Well, that's a relief!"

The dog sniffed my leg and, gently, I stroked his silver-grey velvety head. "You're a handsome boy," I said softly. The dog pushed his head strongly into the palm of my hand.

"You didn't tell me you had dogs!" I called out and, instantly, cringed. I didn't know Nick. Why would he have told me?

Nick didn't reply but continued to study me. I took a deep breath, tried to compose myself and walked towards the barn.

"This is fabulous," I said as I approached.

He smiled and moved aside so that I could enter. Baron followed closely behind.

"It's a work in progress. Hopefully it will be fabulous, but not yet." Looking back towards the two dogs still playing on the grass he called, "Casper, Tilly. Come!"

The German shorthaired pointer paused in its rough and tumble game with the golden retriever and obediently came towards the barn.

"Tilly come!" Nick called again. "My sister's dog. Tilly comes to stay with the boys when Helen goes away."

I smiled and looked around the amazing space. I was standing in an open-plan living area about fifty feet long with an open kitchen at the far end. Substantial oak beams rising to the atrium and floor to ceiling glass along the full front elevation created a definite 'wow' factor. I could see, however, that it was indeed a work in progress and there was still some way to go before the finished product emerged.

"Would you like a coffee?" Nick asked. "The kettle's just boiled."

"Thanks."

He walked to the kitchen, at ease in his surroundings, the Weimaraner at his heels. The Pointer had settled down on a well-worn, brown leather sofa and his sister's dog had disappeared through an open doorway to my left.

"Make yourself comfortable," Nick called over his shoulder.

"How long have you lived here?" I asked as I removed my scarf and jacket.

"Approaching two years. I should have finished by now but work's been taking up a lot of my time recently. Not complaining, though," said Nick, as he opened the fridge door.

"It's a great spot," I complimented him.

I sat on the sofa next to the dog.

"I was very fortunate," he said modestly. "Kate and Simon up at the house are good friends of mine. When they heard I was looking for somewhere they sold me this barn and a couple of acres."

Friends indeed!

"The planners needed a little more persuasion, though." He walked towards me, a mug of coffee in one hand and a packet of biscuits in the other. "But once I'd explained the plans and shown them how low a carbon footprint the whole project would have, they soon rolled over."

He laughed, that lovely soft laugh and my heart went into free-fall.

Handing me the mug, he placed the packet of biscuits on a chunky wooden coffee table and invited me to help myself. I told him I would like to take photos to accompany the article I planned to write.

"Good idea. It's a great day for photos," he said. "We get challenging weather here being so high up. It rolls in from the sea and sweeps across the valley, but this barn has withstood many a storm."

I looked up at the glass atrium two floors above me. "Isn't it noisy in the rain with all this glass?"

"No, not noisy, more muffled. We've used two sheets of glass, seven millimetres thick, bonded together with a specially formulated resin for the atrium and glass roof panels. It dampens the vibrations and sound waves by forty percent. It also blocks eighty six percent of ultra violet light and transmits sixty six percent of visible light. It also has very low solar heat gain, which helps to keep the barn cool in summer and indirectly warm in winter."

He smiled at me and then teasingly asked, "Got that?"

I laughed. "I have, actually."

"I'd say the rain's more of a comforting sound," he continued softly. "Especially when you're lying in bed looking up at the night sky."

Oh! The thought of lying in bed with him. I couldn't look at him and concentrated hard on supressing the embarrassing blush which threatened to break out. Why did he have this effect on me?

"I'll show you around when you've finished your coffee."

I said I'd like that very much and, as a distraction, patted Baron who had come up looking for biscuits. I sensed his amusement at my disccomfort.

We chatted a while longer and I started to take notes. He told me he had carried out most of the work himself with the help of a few friends in the initial stages. His idea was that the barn would be sympathetically restored using natural materials, where possible, with the ultimate goal being it would be carbon-neutral and as economical to run as was practicable. I loved hearing him talk. He was

The Forgotten Promise

so passionate about the project. When he later showed me around, it was obvious that the craftsman in him had cut no corners and even the walnut dining table had been lovingly crafted. It was a unique building and one that was being renovated with great thought.

We started the tour on the ground floor and Nick laid out his vision for me. I took photographs and wrote furiously on my notepad, trying to keep up with his enthusiasm. It was a large L-shaped stone barn with enormous timber roof trusses. He explained that the doors we had entered through were once where the original threshing doors had hung. These had been replaced with glass panels within a steel framework which rose two storeys to the roof line. Very contemporary and a huge statement.

"These doors face due south," he explained. "They're on the sunniest side of the barn so we've used tinted, toughened glass as this absorbs more solar radiation than clear glass."

The large open-plan living space had been divided into study and living areas, both of which had oak flooring, with a galleried area above. A crisp slate flagstone floor defined the dining area and the bespoke kitchen units he had handcrafted from oak. The barn was warmed through under floor heating, powered by an individual ground source heat pump and Nick explained that both warm and cooling air was distributed around the property through an energy efficient, whole-house system of ventilation.

At the far end, beyond the kitchen, a door opened to what would be a utility room and downstairs bathroom. A staircase led up to two guest bedrooms with large Velux windows taking in the view down the valley to the sea. This part of the barn was still in the early stages of development and Nick informed me he had designed it so that it could be used as a separate annexe, if required. The utility room would double up as a kitchen and one of the bedrooms could act equally well as a living room.

At the other end of the main living area, centrally situated beside the door leading to the study, a beautiful wooden spiral staircase led up to the galleried area. A door to the other side of the staircase led through to a large side entrance porch with a door opening to a downstairs cloakroom.

As I followed Nick up the spiral staircase, he explained how it was made from the yew tree donated to him from The Hyde; the same tree from which he had created the sculpture in the courtyard at his shop. I was about to say "I love yew," when I realised how it would sound and managed to swallow the words just in time!

We emerged out onto the galleried area; an open-plan master bedroom that overlooked the lounge and dining areas. It was a fabulous room. Exposed A-frame trusses rose up to a glassed roof area and one wall was completely glazed with floor to ceiling windows taking in those fantastic panoramic views down the valley and out over the English Channel. A glass door within the windows led out onto a wooden balcony above the porch area.

I studiously avoided staring at the large king-size bed positioned under the glass apex but when he showed me the en-suite shower room, I could not ignore the tell-tale signs of a female presence. Neatly arranged on the counter was a selection of make-up, face creams and straightening tongs. I did my best to ignore the obvious confirmation of Sarah in Nick's life and commented on the travertine tiling to the floors and walls and the clever use of neutral colours. The only window in the room was a glazed arrow slit, but there was plenty of light as the sloping ceiling was

The Forgotten Promise

clear glass. Gazing at the large double walk-in shower, I thought how wonderful it must be to wash under the stars and then immediately had a vision of Nick and Sarah enjoying steamy showers together.

Flustered and with despondency nipping at my heels, I asked if I could have a look around outside. As we descended to the living area Nick called to the dogs and, accustomed to their master's voice, Baron and Casper immediately rose and waited patiently at the bottom of the stairs. Tilly, however, remained seated by one of the sofas, enthusiastically wagging her tail.

"Come on Tils, old girl. You'll get left behind!" Nick called again.

She got to her feet and followed him through to the porch where he took a refer jacket from the coat rack. Retrieving my jacket and scarf from the chair, I picked up my camera and followed him outside. Even though it was a sunny day there was a cold nip in the air and I threw the scarf around my neck and zipped up my jacket.

We ascended steep steps to the rear of the barn, which brought us to a terrace above roof level where two storage tanks were located. Nick explained that private well water was pumped into the tanks before gravity delivered the water to the property and there was also a rain butt at the far end of the barn that collected water from the roof. The light had a wonderful quality to it on that January afternoon and I took several photos and thought that even by my amateur efforts the pictures would look pretty special.

Following Nick down a side track, I observed how Baron always kept one eye on him and, though the dog would run off with the others, he never let Nick out of his sight. I commented on this.

"Weimaraners are a one-person dog," he said. "They'll be friendly towards other people but tend to be loyal to just one person. And Baron's been with me eight years so we know each other's foibles quite well!"

We crossed the driveway where the cars were parked and walked towards a log cabin positioned a short distance from the barn. This housed a diesel powered generator which Nick explained provided power to both the dual 240v and 12v lighting/electrical systems. And beyond the cabin was a wind powered generator.

"The barn stands at seven hundred feet above sea level and it's often windy up here," he said. "In fact, there's so much stored energy from the wind turbine that we give some back to the national grid!"

We? I had tried to ignore it up until then. Was that simply a figure of speech or was it a reference to Nick and Sarah? It sounded cast in cement.

I was trying to make notes as he spoke and take photos at the same time and, although I was agitated at the thought of his long-term relationship, again I was aware that in Nick's presence I experienced a delicious calming of the soul.

Walking down some roughly hewn steps from one terrace to another, I noticed life-sized animal sculptures dotted around. There were a couple of pigs rooting through the trees; a preening cockerel and a scratching hen on the middle terrace; and on the bottom terrace, a hissing goose at the edge of a large lake. I took photographs of the wooden sculptures and said that I would like to include them in my feature on the barn.

"Just some samples I did for my students," Nick commented.

"How long have you been tutoring?"

The Forgotten Promise

"This is the third year I've run the evening class for Bridport. It's a general carpentry course but last year's students wanted to concentrate on more creative aspects, so I produced these to show what could be achieved."

"They look great in this setting," I enthused.

"Yeah. I didn't think they looked out of place."

At that moment, Casper tore past us and leapt straight off the terrace onto the terrace below before bounding into the wet, reedy area at the edge of the lake. Tilly followed closely behind.

"Look at that mad dog," Nick exclaimed. "I swear he thinks he's a water spaniel!" He laughed, that good-natured, infectious laugh. "Casper get out of there!"

Jumping down to the terrace below he called to his dog. Casper turned and immediately responded. Tilly, however, waded up to her belly amongst the reeds and was reluctant to leave the lake. Eventually, and after much persuasion, she emerged draped in weed and vigorously shook herself, causing Nick to jump out of the way of the shower.

"Argh! Bad girl Tils," he said, but he was laughing as he said it.

The dog looked up at him with soulful eyes.

"I'll explain the significance of the reed lake, Maddie, and you'll understand why it's not good for these rebels to go wading around in it!"

He looked up at me standing on the terrace above him and held out his hands. I felt that we were about to take a momentous step and, as I placed my hands on his shoulders and looked into his open, tanned face and clear blue-grey eyes, I experienced the strongest sensation that we had done this before. Holding me under my arms, he carefully lifted me down to the terrace below and, as he did so, a great hush descended—a deep silence, like a held breath. I became aware of an incredible light shining from my body and as our eyes locked, I knew that this was how it should be. It was as if time had stopped. Somehow we had stolen back time. We were in a place where there was no time; the normal laws of the universe did not apply.

And then words came to me which I did not fully understand. 'Oh, such joy to look upon your face again and feel once more a touch long still . . . '

But then the moment had passed and Nick was busy explaining how connecting to the main sewer had worked out to be prohibitively expensive, as well as impractical, so a reed bed purification lake had been created that naturally filtered all waste water from the barn.

"The pond naturally balances and recycles the waste water and, once processed, it's then pumped back up to one of the storage tanks above the house for re-use."

As he talked I wondered if he had experienced anything just then; noticed any slight shift in the order of things? He didn't appear to have. But I was sure that when our eyes locked I had seen a flicker of emotion; a question in his eyes.

I was still pondering this when Nick interrupted my thoughts.

"How are you for time, Maddie?"

I glanced at my watch—12.30pm. "OK. I'm working the evening shift."

"Would you like to stay for lunch?"

We were standing next to each other but looking straight ahead at the view.

My heart, thumping loudly, cried, *'Stay!'*

My mind sternly advised, *'You're heading into unchartered waters, Madeleine. Go!'*

Nick turned to me, smiled and said, "Nothing special I'm afraid. My skills lie more in wood than food, but if you'd like to stay I can rustle up something."

'*Stay,*' whispered my heart.

'*Go!*' shouted my mind.

And so I stayed.

Sitting at the dining table chatting companionably while he prepared lunch, I noticed how capable he was in the kitchen. Someone who could look after himself, I thought, but instinctively knew that there had been very few times during his life that he had needed to.

I felt myself falling deeper into the abyss and knew that my heart should not have won the argument. I should have put some distance between us and headed back to Walditch. But I was powerless, some greater force directing me, and I was merely an actor with but a small part to play.

Early February

I spent the following week working hard on the article that I planned to submit to Richard for EcoWorld magazine and was pleased with the way it was coming together. I had several good photos to choose from and I wanted to get it finished in time for Nick's visit on Thursday when he was coming round to fit the oven door. I wasn't sure if it was an extra service he had offered me or whether it simply fell in with his normal work ethic. Either way, it was a generous gesture.

I had just returned from a shopping trip to Bridport and was parking the car when I saw Janet walking towards me from the direction of the Blacksmith's Arms. She was holding a small brown paper parcel and waved it at me. I switched off the ignition, got out of the car and opened the boot, grabbing a couple of bags of shopping.

"Hi Janet. What's up?"

"This came for you at the pub." She held out the package. "Brian said Mrs McKendrick's son-in-law dropped it in yesterday 'cos he thought you might be working."

I took the package from her. It was addressed to The Olde Smithy.

"He said his mother-in-law's been dispatched upstairs."

I looked at her, wondering what she meant. Then the penny dropped. "Oh! You mean she's passed away."

I was taken aback by the way the man had referred to his mother-in-law's death.

"S'pose so."

"Thanks for bringing it over, Janet. See you Friday."

I turned and walked towards the cottage, saddened by the news and wondering what the package contained. Having emptied the shopping bags and lit the wood burner, I made myself a coffee and settled down in the chair by the fire before Storm had a chance to monopolise it. Then I opened the package. Inside was a small, sealed envelope addressed to Mary and a well-read hardback entitled *'Dorset—the effect of the Civil War'*. Carefully I opened the envelope, unfolded the letter within and read the small shaky handwriting.

My Dearest Mary,

I am so thankful to have met you. I should have liked to have talked with you at greater length but the good Lord has told me I am approaching the end of my time, although my daughter assures me otherwise (she WILL try to protect me from the natural passing of time, bless her!) I am so very tired these days and I do look forward to being reunited with my husband. As you and I know, Mary dear, life goes on.

I was very happy living in your cottage for over 30 years, once I had learnt to accept its special ways (Hugh was always unaware and lived within its four walls in blissful ignorance).

I wish you every chance of happiness and fulfilment in this life and enclose something which may assist you in your search. Don't give up!

God Bless.
Joyce McKendrick

I sat there for several minutes re-reading the letter, wondering what it could mean. I knew that if her daughter had read the letter she would have dismissed it as merely the ramblings of an old woman with increasing dementia but I recognised that these were true and honest sentiments, however obscure.

Turning the book over, I read the back cover. The book appeared to be an account of the role Dorset had played during the English Civil War. I opened the book and started to read, not noticing the passage of time until I became aware of a deep stillness. A log in the wood burner caught my eye. Almost burnt through, it shifted and threw up sparks and yet I heard not a sound. And then I noticed the dense, fog-like mist around the opening to the bread oven which shifted shape but never took form. I was not frightened but simply accepted it and watched closely. Rising from the chair, I moved closer to the mist and, as I did, it withdrew, compacted and appeared to view me as I viewed it.

"Show me your secrets," I whispered.

The fog swiftly surrounded me, seemingly investigating me before dispersing and suddenly disappearing. Once more, the sounds of my world returned.

"Oh please show me your secrets," I whispered again.

I read late into the night. I felt that Mrs McKendrick had given me a key to a mysterious, closed door that had opened a fraction. If I could prize it open a bit more, I might be able to see more clearly the way ahead. I finally went to bed at around midnight, the stack of wood beside the wood burner having been reduced to a single log by the time I turned in.

That night I, again, dreamt of dark claustrophobic tunnels and a desperate need to discover something important. Only this time, once I came close to its discovery it did not instantly turn to sand; I was getting closer to the heart of the riddle. I awoke the next morning feeling as if I had been on a long journey, but with a calm acceptance of all that was happening to me.

Shortly after 4pm Nick arrived. I was working at the computer when I heard his van pull up. Looking out of the window, I saw him speaking into his mobile. He appeared exasperated and I watched as he distractedly dragged a hand through his hair. I turned away, not wanting to pry, but a minute later I couldn't help but steal a glance. I could tell it was a heated discussion that was taking place. Suddenly he threw the mobile on the seat beside him, thumped the steering wheel and sat staring straight ahead. I turned away and concentrated on the article, which I had entitled '*Eco Magic in the Black Down Hills*'. Some minutes later there was a knock at the door.

As I walked through the doorway into the hall, I noticed that the driftwood mirror no longer reflected the colours of the stained-glass room divide but appeared to be a mass of swirling grey smoke and shadows. I thought it strange but assumed that it must be something to do with different lights at different times of the day. I didn't dwell on it further as these thoughts were immediately put out of my mind when I opened the front door and saw the strain on Nick's face.

"It's really good of you to come round," I said, as he walked into the hallway.

He acknowledged this with a quick nod of the head and set his toolbag down on the hall floor.

"I've almost finished the article on your barn," I continued lightly. "Come and have a look and tell me what you think."

He hung his jacket on the coat rack in the hall before following me through to the dining room. I sat at the computer again and motioned him to pull up a chair. When he sat down, he was so close to me that our legs almost touched and I could feel the heat emanating from his body. I tried to concentrate.

Scrolling down the page, I started to read from the screen. "'*If you are prepared to invest in great ideas, just look at what you can achieve! Recently, I visited a unique property that features the latest in contemporary design with extensive use of natural and locally sourced materials'.*"

I continued reading the article aloud, acutely aware that Nick had casually put his arm along the back of my chair and was now leaning in to look at the screen.

We were very close and the voice inside my head mocked, '*So near, and yet so far!*'

I read to the end of the article and was suddenly overcome with shyness.

"Well, what do you think?" I asked tentatively.

"I'm blown away Maddie!" he answered generously. "If it wasn't already my place I'd want to go out and create it straightaway."

I smiled and relaxed a little. Explaining that I had started to choose some photos to accompany the piece, I suggested he took a look at them to see if he agreed with my selection. I opened the photos in thumbnail format and rose from the chair.

"Would you like tea or something stronger?"

"Something stronger sounds good."

He shifted into my seat.

I poured him a beer and a wine for myself, and then returned to the table. Nick was engrossed in choosing the photos. We decided on ten including a picture of the magnificent view from the terrace and a photo of the dogs around the lake; the hissing wooden goose in the foreground.

Pointing to the goose, I said, "You never know, you might get some commissions out of this."

He smiled at me, a gentle look in his eyes replacing the earlier strain. "We seem to be good at helping each other out."

I quietly held my breath, aware that this was the first time he had made any personal reference to the two of us.

"Talking of which, let me sort out your door," he said, getting up from the chair; practical once more.

He fetched his toolbag and set it down in the inglenook.

As he straightened up my inner voice again mocked, *'He looks so right, as if he belongs.'*

I ignored it and walked to the kitchen to fetch the bolts and hinges I had bought for the bread oven door.

"I'd say this is the original opening," Nick said as I re-entered the room. He was feeling around the smooth entrance to the bread oven. "Hopefully the stonework's solid enough to get a purchase."

He felt inside the entrance and then leant in futher. "What's this? There seems to be a ledge."

He balanced himself against the outer wall and inserted his arm deeper into the opening. "There's something here."

Straining to get a better angle, he suddenly withdrew his arm, a wooden box in his hand.

"What is it?" I asked, aware of an intense, mounting excitement and I remembered the anticipation I'd felt when Dan had first discovered the opening.

He placed the box on the coffee table and carefully opened the lid, which was stiff with age. There, sitting within, was a pendant and a ring. Carefully he picked up the pendant and placed it in the palm of my hand. It was an exquisitely crafted 3D heart made up of badly discoloured, interlocking metal strands. I was immediately overcome with a rush of such happiness and pure joy that it took my breath away. As if in a trance, I heard Nick tell me to turn around and hold my hair aloft and, as I did so, gently he fastened a silk ribbon around my neck. I glanced down and was surprised to see that I was wearing a blue dress with a deep neckline trimmed in white lace, a shiny silver heart pendant nestling just above my breasts. I felt a tender kiss on my neck and heard the whispered words, "I made this for you . . . a token of my love."

Astonished, I made to turn back to him but then saw two children watching and giggling at us from the open archway between the two rooms. A little boy with a mop of curly blonde hair stood next to an older girl and peeped through the opening where the stained-glass window should have been. The cottage, though familiar, had altered and I could see a rustic wooden table and bench seats in the other room and a crude staircase rising to an upper floor. Propped against the front wall was a large stained-glass panel, the lead crisp and gleaming, the small glass panes glistening in the firelight and filling the rooms with a subtle kaleidoscope of colours.

I watched as I stretched out my arms to the children. The boy was no more than three or four years old and I recognised him as the child in the cot. Immediately, they

The Forgotten Promise

ran to me and caught hold of my hands. Together we danced around and around, my skirts swirling as we spun ever faster. I had never been so happy and we laughed with sheer joy and abandonment.

Glancing over at Nick standing in the inglenook in front of an open log fire, I was taken aback by the look of such wonderment on his face, his blue-grey eyes soft and tender and I felt my heart shift into meltdown. And then I noticed that his appearance had altered and though the eyes were Nick's, his features were those of that other, more feral man I had previously seen in the cottage.

And then the dizziness and nausea kicked in. I let go of the children's hands and closed my eyes, willing the room to stop spinning. When I opened them again, in a glance I took in the familiar pictures hanging on the walls and the IKEA sofa I had bought from the Croydon store two years before. I looked down at the dirty pendant still cupped in the palm of my hand and quickly glanced up at Nick.

"Did you see that? Did you?" I demanded in an urgent, breathless whisper.

The look of wonderment was still on his face. "I don't know what I saw, Maddie, but I saw something."

I sat on the sofa, cupping the pendant tenderly in my hand. What had just occurred? I leant forward and carefully placed the pendant back in the box and picked up the ring. Turning it lovingly between my fingers, I resisted an overwhelming urge to slip it onto my wedding finger. It was exquisite, like an Irish Claddagh ring. The shank was decorated with swirling motifs, fancy sleeves out of which came a pair of hands that encompassed a piece of red glass shaped like a heart.

"Oh this is lovely!" I cried. "But why are they here?"

Nick knelt in front of me and cupped my hands in his as he carefully picked up the ring. I was acutely aware that this was the first time he had made contact with me from choice and somewhere deep within me there was recognition, like the muffled sound of a bell of distant memory. I sighed, feeling that a great many years of angst had just lifted from my heart.

"These are love tokens," he said, looking very directly at me. "But how they came to be inside your bread oven, I don't know."

"But whose are they?"

He shook his head. "They appear to be very old. You should get someone to take a look at them. Perhaps the museum?"

I agreed and he handed the ring back to me.

Taking the pendant out of the box again, he said, "This is very well made. The work of a true craftsman." A frown furrowed his forehead and, as if to himself, he murmured, "I wonder who?"

Suddenly he became business-like. "This isn't getting anything accomplished. You sit there Maddie and I'll get the door fixed."

He worked quickly and competently and made surprisingly little mess. Within half-an-hour the door was in place.

"Looks like it's been there hundreds of years," he said, standing back to admire it and I agreed. "Now, what about this window?"

"Well, it's been fine over Christmas."

"Let's have a look at it anyway."

He offered his hand and pulled me to my feet with such strength that I bowled straight into him. I laughed out of nervousness as he steadied me, but when our eyes met it seemed to me that I had known this man forever and there was no need for embarrassment. He smiled and followed me upstairs.

I was walking on air but my inner voice taunted, '*He's only going to look at your window.*' I shut it out.

Nick checked his repairs. "It's up to you, Maddie, but this window could last you a while longer as it is."

I thought of all the costs I had incurred since moving in plus the fact that I was currently earning very little and my sensible, fiscal voice told me to make do.

"Well, I have had a lot of expenditure recently . . ."

"Then see how it holds up through the year and when you're ready we can discuss it again."

He looked at me across the yawning expanse of bed. With dismay, I realised that there was now no longer any practical reason for me to see him again.

"How are you for time, Nick?" I chose the same phrase he had used when I'd visited his barn. "Would you like to stay for supper?"

He looked at his watch and frowned. "Better not."

My heart sank.

"It's getting late and I shall be missed."

My disappointment was palpable but, as casually as I could, I said, "Your loss. Not only do I pull a mean pint but I can also rustle up a terrific shepherd's pie!"

He smiled. "Some other time Maddie. Thanks."

'*Some other time—never!*' mocked my inner voice.

And so, once again, I said farewell to Nick and watched as he walked across the village green and climbed into his van. I stood at the front door feeling sad and lonely. Putting the van into first gear, he looked back towards the cottage and acknowledged that I was still standing there. This time, however, there was a troubled look upon his face.

The following morning I emailed the article to Richard and was pleased to receive a return email later that afternoon. He was happy with the copy and confirmed that it would appear in the May issue of EcoWorld. My spirits lifted when he suggested that I might want to retake some external shots, should the landscape take on a more spring-like appearance between now and publication date. Here was another valid reason for contacting Nick. Richard also asked me to source other eco projects and to submit further articles as soon as possible. He signed off with: *Seen anything of Dan recently? He seems to have gone to ground.*

I was still incensed that Dan had not bothered to contact me since he had come to stay in early December with Lucy in tow. Surely eight years of a very close friendship should count for something? I thought angrily. However fantastic Lucy might be, he could at least maintain some contact!

Feeling restless, I decided to find out more about the jewellery. I had placed the wooden box on my bedside table the previous night, curiously reluctant to be apart from it, and it was the first thing I had looked for when I awoke. I brought it downstairs and placed it carefully on the dining room table. Why had it been placed on a ledge inside the bread oven and who had put it there? And why had the oven then been sealed up? What dramas had The Olde Smithy been privy to?

I fetched the book Mrs McKendrick had sent me and re-read her letter, wondering again what she meant. But the meaning was no clearer on second reading.

The Forgotten Promise

I took the contents out of the box and placed them on the table, as if they were the most precious objects in the world to me. Again, I had the strongest urge to slip the ring on my finger and I marvelled at the fine craftsmanship and delicacy of the heart pendant. Even in its sorry, blackened state it was obvious that it had been carefully crafted with dedication. '*A love token*', Nick had said. I recalled the look in his eyes as he had spoken the words and a thrill of excitement coursed through my body.

"What story do you have to tell?" I asked out loud.

Silence.

I logged onto the internet. Dorchester County Museum's telephone number was easy to find and I quickly made the phone call. On the third ring a woman answered. I explained my find and asked if there was anyone she could recommend to look at the jewellery and perhaps date it.

"Just a moment," she said and I could hear her rifling through a folder. Eventually she returned to the phone. "Professor Stephens, Head of Archeology at the University of Southampton. He may be able to help."

As soon as we'd finished the call, I dialled the number she had given me but there was no reply, so I left a brief message outlining my request for his services together with my telephone number.

It was early evening and I realised that I needed to get a move on if I was going to get to work on time. Even Brian, however amenable a disposition, would not accept a 'got held up in traffic' excuse from the other side of the village green! I opened the back door and called for Storm but there was no sign of him. I rushed upstairs to change my clothes and found him curled up on the bed.

"You!" I scolded jokingly, as I hurriedly put on a clean pair of black trousers. "Sneaking up here when I'm not looking!"

He yawned, stretched, opened one eye and surveyed me. I rubbed the underside of his belly. "Yes, you. I'm talking to you!"

Hurriedly rummaging through one of the boxes stacked at the side of the room, I found a clean sweatshirt and was pulling it on over my head when, from behind me, I heard a voice whisper urgently, *"Mary!"*

I spun round. There was nobody there.

"What?" I called out loudly.

I was surprised at the fear I felt; it was more than just the sound of the voice.

"What is it?" I asked again. "Tell me."

A faint breeze on my face. I glanced over at the window to see if it could be coming from there, but the window was fastened tight and the weather outside was still. I sat down on the bed, frustrated. Storm got to his feet and rubbed against my arm.

"How are we going to find out more Storm?"

I stroked his head and then I heard it again. A loud, urgent whisper. *"Mary. Come!"*

By the door was a suggestion of the mist I had previously seen in the living room. As I reached out my hand, it quickly dispersed and evaporated. The moment had passed.

Glancing at the digital clock, I realised that I was now definitely late for work.

Valentine's Day

The following Wednesday was Valentine's Day. Brian asked me to work the evening shift, which I enthusiastically agreed to knowing that I would feel wretched if I was sitting in on my own that night. Not that I was a great advocate of the event, but I was currently feeling vulnerable and a little sorry for myself. The Blacksmith's Arms had advertised a Valentine's Special and the restaurant was fully booked. Brian advised me that he was prepared to risk his reputation once more and said that he wanted me to waitress as well as cover the bar. He and Vera had decided the pub would have a red and silver theme and had asked that we all dressed accordingly. I wore my comfortable black work trousers, dressing these up with a silver blouse I had found in a charity shop in Bridport, and I tied my hair back in a matching silver ribbon. The requirement for red needed some thought but I searched through my jewellery box and found a red bead surfer's choker and matching bracelet, purchased on a weekend trip to Newquay with Dan early on in our relationship. I finished the outfit off with my favourite native North American, bear paw and feather, coral and silver earrings.

On my way out I stopped to check my appearance in the driftwood mirror, childishly sticking my tongue out at my reflection. The glass, once again, appeared dark and smoke-like, as if it needed a good clean and even though the lights were on in the dining room across the hallway I could see none of this detail. There was also something odd about the image reflecting back at me. I moved in to take a closer look and gasped. The face that serenely observed me was mine, but it was not. In the mirror my hair tumbled around my shoulders, yet mine was tied back, and in the reflection I was dressed in a dark blue cloak. Quickly I glanced down at my open-necked silver shirt.

"Who are you?" As soon as I spoke the words the vision began to fade. "What do you want from me?"

Was there a suggestion of a smile on the rapidly vanishing face?

Swirling grey smoke gave way to clear glass. In the mirror I now clearly saw the laptop open on the dining room table with the stained-glass window divide on the far side of the room. The moment was gone and I noticed the look in my eyes was not altogether calm.

Closing the front door purposefully behind me, I walked briskly across the village green, beneath the boughs of the old oak tree and entered the pub. Janet was already there and Gayle arrived shortly afterwards with Danielle, a girl Brian employed on a casual basis. I threw myself into work and forgot about that 'other' woman. We dressed the restaurant with helium-filled silver balloons and adorned the beams with silver and red streamers.

A local band had been hired for the night and the four musicians were busily setting up their equipment and carrying out sound checks. Each table had been laid with a red tablecloth and we arranged silver coloured napkins in wine glasses and placed a vase with a single-stem red rose in the centre. Standing back to admire the room, we unanimously agreed that the end result was warm and welcoming with a hint of stardust magic.

Before the evening got underway, Brian gathered us to the bar and explained that he had put Janet in charge of the restaurant, which he had roughly divided into four. I was responsible for the three tables closest to the entrance so that I could also keep an eye on the bar and help out there when necessary, and the remainder of the tables were divided between Janet, Gayle and Danielle. I saw the girls exchange meaningful looks—there were a lot of customers to keep happy—but Brian pointed out that Janet would not be needed in the kitchen as Kevin, the replacement assistant chef, had survived his baptism of fire. He was now a fully fledged member of the team and would be working alongside Vera in the kitchen.

"Any questions?" he asked.

We shook our heads.

"Good. Then let's make this evening a success."

I checked the restaurant booking sheet and saw that table ten was booked for four people in the name of Corbin and a mixture of emotions coursed through my veins. As fate would have it, table ten was my responsibility.

"Janet, I don't suppose you'd swap your table three for my table ten would you?" I asked quietly.

She was about to agree when Brian interjected, "No, I want you to be free for the bar, Maddie. Table ten is closer."

I resigned myself to the fact and then thought that it probably wouldn't be Nick anyway. After all, he had told me his family came from the area so it could be anyone.

As the musicians ran through a couple of numbers, I helped Brian prepare the bar. With mounting nervousness, I watched as the first of the Valentine's night customers arrived and poured drinks as they congregated around the bar before moving through to the restaurant. At 7.15pm my table one arrived, a sweet young couple who couldn't have been much more than eighteen. They ordered drinks and then followed Janet as she showed them to their table. A few minutes later, I walked through to the restaurant with their drinks and left them with a couple of menus.

I was walking back to the bar area when I saw Sarah and a woman I hadn't seen before enter the pub, closely followed by Nick and another man. I watched as Nick instantly scanned the room and his eyes met mine. I swallowed hard, managing a smile, despite my nervousness, which had now developed into nausea. He looked fantastic dressed in a white shirt, which set off his tan very well, grey moleskin trousers and a dusky blue casual jacket. Sarah looked freezing in silver strappy sandals, a thin jacket and a short black dress, obvioulsy worn to show off her deeply tanned, bare legs. She was talking animatedly to the other woman as they all moved towards the bar. I was relieved when Brian moved to serve them and I could escape to the restaurant and take the young couple's order. However, as I returned to the bar, Nick's party were coming through to the restaurant, following Janet to their table. Sarah glanced at me, her face an expressionless mask, but Nick hung back and stopped me with a light touch. The look in his eyes made the butterflies explode.

"Hi Maddie."

"Hi!"

"You look really good to me," he said softly.

"You don't look bad yourself," I responded, amazed at how strong I sounded because the room had suddenly become terribly hot and I was having trouble breathing. Was this swooning, I wondered.

The Forgotten Promise

He smiled.

To cover my confusion I hurriedly said, "You'd better brace yourself. I'm your waitress tonight."

"Oh no!" he groaned teasingly. "What have I done to deserve this? Twice in less than three months!"

I laughed and promised to do my best not to stab him.

"That would be greatly appreciated!" He still had his hand lightly resting on my arm. "I'd better go and join the others."

He turned and walked through the open archway into the restaurant.

The pub soon filled up and before long I was too busy to worry about anything. As I showed customers to their tables I was aware of Nick's eyes on me and I basked in the spotlight of his gaze. Eventually, I had to approach his table to see if they were ready to order.

Without any thought for my sensitivity, Nick teasingly said to the other man, "I warn you now, Peter, this girl's lethal! She does a mean trick with flying cutlery."

The man laughed and the woman sitting at his side smiled sympathetically at me.

Nick continued, "But we can excuse her that because she more than makes up for her waitressing shortcomings with her Irish charm."

Sarah surveyed me coldly.

"Don't listen to my brother," the other woman said kindly. "He's a big tease. I'm sure you're a fine waitress."

I smiled at her thinking how like Nick she was, possessing the same open, friendly face. Maybe this was a family trait.

Nick laughed. "No Helen, I warn you now! Maddie is *not* a fine waitress but she *is* an excellent journalist."

I saw Sarah set her jaw and purse her lips into a thin, mean line; her eyes narrowing.

"Ah," exclaimed Peter in a friendly manner. "You're the one Nick's been talking about!"

"And I understand Tilly made sure she was centre stage in all the photos," Helen added in a gentle Dorset lilt.

I smiled. She had the same inflections as her brother.

"Even though the barn's fantastic in its own right, having the dogs in the shots has added a homely touch. It will enable readers to imagine themselves living there," I responded.

"I must get a copy of the magazine," said Helen. "When is the article being published?"

"It's scheduled for the May issue of EcoWorld," I replied.

"It's a new title," explained Nick to his sister.

Turning to Nick, I said, "Richard has asked me take some more external photos before publication deadline."

I was acutely aware that Sarah was looking daggers at me. Pointedly, she said, "We can take the photos and email them to you."

An awkward silence descended upon the table.

Nick was the first to speak. "Don't be silly, Sarah. Maddie's got to take them. It's her job!"

Sarah glared at me.

"I'm starving," said Helen, concentrating hard on the menu. "Let's order. I'm sure Maddie has better things to do with her time than talk to us."

Not really, I thought. I love talking to you because you're part of Nick's life.

I took their order and rushed it through to the kitchen and advised Brian that they had requested a bottle of

The Forgotten Promise

champagne. I silently prayed that this was simply because it was Valentine's Day and not that there was something else of importance to celebrate.

Brian was on good form. He excelled when he threw a party. The band were great, playing romantic songs spanning several decades and the evening went with a swing. I was amazed that I didn't drop any cutlery when clearing away the dishes from Nick's table, especially as I felt him watching my every move. Each time I approached his table I had to will my legs to move, my knees had turned to jelly, and it was all I could do to refrain from jumping into his arms. Helen and Peter seemed a nice couple, open and friendly, and I liked their company. Sarah, however, was interesting to observe. When I was elsewhere in the restaurant serving other tables, I noticed that she joined in with their conversation but each time I approached she fell silent, her mouth pursed unattractively. She leant into Nick and made sure I noticed their intimacy, all the while shooting me challenging looks. I remembered to look and noticed that there was still no ring on her finger. Mo would have been proud of me. Mo, whose man had flown to Paris from New York to share a romantic Valentine's meal with her before flying back across the pond the following morning!

I was serving coffee and heart-shaped chocolates to the young couple on table one when I heard Sarah exclaiming loudly and excitedly from the next table. Even the young couple looked over at the neighbouring table and we all watched as Sarah hugged and kissed Nick. Helen and Peter smiled happily at the couple.

Oh God, I thought, surely he hasn't proposed? I felt as if I'd been kicked in the stomach.

'See, he belongs to her. Not you!' mocked my inner voice.

Interrupting my rising panic, the young girl said, "Excuse me, but I think that man is trying to attract your attenion."

I looked over to where she was pointing and saw Brian beckoning me over.

"What's up?" I asked as I approached him.

"Your mate's here." He jerked his head over his right shoulder.

"What mate?"

"The one from the film company."

"Dan?" I asked incredulously.

"That's the one."

I rounded the corner and there he was, sitting at the bar.

"Dan!" I rushed up to him, forgetting how annoyed I was with him. "What are you doing here?"

I hugged him hard then quickly checked to see if Lucy was around, but he was on his own.

"Wow, you look hot!" He hugged me back. "Didn't know what sort of reception I'd get."

Then I remembered that he hadn't been in contact for ages.

"But what are you doing here?" I repeated the question.

He looked thinner than I remembered and there were dark shadows under his eyes. Dear exhausted Dan!

"Just had to come and see you."

Brian set a beer on the bar in front of him and Dan quickly stood up, delving his hand deep into his jeans' pocket searching for loose change.

The Forgotten Promise

"On the house, mate," said Brian. "Looks like you could do with one."

Dan smiled thinly.

"Have you had anything to eat?" I asked.

"Yeah. Had a bite on the way down." He looked at me and his eyes alighted on my choker. "Hey, you're wearing the surfer beads I gave you. Didn't think you still cared!"

"Well, you know me Dan, a sentimental old fool," I said, slipping easily into the casual banter we had always shared.

"Fistral Beach. Yeah, I remember that weekend well."

"Look, I've still got some tables to serve but I'll be back in a bit."

I returned to the restaurant wondering where the fantastic Lucy was, tonight of all nights. I served coffee and chocolates to table two and then Peter called me over and asked if they could have coffee and liqueurs in the bar area. I told them to come through when they were ready.

Sarah was talking vivaciously to Nick. He laughed and put his arm around her and, instantly, she looked at me with something like victory in her eyes. I tried to shut out the stab of jealousy, reminding myself that they were a couple after all.

Concentrating on the job in hand, I walked back to join Dan and as I approached, I noticed that Brian, who had been talking to him, discreetly withdrew to the other end of the bar. I sat on the bar stool next to Dan and put my hands on his knees.

"So, why did you *have* to come and see me after all this time?"

He looked at me, searchingly, making me feel as if I had done something wrong. "Well, that's just it—after all this time! You haven't been in touch for ages. I needed to know you were all right."

"What do you mean I haven't been in touch?" Indignantly I sat bolt upright, removing my hands from his knees. "It's you who hasn't returned any of my calls!"

"What calls?" he asked, looking at me in confusion.

"And you didn't even bother to send me a Christmas card," I added sulkily.

"I did send a card, it's you who didn't! At least, Lucy told me she'd sent it . . ."

We looked at each other for a long moment.

"I think someone's been making trouble for us," he said.

"I think you could be right."

"Come here."

Dan leant forward and drew me to him in a warm embrace; a safe, comforting, familiar act I knew so well. Glancing over his shoulder I saw Nick and Sarah standing at the bar a few feet away. Nick was watching us and I could have sworn I saw a fleeting look of hurt in his eyes before he quickly looked away.

Surely not? I thought.

'No, just your pathetic, hopeful imagination,' answered my unrelenting inner voice.

I extricated myself from Dan.

Brian placed four liqueurs on the bar and, as Sarah took them over to the alcove where Helen and Peter were already sitting, I called over to Nick.

"Nick, this is Dan. A good friend of mine from London. We used to work together."

"And play together . . ." said Dan, as he shook Nick's hand.

"Pleased to meet you," Nick responded politely. "Nick Corbin."

"Nick's helped me in the cottage," I explained to Dan. "He's sorted out the window for me."

"No more draughty nights and puddles on the floor then?" Dan laughed.

I watched Nick's face and there was that flicker again, however fleeting.

"He's also fitted the bread oven door, which looks great," I continued.

"Swell," said Dan.

"Oh, I've got so much to tell you!" I said excitedly and Dan laughed at my enthusiasm.

I sensed that Nick was uncomfortable and wondered whether he thought I was being presumptuous, that I had overstepped the mark and was assuming a friendship between us when, in fact, there was none. I was just considering how to proceed when Sarah returned.

"Helen and Peter want to know if you'll join us?"

Putting her arm through Nick's, she looked up at Dan with a coquetish look in her eyes and smiled brightly. Nick shifted awkwardly and I quickly made an excuse.

"I'm still on duty so I can't. But thanks anyway."

"That's OK Maddie, you've served coffees," said Brian, without looking up from the bar. "You don't have to do anything for a while. Go on and enjoy yourself."

I looked at him sharply. Was he enjoying this at my expense? But he turned away and started to stack the glass-washer and I couldn't see the look on his face.

And so I found myself sitting at the Corbin table, feeling as uncomfortable as Nick, while Sarah flirted with Dan. Helen and Peter appeared to be oblivious to any undercurrents. When Sarah learnt that Dan was a cameraman with a film company she was so excited I thought she was going to burst a blood vessel. Although she appeared to be only a few years younger than me, she seemed quite unworldly and immature. She fell quiet when Dan told her that I had been the assistant director before giving it all up to come and live in Walditch. I might have imagined it but I thought I noticed a look of pride, tinged with sadness, creep into Nick's eyes. Helen—lovely woman—congratulated me on having the courage to give up an established career to follow my dreams.

"Maddie will always be OK wherever life takes her," Dan commented.

If only he knew, I thought, taut with the strain of it all.

He smiled at me, such a warm dear smile, that it caught me off guard and for one awful moment I thought I was going to burst into tears. Frantically I searched around for some form of distraction and, luckily, Peter provided me with one.

"Will you concentrate on journalism now?" he asked.

"Well I have been commissioned to write some more eco-based articles but first I've got to find some subjects!"

"I could put you in touch with a work colleague," he suggested amiably. "He runs an organic smallholding and, what with the oil crisis looming, he's turned part of it over to sustainable woodland."

How strange life is, I thought, just when everything seems to have reached a dead-end something turns up.

"Charlie?" asked Nick, the first words he had uttered for quite a while.

"Yes, my partner," Peter explained.

"Charles Bosworth is a loveable rogue," Helen told me. "I swear that if he hadn't been ordered by his father to be a solicitor he would have found himself on the wrong side of the law by now!"

"He sounds quite a character. Thanks, Peter, that would be great. Perhaps you could introduce us?"

Sarah, moving closer to Nick, lay her head on his shoulder and looked up at Dan with big, wide, innocent eyes. "How long have you two known each other?" she asked.

Dan answered cheerily, "Oh years! As soon as I saw Mads, fresh-faced off the plane from Dublin, I just knew we were going to have history together. She was like a breath of fresh air!"

Nick was watching Dan with an impenetrable look on his face.

"'History' being the operative word," I said archly.

"Well, history has a way of repeating itself," countered Dan gently.

Suddenly I felt icy cold and shivered.

"Here, come here." He drew me closer and, looking deep into my eyes, twisted a loose tendril of my hair between his fingers, totally ignoring the others around the table.

I was incensed. How dare Dan assume that he could simply pick up where he had left off just because something might have happened between him and Lucy. And where was the amazing Lucy anyway? Abruptly, I got to my feet and apologised to the rest of the table saying that I had to get back to work.

I cleared away my tables and then started to help the other girls clear theirs. A short while later Helen and Peter appeared in the archway and said goodbye and promised to be in touch regarding Peter's partner. I followed them through to the bar and watched as they collected their coats from the alcove. Sarah was talking to Nick and he smiled down at her, holding her jacket open for her. I tried hard not to stare as she slipped her arms into the sleeves, turned in the circle of his arms and smiled up at him, a look of adoration in her eyes. With difficulty, I averted my eyes from this private display of affection.

Quickly, I joined Vera and Dan who were sitting at the bar drinking and as Nick's group walked by, they complimented Vera on her cooking before continuing on towards the door. I willed Nick to cast me a last brief glance but Peter had engaged him in conversation and, although he hesitated at the door as if to turn around, the next minute they had disappeared together through the doorway. The room suddenly felt very empty.

"The evening seems to have been a success," said Brian, returning from the restaurant. "People are on the dance floor."

He slipped behind the bar, poured a gin and tonic and pushed it towards me. "Here, get this down your neck, Maddie. You deserve it."

I took a large swig but it did nothing to quash my despair.

"These evenings are turning out well," he said. "Maybe we should think about doing a St. Patrick's Day meal?"

Well used to her husband's enthusiastic approach, in a long-suffering voice Vera said, "Let's recover from this one first, Bri love."

"Yeah, OK Vera. But we've got our own resident Irish lass right here in front of us. I bet she could tell us a St. Patrick's Day tale or two!"

But, before I could reply, Dan recounted a visit we had made together back home a few years earlier for the festivities during which I had first introduced him to the wider O'Brien clan.

"That was an experience and a half I can tell you," he said. "I thought I'd died and gone to heaven. Every which way I looked I was surrounded by stunners!"

"Having met Maddie's sister, Mo, I can well believe that," Brian agreed. "Bet there wasn't a Dublin lad safe during their teenage years!"

"You should see the older sister," said Dan, warming to his subject. "And as for Mrs O'Brien—phew!"

He had obviously had one too many.

"I will always hold Finn O'Brien in the highest esteem for being able to handle that family and yet still maintain some semblance of sanity."

The two men laughed and Vera looked at me over the rim of her glass and raised her eyebrows.

Deciding enough was enough, I quickly downed my drink. "Come on, Daniel Carver, I think it's time to go," I said in a prim, schoolmistress voice.

We said goodnight and I went through to the restaurant and waved goodbye to Janet, Gayle and Danielle who were now dancing together in front of the band. Dan collected an overnight bag from his car and we walked across the village green towards The Olde Smithy. It was past midnight and I was bushed but Dan seemed to have found a second wind and wanted to talk.

"Dan, I need to sleep. I've been on my feet all evening," I pleaded. "Look, let's make up a bed for you in the spare room and you can talk while we do that."

He agreed and followed me upstairs. He set his bag down by the window while I found sheets and pillowcases from the airing cupboard.

"Why didn't you phone me to let me know you were coming?" I asked, as we wrestled the duvet into its cover.

"I did," he said. "There was no reply so I left a message."

"For all you knew I might have been out of the country," I countered, thinking of Mo and Jeff. "Whisked away on some romantic trip to Europe."

"True. But then I figured I'd take the chance."

I plumped up a pillow. "So, where's Lucy?"

He didn't answer at once. When I looked at him, to my consternation, I thought he was crying.

"I don't know," he said eventually in a small voice.

I sighed, knowing that blessed sleep was a long way off. "Dan, come downstairs and I'll fix us a drink. Do you want tea?"

He said he would prefer whisky and I decided that I probably needed one as well. I ordered Dan to pour the drinks as I produced ice cubes from the freezer. Opening the back door to let Storm in, I was pleased that I managed to make it to his favourite chair while he was still checking out his bowl in the kitchen.

I glanced at my watch—12.45am. It was going to be a long night. "So, tell me what's happened," I said.

It transpired that Lucy had moved in with Dan the minute she'd arrived in London. He had not been aware that this was the arrangement until he'd woken up one weekend to realise that she'd been living with him for over two weeks but when he asked himself if he wanted her to go, he'd found the answer was 'no'. As he was telling me this, I thought how unfair it was that some women could move in on a man and get what they want when it seemed an impossibility for me. Pulling myself back to Dan's tale, he said he was OK with the invasion on his, up until then, mainly independent, bachelor lifestyle.

"It was great," he said. "She fitted right in."

Storm jumped onto my lap, circled twice and settled down, purring.

"We didn't go out for weeks, we were just happy to stay in."

"Yes, both Caro and Richard said they hadn't heard from you for ages," I said bluntly, not sparing his feelings.

He looked guilty. "As you know, Lucy's full on. She doesn't leave much time for anything else," he said.

As if that's an explanation, I thought.

Pointedly, I said, "And we're your friends!"

He held his hands up in surrender.

"Peace, Mads, please! You have no idea what it's like. She bowled me over completely. She's like a drug." He raked his hands through his hair.

I looked at him with pity. Dan had always been so laid back and easy company, I could see that he was being torn apart by whatever had happened between them.

I took a long sip. "Go on."

He downed his drink in one. "Do you remember asking what baggage she came with?"

I nodded.

"Well, it appears the 'ex' is not so much of an ex."

"Oh Dan. I told you to be careful."

"I know Mads. Don't preach!" he whined.

"How did you find out?"

He then described how Lucy always had always made sure she got to the phone first before he had a chance to answer it.

Probably fielding my phone calls, I thought cynically.

"On the few occasions I did get to answer no-one ever spoke, but I could hear breathing down the line."

"Did you ask her about it?" I asked.

He nodded and said that she had quickly explained it away by saying that she, too, had experienced similar phone calls but had dismissed them as probably a girlfriend of his who didn't want to talk to her.

Devious, manipulative and well practised, I decided.

"I had no reason to doubt her . . . then," he said.

"So what made you?"

"Lucy hasn't been able to find work since arriving in London. When I leave for the studio in the morning she's at the flat and she's always there when I get home. Well, one day I finished at lunchtime and thought I'd surprise her. I got home and let myself in but she wasn't there. I looked on the calendar thinking that she might have an interview, but the date was empty. I thought maybe she'd gone to the shops or something and would be back soon, so I decided to wait for her in bed."

He looked at me guiltily. "We're like that . . ."

"No need to explain," I said hurriedly, having no desire to hear the intimate details. I tickled Storm under his chin. "Go on."

"Well, as soon as I entered the bedroom I knew someone else had been there. The sheets were all rumpled and there was a strong smell of aftershave."

"Are you sure it wasn't perfume?" I asked. "And Lucy could have just had a restless sleep-in."

"When I left for work she was dressed and making the bed."

"Oh!" I looked at Dan. He looked wretched. Lucy must be amazing to have this effect on him, I reflected ruefully. "What happened then?"

"I waited all afternoon and she came back at 4.30pm. I know because I was sitting in the lounge timing her, to see if she'd make sure she was back before I was due home."

"Did you tackle her about it then?" I asked.

"No. I didn't say anything. She didn't notice me at first. She had a secret smile on her face."

I knew that smile; I had seen it in my kitchen.

"She looked shocked when she saw me sitting there but said she'd been touting around the agents and that she was tired and needed a shower. I let it ride, even when she stripped the bed saying that we needed clean sheets though she'd changed them only a few days before."

"So, then what happened?"

"Nothing really. She was always there when I got home and our sex life was as fantastic as ever."

"What about the phone calls? Did they continue?"

"They stopped but she was always texting. And then, last Tuesday, Tom asked if Lucy's brother had got the job. When I asked him what he meant he said he'd bumped into her coming out of the Hilton with a man one afternoon the previous week. She'd introduced him as her brother. Said he was in London for a job interview. When I told him I didn't know anything about a brother, Tom looked awkward and said he must have got it wrong."

Tom, the stunt co-ordinator at Hawkstone, was diplomacy personified. I knew how awful he would have felt if he thought he had caused trouble.

"When I got home that evening she was there as usual," Dan continued. "But I noticed yet another change of sheets and that made me see red. Over supper I asked if she was free the next day to meet me for lunch. She made some excuse saying that she had to meet some producer about a costume drama and when I asked for more details she was fairly vague and changed the subject. A while later her mobile went off and she started texting."

"How could you let her continue living in your flat if you were so suspicious of her?" I asked incredulously. "The pressure must have been unbearable."

Dan looked so sad.

"If I hadn't come home that lunchtime, I wouldn't have known anything was amiss. Everything—and I mean everything—was exactly as it had always been. She has a voracious appetite." He leant forward with head in hands. "I tell you, she's like a drug!"

This superwoman was really pissing me off.

"How did you find out it was her ex?" I asked as kindly as I could.

He sighed deeply and sat up again.

"I left the flat the next day as if to go to work, but phoned in sick. I sat in the car just around the corner in Gladstone Street. I had a good view of the front steps and I didn't have to wait long. A man turned up and Lucy opened the door to him. She was just wearing a T-shirt!"

I remembered her standing in my bedroom wearing a T-shirt with those long, slender legs seemingly going on forever.

"Could have been her brother," I suggested.

Dan gave me a withering look—justly deserved. "She kissed him and pulled him into the flat."

OK. Maybe not!

"So what did you do?" I asked.

"I waited about ten minutes and then quietly let myself into the flat. They were going at it hammer and tongs in *my* bed," he said outraged. "I stood in the doorway and watched them."

I could see it now, Dan coolly watching the cavorting couple.

"They were so preoccupied she didn't notice me for several minutes."

I could imagine her shock when she eventually saw him.

"What happened then?" I asked.

Dan rubbed his forehead, as if trying to eradicate the vision. "She tried to cover herself up. Kept saying she was really sorry but could explain."

"And the guy? What was he doing?"

"What blokes normally do in those circumstances. Looking foolish, hopping around the room trying to get into his underpants."

I laughed and Dan shot me a glance. Quickly, I recomposed my features into concern whilst idly wondering whether Lucy's tousled hair look—as if she'd only just got out of bed—was because more often that not she just had!

"I told him to leave my flat, which he did," Dan continued. "I asked Lucy what was going on and she started crying, saying that when I first met her this bloke, Tony, had just left her and gone back to his wife and two kids. They'd apparently been having an affair for four years and he suddenly felt guilty about it. She said that she couldn't believe it when I started paying her attention as she thought a bloke like me would never be interested in someone like her."

Oh spare me the violins, I thought.

"She said she dreamt of making a new life with me and was overwhelmed when I'd appeared to want the same thing."

I was appalled at how gullible Dan had been.

"She was full on from the start, Mads. I know I should have heeded your words but she's like a drug. I can't . . . couldn't get enough of her."

"Putty," I said.

He had the decency to look sheepish.

"So why did this Tony come back into her life?" I asked in a no-nonsense voice.

"Apparently he was never out of it," Dan said bitterly. "As soon as Lucy told him she'd met someone else his interest was rekindled."

Oh very clever, I thought.

"And once she'd moved to London he called her and told her he couldn't be without her."

Dan looked so deflated, he seemed to collapse in the chair.

"He's a salesman," he continued. "Made sure he spent a lot of time in London and the Home Counties."

He looked so lost that I removed Storm from my lap and went over to Dan and hugged him.

"And do you know what the most galling thing is, Mads?"

I shook my head.

"He's spent about as much time in my bed as I have over the past four months!"

It hadn't been all fun for Lucy, though, I considered. She must have had one hell of a lot of laundry.

"When did all this happen?"

"Day before yesterday. I told Lucy to go and she pleaded with me to give her a second chance. I almost gave in."

I groaned. "But you didn't, did you?"

He shook his head.

I had never seen Dan like this before. He was always so level-headed and in control. It shook me to the core to see him falling apart.

"Come on Dan," I said gently, pulling him out of the chair. "It's past 3am and I'm knackered. Let's go to bed."

The look of panic that swept across his face made me want to burst out laughing.

"In separate beds, Dan. I don't want to jump your bones tonight."

Embarrassment replaced the panic.

"Mads, you know you're really special to me but what with all this, I . . . I'm a mess," he stuttered.

"You don't need to explain, Dan. We're good friends. Let's just get some sleep. It'll all seem so much better in the morning. When do you have to go back to work?"

He said he'd taken a couple of days off so I suggested we slept in and got up when we fancied. I glanced in the hall mirror on the way upstairs, steeling myself in case I saw the 'other' woman watching, but the glass was clear and simply reflected Dan following me. On the landing I turned to him, stood on tiptoes and kissed him lightly on the mouth. His lips responded out of familiarity but the look in his eyes was one of sheer terror. Poor Dan!

I lay in bed thinking about everything Dan had told me. I was so angry with Lucy. He didn't deserve to be treated so flippantly. Dan was a decent man and I resolved that should our paths ever cross again Lucy would definitely get a piece of my mind.

Sleep came to me eventually, but it was a fitful sleep and I dreamt of shadowy figures coming and going in the night and horses—many horses—below in the courtyard. I awoke and looked at the clock—4.33am. I sighed, opened the bedside cabinet drawer, checked that the precious jewellery was still in the wooden casket and then turned over, instantly drifting off to sleep and immediately returning to my dream.

In the corner of the room stood the large, rustic cot and I could hear crying emanating from within. I climbed out of bed and walked cautiously towards the cot, peered in and saw the little boy who had danced with me in the sitting room. He was red faced, hot and flushed with fever, crying and whimpering all the time. He looked up, stretched his arms towards me as I leaned over the cot and picked him up. I tried to comfort him as he desperately clung to me.

Aware of another presence, I glanced across to the other side of the room and saw the girl standing there, looking out of the window that overlooked the village green. She was aged about seven and had long, curly, auburn hair, not dissimilar to my own.

"Come away from the window Elisabeth," I whispered urgently. "Come away now."

She moved slightly but stayed within range of the window. That daughter of mine is so headstrong, I thought, it will get her into trouble one of these days. Daughter of mine? What was I thinking? And yet I knew it to be true.

"Elisabeth, come here!" I hissed in a louder whisper.

She ignored me and continued to look out of the window. Leaving the boy crying on the bed, I got up, crossed the room in three strides and roughly grabbed her by the arm. She cried out in pain with a hurt look in her eyes. I pulled her away from the window but not before one of the soldiers below looked up and saw us standing there. He had a round, not unkindly, ruddy face and wore his hair short under a metal helmet. He stared up

The Forgotten Promise

at us in surprise and I noticed his leather tunic and metal breastplate. He turned to say something to the soldier standing next to him but did not and, as we withdrew, he glanced back up at the bedroom window.

It was dusk and raining hard. From the safety of the room I looked out at the village green. It was full of soldiers and horses, the ground trampled and poached. A huddle of men stood sheltering beneath the boughs of the oak tree and, with surprise, I saw how immature and small it was. Across the other side of the green stood the Blacksmith's Arms, only it wasn't. It was a tavern—a sign swung from its stone front elevation—but whereas the Blacksmith's roof was tiled, this roof was thatched and there were stone mullions at the windows. An archway lead through the centre of the building and I could see a stable yard beyond.

"When I say come, I mean come!" I scolded Elisabeth, who pulled a face at me.

Returning to the bed, I cradled the boy once more in my arms. He was covered in an angry rash and burning up. Lovingly, I stroked his forehead.

"Hush my child. Hush . . ."

I was frantic with worry and the girl sulking in the corner of the room was not helping matters. I could stand it no longer. "Elisabeth. Go to bed!" I said angrily.

She stood and glared at me before stomping off to the opposite corner of the room. With a dramatic flourish, she threw aside a sackcloth curtain that hung from the ceiling before disappearing behind it.

"I was only looking at the horses," she said in a sulky voice.

"I know," I replied more gently. "But it's best that the soldiers don't know we're here."

I knew I had to be strong for the children but I was gripped with a deep sense of dread. The boy moaned and wriggled in my arms and tried to sit up, then started to thrash around. I felt so helpless. Tears of frustration pricked my eyes.

"What's wrong with Francis?" asked the girl, peering out from behind the curtain.

"I don't know," I said. Briskly, I wiped away a tear.

"Mother, are you crying?"

"No. Now go to sleep."

She mumbled something which I didn't catch, but I could hear her getting into bed without further ado.

I gently stroked the boy and started to sing quietly to him. It was a pleasant, rhythmic melody with a distinctly old-fashioned lilt and, eventually, he slipped into a feverish sleep. I lay there on the bed with the little boy and listened to the rain. An acrid smell lay thick in the air and I heard the rhythmic clang of a blacksmith's hammer on anvil. Above the constant murmur of men's voices, one voice, louder than the rest, suddenly issued an instruction. There followed a series of shouts and the next minute I heard horses hooves clattering down the stony road.

As I lay there with my son in my arms I tried to block out all around me. A while later I heard weary footsteps on the stairs—six, seven, eight and nine—and I became suddenly alert. Then whispering from the other side of the cloth curtain.

"Goodnight father." Elisabeth's clear, sweet voice drifted across the room as someone climbed onto the bed next to me.

"Be careful, Mary. We must be vigilant," a low voice cautioned. "Those men have thunder in their hearts."

The Forgotten Promise

I turned and looked into the face of the man I had seen at the graveside. The minute I saw him I was filled with such intense emotions that I found it hard to breathe. His face was sweaty and grimy and filled with misgiving.

"The boy is sick," I said. "I've tried Culpeper's herbs to no effect. He needs a doctor."

The man leant across me and placed his hand on the, now, sleeping boy's forehead and nodded. He looked at me and the soft, tender eyes that gazed into mine were Nick's and yet his features were more pinched and angular, brought about by an altogether tougher existence.

"Try and sleep a little, Mary."

Gently he kissed my cheek and I sighed. The fear still lurked within the darkest corners of my mind but, with this man by my side, maybe—just maybe—it was not so oppressive as it had first seemed.

As I relaxed under his loving touch I whispered, "I love you Nat."

He swallowed hard and when he spoke his voice was husky with emotion. "And you, my love, are my life."

15th February

I awoke the next morning to the sound of the phone ringing. As I sat up a splitting headache took hold. I felt truly awful and decidedly nauseas. Heaving myself out of bed, I threw on a dressing gown and rushed downstairs, reaching the phone just before it rang off.

"Hello," I said breathlessly.

"Miss O'Brien?" a man's voice enquired.

"Speaking."

"Professor Stephens. Returning your call."

"Oh Professor Stephens, thank you so much for phoning!"

I explained how Nick and I had found the jewellery in the bread oven and that we both thought it was old. He agreed that it sounded intriguing and was keen to examine it further.

"No time like the present," he stated. "I have a rare afternoon off today. Would that be convenient?"

"Yes," I said, excitement bubbling. "Yes, that would be just fine."

He proceeded to give me his address which I scribbled down on the notepad by the phone. He said he looked forward to seeing me at 3pm, in time for tea.

I filled the kettle, threw teabags into a couple of mugs and put some food in Storm's bowl, although he was still curled up asleep in his favourite chair. While waiting for the kettle to boil, I drank a glass of cold water hoping

The Forgotten Promise

that this would quash the nausea rising in my stomach. I glanced out at the courtyard and remembered my dream. Last night, it had been full of horses and as I looked more closely at the outbuildings I wondered at their original use. And then I thought of that other man, the man who seemed to mean the world to me, and then my thoughts turned to Nick.

With dismay, I remembered how Valentine's evening had not been a success for me and it was apparent that Nick and Sarah were very much a couple. I also recalled that Dan had intimated very strongly to them that he was hoping to get back with me—although I very much doubted that now, having heard his sorry tale—and I remembered the inscrutable look on Nick's face when he had heard the news. Nick confused me. He was friendly and open and, yet, each time there was the slightest chance of us getting closer, the chasm between us yawned deep and wide.

I made the tea and carried the mugs upstairs, being careful not to spill any, and knocked softly on the spare bedroom door. I heard a groan and entered.

"Morning Dan," I said, as cheerily as I could muster.

Dan lay on his back, one hand covering his eyes. "Can't be that time already? God, I feel rough!"

"Snap. I've got some Resolve somewhere."

He groaned again, pushed himself up into a crumpled sitting position and took the proffered mug of tea from me. He did look awful and I suspected that it was more than just a hangover he was suffering from. No doubt he'd been beating himself up over Lucy for most of the night.

I sat on the bed beside him and asked whether he planned to stay another day or two or immediately head back to London. He fumbled for his mobile phone. There were no messages or missed calls.

"I'll stay on, if that's OK?"

"No trouble. But I've got an appointment with Professor Stephens this afternoon. You can drive me there."

He agreed. When he didn't ask who Professor Stephens was I knew he was still in the doldrums and hadn't really been listening.

"Shall I run you a bath?" I asked.

He stared straight ahead and then, turning to me, smiled a sad smile. "You're a good friend, Mads. Caro always told me I should have made our arrangement permanent."

"It wasn't meant to be, Dan, however well your sister means."

I thought he was going to cry, so gave him a friendly nudge.

"Missed opportunity," he said quietly.

However fond I was of him the days ahead were going to be very long if this sombre mood didn't lift. I finished my tea.

"I'll find that Resolve and run you a bath," I announced, more brightly than I felt. "There's plenty of hot water. Take as long as you want."

I took some Resolve as well, for good measure.

By the time Dan emerged from the bathroom it was past noon. I made toast and tea—neither of us could face more than that—and then found a map of the area and checked out the route to Professor Stephens. He lived at The Manse in a village called Hermitage and this proved to be a pleasant drive of some twenty miles amongst Dorset's rolling hills. During the journey I read extracts from a book I had on the area and it wasn't long before Dan's inquisitive nature shook him out of his gloom and he began to notice the countryside we were driving through.

"Listen to this, Dan. *Although situated only four miles from Cerne Abbas, Hermitage seems to delight in being a forgotten place. In Sir Frederick Treves' book, 'The Highways and Bye-ways of Dorset', it is described as a Rip Van Winkle village lying at the foot of the grassy slopes of High Stoy, a lovely hill 860 feet high, about six miles south of Sherborne. One cannot imagine a greater solitude for the Order of St. Augustine whose hermitage once stood here, yet the monks left as long ago as 1460. In 1583 a landslide caused three acres of land to slip and block the highway to Cerne Abbas. Treves, with dry humour, comments: Since this date nothing in Hermitage has moved and it is a question now if even an earthquake would rouse it'.*"

I glanced at Dan who had a faraway look on his face.

"I wonder if Professor Stephens will be roused by my find?" I concluded loudly.

"What find?" Dan asked suddenly.

So he was listening.

"Why are we going to see this bloke?"

"Took you long enough, Daniel Carver," I said firmly.

He acknowledged the truth in this and looked at me sheepishly. "Sorry Mads. I must be terrible company."

"Not exactly terrible . . ."

We crossed the A37 and followed a country lane until reaching the crossroads in the middle of Hermitage which, as Sir Frederick Treves had stated, did appear to be a sleepy, untouched, Rip Van Winkle of a village. Immediately ahead was a no through road and, following Professor Stephens' directions, I instructed Dan to drive to the end. We spotted The Old Manse straightaway; a tall, imposing property set in manicured grounds with plenty of shingled parking in front of the house. Dan drove through the open wrought iron entrance gates and onto the sweeping driveway, coming to a halt in front of the house. He parked alongside an immaculate black Porsche. Belying my earlier consideration that he might be slow to rouse, Professor Stephens was obviously a man of speed!

As I stepped out of the car, precious casket in hand, I heard a muffled bark from somewhere deep within the house. Suddenly, the large, freshly painted front door swung open and a tall, casually dressed, grey haired man, aged about sixty, appeared on the doorstep. He was attractive, in a boffinish sort of way, and steely blue eyes peered at me over a large, prominent nose which was suitably offset by a wide, generous mouth.

"Madeleine O'Brien I presume?" he enquired, the upper-class accent in keeping with its surroundings.

I walked up the tiled steps, shook the extended large hand and introduced Dan.

"Nice bit of metal on the front drive," Dan murmured appreciatively, looking back longingly at the Porsche.

"My little indulgence, dear boy. I have so few these days."

"911 Turbo. Top speed 193mph!" swooned Dan.

"Ah, you know your stuff, young man," replied the professor. "And 0-62mph in less than four seconds. Not that I tell the Dorset police that, you understand."

He beckoned us into the hallway.

It was cool in the house. Looking around, I observed the original black and white floor tiles, the high ceilings with their ornate cornicing and the dado rails that ran the full length of the hall. A house of substance, befitting a man of Professor Stephens' obvious authority and status. Nothing fake about this man, I decided, and a sense of excitement began to take hold. Perhaps there would be some answers for me today.

"Shall we go through to the sunroom? I will ask Janice to bring in the tea."

We followed him through a doorway at the end of the hall that led into a Victorian orangery filled with plants. Some sunroom! Inviting us to sit at an ornate cast-iron table, the professor then disappeared into the house to organise the tea. Dan looked at me with raised eyebrows.

"There's obviously money in archaeology. I should have considered that when I was thinking of a career."

"Shhh. He'll hear," I whispered urgently.

It was a pleasant view from the orangery. The garden, stocked with a large selection of mature shrubs and specimen trees, backed onto open fields that ran into woodland. In the centre of the lawn was a pond built from mellow Dorset stone and a substantial rockery to one side supported a waterfall feature that cascaded into the still waters of the pool. The grass, I noted, comparing it to my own sorry patch, was mowed to within an inch of its life. Not a weed dared peep its head above the bowling green that masqueraded as a lawn.

Presently, Professor Stephens reappeared clutching a pair of spectacles in one hand, followed by a black Labrador who was as grey around the gills as his owner.

"You don't mind dogs, do you?" he asked. "Bertie is no trouble these days though in his youth he led me a merry dance, I can tell you. Always running off after any bitch, so to speak." He shot me an apologetic glance and smiled conspiratorily at Dan.

I assured him that I loved dogs, thinking of Baron and Casper in particular, and suddenly I flushed, which had nothing to do with the warmth of the orangery.

"Fabulous garden," Dan complimented.

"Another of my indulgences, dear boy. This has been twenty years in creation. I think it passable now, don't you?"

"Very," agreed Dan.

The professor shot Dan an appreciative look.

"Ah Janice. Thank you."

He rose to his feet as a plump, bustling, sweet-faced woman appeared with a large, heavily laden tray set with a silver tea service, fine bone china and a homemade fruitcake. Obviously a bachelor, I wondered if 'tea' was a ritual for the professor. He took the tray from the woman.

"Would you like some biscuits to go with Marjorie's cake, professor?" the woman asked in a broad Dorset accent.

"Oh I think so, Janice. That would be most appropriate."

She disappeared through the open door.

"Janice is yet another of my indulgences," he explained, as he set the tray on the table. "So I guess one could say I do have quite a few these days after all!"

He chuckled to himself. "I think it such a shame that more people don't indulge in a 'lady who does'."

Dan's eyes sought mine, his left eyebrow twitching ever higher, and I shot him a warning glance.

Janice reappeared with a plateful of biscuits which, to my delight, included my particular favourite—chocolate Hobnobs. In fact, these could be referred to as 'my little indulgence' I thought in amusement.

The Forgotten Promise

"I'll be off now professor" Janice announced. "I've hung the freshly ironed clothes in the wardrobe and the silver's all been cleaned and put back in the sideboard."

"Thank you, Janice. Most kind. I'll see you next Friday then."

Janice bade us farewell and diappeared through the open door once again.

Pouring tea into the china cups, the professor waved at the cake and biscuits and invited us to 'tuck in'. Dan picked up a plate and selected a large slice of the fruitcake and the professor congratulated him, saying it was an excellent choice. I helped myself to a biscuit.

"Take two, dear girl. You look as though you could do with a square meal."

I did as I was told.

Choosing the fruitcake himself, the professor broke off a piece and gave it to the Labrador sitting patiently at his feet. The dog wolfed it down, licked its lips and looked hopefully at the man for more, but Professor Stephens had turned his attention to me.

"Now, young lady, what's all this about a treasure trove?"

I explained how Dan and I had discovered the bread oven and, on further investigation, I had unearthed a wooden box, which I now placed on the table before me. Carefully, I opened the lid and showed him the pendant and ring lying within. As he leant forward to examine the contents, without warning, I was overcome with a curious sense of possession and when he picked up the ring I had to sit on my hands to prevent an overwhelming urge to snatch it away from him.

With careful deliberation he put on his glasses, resting them halfway down his prominent, bony nose. Tilting his head back, he peered through the lenses and turned the ring in his fingers.

"Intriguing," he said. "Very intriguing. What age did you say your cottage was?"

"The estate agent said part of it dates back to around the 17th Century," I replied.

"I would say they are probably right judging by this."

Excitement caught at my throat.

"I won't be a minute." The professor replaced the ring in the casket and strode from the room, the Labrador hauling itself to its feet and following a few steps behind. Dan shifted in his chair and leaned forward to pick up the ring.

"Don't touch!" I snapped.

He looked at me in surprise and I wondered why I had shouted at him in such a cross, irritated manner.

"I wasn't going to damage it!" he replied defensively. Justifiably peeved, he sat back in the chair and helped himself to a biscuit.

"Sorry Dan. I just think the least we contaminate the jewellery, the better," I said feebly.

He didn't look at me and chewed furiously. I could tell he was sulking.

Professor Stephens reappeared with an eyeglass and, placing it to his left eye socket, proceeded to examine the ring. I knew it was childish but when people used eyeglasses it always made me think of cyborgs. I wanted to laugh but managed to swallow the smile.

"Yes, very intriguing." He placed the ring on the table and took the pendant out of the box.

Nick's voice rang in my ears. '*A love token*' he had said.

Professor Stephens carefully turned the heart pendant over. "This has been very cleverly crafted. It's not the work of a professional, you understand, but whoever created it was a very talented craftsman nonetheless."

He carefully placed it on the table and, once again, picked up the ring. Holding it lightly between his forefinger and thumb, he started to apply a constant pressure. "If I'm not mistaken, this is a ring in three parts," he explained.

He continued the pressure but nothing happened. "I wonder if you would mind if I showed these to a colleague of mine, a jewellery specialist?"

He replaced the jewellery in the box and removed the eyeglass, which now left a red rim encircling his eye.

"Oh, I'm not sure I want to let them go. I don't know . . ." I was consumed by panic and Dan gave me an odd look.

"Go on Mads, let the professor show them to the specialist."

"I assure you young lady that no harm will come to these pieces."

I hesitated, unsure what to do.

"I will write you a receipt," continued the professor. "If they are what I think they are, well, they are a marvellous find."

I was racked with indecision but I did want to discover more about the jewellery. Even this visit had not produced the answers I had hoped for.

"Do you know what metal they are?" I asked, stalling for time, still trying to decide whether I wanted to leave these precious objects with this man.

"Oh, I should say that the ring is enamelled gold and if I'm not mistaken the stone is a ruby."

I peered at the contents of the wooden casket in astonishment. "Ruby? I thought it was a piece of coloured glass!"

"Ah, just you wait." Professor Stephens grinned at me. "Philip is one of the best restorers I know. He has a very sympathetic touch. Then you will see what a beautiful piece it is. The pendant, on the other hand, is not gold."

Dan seemed to have forgiven me my earlier outburst and was no longer sulking. Once more, he was intrigued. "Can you date them precisely?" he asked.

The professor smiled at Dan in such a way that it suddenly occurred to me he might swing the other way, which would explain his bachelorhood.

"Well, dear boy, the heart became a very popular design during the 17th Century and if the ring is what I think it is, that would date it to around the same time. I would say early to middle 1600s."

I shivered. Someone had just tiptoed upon my grave.

"Mads, you've got to let the specialist look at these," Dan said enthusiastically.

I looked from one man to the other: the older fired up by the love of antiquity; the younger excited by the mystery of the unknown. Reluctantly, I agreed.

Professor Stephens wrote out a receipt and handed it to me. "I should think it will be another couple of weeks before I have some answers for you."

I looked back at the wooden box on the table, still unwilling to leave it, and then followed the two men to the front door. We thanked the professor for tea and headed towards the car, the deep gravel crunching beneath our feet. Dan paused enroute to look through the darkened glass windows of the Porsche.

The Forgotten Promise

"Next time you visit, young man, I will take you for a spin," promised the professor.

I looked over at Dan, raised my eyebrows and saw him uncharacteristically blush. The professor's interest in him had obviously not gone unnoticed.

That evening I felt agitated and couldn't settle. I was fretting about the jewellery no longer being in my possession. Dan was amused by my agitation.

"Why does it mean so much to you?" he asked.

"I don't know. It just does."

I didn't want to discuss it.

He lay on the couch, Storm draped across his chest. The cat was totally relaxed, purring contentedly as Dan stroked him. Having been so nervous and wary at the beginning, it amazed me how trusting Storm's natural character was and how he befriended everyone. Not for the first time I wondered what circumstances had caused him to happen upon me.

I was sitting at the dining room table trying to access the internet and intending to do a search on Professor Stephens and his specialist friend, Philip Harcourt-Jones.

"Oh damn, why can't I connect tonight?" I said in exasperation.

"Try turning your router off and on," Dan suggested.

"Good thinking."

I got up to walk to the wall where the router was plugged in but, as I bent down to switch it off, I noticed a shadow pass across the glass divide between the two rooms. Straightening up, I watched as the man, Nat, walked across the living room and out through the doorway into the kitchen. Quickly moving to the archway, I saw him walk straight through the rear kitchen wall. I glanced over at Dan who was still languidly reclining on the sofa, oblivious, but Storm was now sitting bolt upright looking intently at the kitchen doorway. I hurried to the kitchen and peered out of the window but there was nothing to see. Nat was not in the courtyard.

"What's up Storm?" I heard Dan say. "Seen a ghost?"

Walking back to the doorway, I stared at Dan.

"Why are you looking at me like that?" he asked, moving Storm off his chest and sitting up.

"Like what?"

"Like you're expecting me to do or say something."

"Didn't you see it then?"

"See what?"

I had always believed Dan and I could talk about anything. We had always appeared to be in tune with each other, but since Lucy had got inside his head we seemed to have lost that connection.

"I thought I saw something," I said. "Never mind. Do you want a drink?"

"Jack Daniels would be good," he said, as his mobile rang.

I turned back to the kitchen. Stretching up for the glass tumblers on the top shelf, I decided that if I was going to start making a habit of drinking shorts I had better move them to a more accessible height. I busied myself pouring drinks and heard Dan speaking intently in a low voice. He had never spoken to me in that voice. I opened the freezer door and pulled out a tray of ice cubes as Storm wandered through to investigate his food bowl.

Suddenly Dan's voice rose in frustration. "But why should I? I don't know how you can ask me that. You obviously don't know me that well!"

The Forgotten Promise

It was impossible not to overhear the conversation. Hesitating, drinks in hand, I wondered whether I should go into the courtyard to give him some privacy.

"Well you'd better shack up with him again then," he said loudly and very firmly.

I left it a couple more minutes, took a deep breath and walked into the room. Dan sat on the edge of the couch, head in hands, his mobile on the seat beside him. I cleared my throat. He didn't look up.

"Here, drink this." I held out the tumbler to him.

"God, Mads, what am I going to do?" He took the glass from me and I sat down opposite him.

"I guess that was Lucy?"

He nodded wearily.

"What do you *want* to do?" I asked, bobbing an ice cube with my finger.

"What I want to do and what I need to do are two different things," he mumbled.

"I suppose she's asking to come back," I said, taking a sip.

"Begging, more like," he replied. "She says she can't believe she's cocked up so badly. She wants to give it another go."

"Oh Dan, you've only known her five minutes! For all you know, this might be serial behaviour."

He screwed his face up and I knew he was hurting. "I thought we had something special. Says she can't be on her own." He looked so troubled. "Says she doesn't trust herself and might do something."

I was so angry with her for playing that particular card. If she had been in the room I would have punched her.

"Dan, listen. I'm going to be brutal. I know I only met her that weekend you came and stayed with me but that's all I needed to understand her. She got into your bed within minutes of meeting you, she knows how to play a man and get what she wants. She's not going to do away with herself in a hurry, if that's what you're worried about. She's not that type! She's a survivor. Don't be fooled by that winsome little girl thing . . ." In full flow now, I couldn't stop, " . . . or manipulated."

He stared at me coldly. "And when did you become such an authority on the subject?"

Ouch!

"Well I am a woman," I replied, keeping my voice steady.

I couldn't believe how defensive he was being. She had really got under his skin and she didn't deserve his loyalty. He knocked his drink back in one.

"I tell you what," I said, taking control. "Let's go to the Chinese in Bridport. They do a fantastic Peking Duck, so I've been told."

He nodded, though I wasn't sure he'd really heard me. I hauled him to his feet, found his jacket and marched him out to the car.

We had a relatively jolly evening and the restaurant was surprisingly busy for a Thursday night in February. There was plenty of noise and laughter from the other tables and I tried to keep Dan's mind off Lucy. I told him how Mo had met a successful airline executive from New York who thought nothing of flying around the world to join her wherever she happened to be.

"Good for her! She deserves some pampering."

He had always liked Mo.

The Forgotten Promise

And I told him about the freelance writing work that was slowly beginning to trickle my way and how the editor of the county magazine had invited me to submit a series of write-ups on places to eat for their 'local eateries' feature.

"Well, at least you won't go without a square meal or two then," he teased, the old Dan beginning to emerge. "Perhaps you should include this place? We could get away without paying."

"I don't want to be seen as some free-loader before I've even started, Dan!"

We split the bill.

It was a cold night and the temperature had plummeted while we were in the restaurant. Dan put his arm around me as we hurried back to the car. As I fumbled in my pockets for the car keys his mobile rang. He answered it, immediately turning away from me, and walked to the far side of the car park. I sighed, opened the door and climbed in. A thin layer of ice had formed on the windscreen.

I switched on the heater.

Dan must be freezing, I thought, as I blew on my hands to warm them. He paced up and down, talking intently all the while and, at one point, stopped and madly gesticulated. He didn't look cold; in fact he looked hot and bothered.

I switched on the wipers and watched as they rhythmically smeared ice in a large arc across the glass.

I switched on the radio.

Ten minutes later Dan returned to the car. As he opened the door a blast of cold air accompanied him.

"Get in quick!"

He jumped in and shut the door.

"OK?" I asked.

He nodded but said nothing and we drove back to Walditch in silence.

I didn't question him further that night. It was up to Dan to decide how to handle Lucy but I fervently hoped he would see sense and not take up with her again. On the landing we said goodnight and went to our separate rooms.

A few hours later I awoke, or was I dreaming? When I thought about it later I couldn't be sure. I was sobbing and quickly sat up, trying to catch my breath. I breathed in slowly and deeply but the ache in my heart was too much.

"Hush . . . Don't fret so," said a warm, kindly voice.

A hand gently rubbed my back.

"The boy's in a much happier place."

A tender kiss on my neck.

I turned towards the voice. In the darkness I could just make out Dan, though he was altered, and I saw that it was Nat. Immediately, I looked across to the corner of the room. It was empty. The cot was not there. A wave of utter despair engulfed me and all at once I understood what it was I had been so frantically searching for. My son.

"He's at peace, my love. Let him be." Nat wiped away my tears and kissed me softly. "I will give you another," he whispered.

Despite my heavy heart, the instant I felt his weight a charge surged through me. I was amazed at how hungry I was for him and the shudders he drew from my body. Our lovemaking that night built to a wild and desperate crescendo, as if our very lives depended on it.

Afterwards, as we lay sated in each other's arms, slipping into sleep, he whispered, "I will love you for eternity, Mary, my love, my life . . ."

The Forgotten Promise

The next morning I came to feeling emotionally exhausted, my eyes sore from crying. Turning over, I saw Dan asleep beside me. The movement disturbed him and he started to wake. I watched as he opened his eyes a fraction and focused on me. He smiled and sleepily closed them again. Suddenly his eyes snapped open and he sat bolt upright.

"What?" he asked in bewilderment. "What am I doing here?"

Now, how do I explain this? I wondered.

"What's going on?" he demanded.

"I'm as surprised as you," I answered innocently.

"But hell! How did I get here?"

"Well, if you can't remember I suppose you might have been sleepwalking or something . . ."

"Oh God!" he groaned, holding his head in his hands; a gesture he seemed to be doing a lot these days.

I decided to be flippant. "Well thanks a bunch!"

He looked at me with an anguished look. "I don't mean it like that. I mean I'm bloody sleepwalking now!"

"Don't worry about it Dan," I said calmly. "It's probably got something to do with being in a strange house." *Stranger than he could ever imagine.* "You'll be fine once you're back in your own flat."

He didn't look convinced.

"I'm going to make tea," I said and I swung my legs out of bed. But he grabbed my arm.

"Mads, we didn't, did we?" he asked, panic rising in his voice.

"Don't think so," I half-lied, unsure whether it had been Dan or Nat that I had made love to so passionately the night before. "But so what if we did? You're not married or anything."

"Oh Christ!" he groaned.

Now I was beginning to feel angry. "For God's sake Dan, it's not as if we don't know each other's bodies inside out!"

"I know, I know. Oh Mads, I'm in such a mess!"

And feeling sorry for yourself, I thought, is so very unattractive. Get a grip!

I headed for the door, stomped downstairs and filled the kettle. Storm, curled up in his favourite chair by the inglenook, watched me through the open doorway. He stretched, jumped down and walked into the kitchen. I opened a tin of cat food and he purred loudly, rubbing around my legs.

"You and me, Storm," I said softly. "That's the way to be. Just you and me. So much less complicated."

I was still irritated as I took the mugs of tea back upstairs. When I opened the bedroom door Dan was on his mobile. I assumed to Lucy. Swiftly, I placed the mugs on the bedside cabinet, turned and walked back downstairs to the bathroom. Peering in the mirror I was stunned by my appearance—swollen face and puffball eyes—and Dan hadn't even noticed! I splashed cold water on my face, soaked a couple of cotton wool pads and placed them on my eyelids, savouring the sweet coolness against my burning skin.

I'd just finished brushing my teeth when I heard Dan coming noisily downstairs. Why did he seem to be such a bull in a china shop these days? He knocked loudly on the door.

"Mads, I think I'll head back to London this morning."

I opened the bathroom door, toothbrush in hand. Dan was already dressed.

The Forgotten Promise

"That was Lucy. She wants to meet up today." He stood back from the doorway as if to get out of the firing line. "And before you say anything, I'm not going to welcome her back with open arms."

"I wasn't going to say anything, Dan," I said crossly.

He looked at me long and hard. It was a cold, unforgiving look, one that I hadn't seen before and I wondered who this person was. Obviously eager to be on the road and away back to Lucy, he said he would make a start on the breakfast.

He left around 11am without either of us mentioning Lucy again or his presence in my bed the previous night. Once he'd gone I breathed a sigh of relief. I was sorry to see Dan so troubled and in such turmoil but the laid back, easygoing man I had known for so long was nowhere in sight.

18th February

I spent Sunday morning working on a piece about the Blacksmith's Arms for the 'local eateries' feature, but by lunchtime I felt claustrophobic and desperately needed to get out. Following Dan's unexpected visit I had been in a strange mood, reflective and quiet, and my usual optimistic outlook had deserted me.

With no pre-planned destination in mind, I drove out of the village thinking it would be interesting to see where I eventually arrived. It turned out to be the Hardy Monument standing tall on the summit of Black Down Hill, high above the village of Portesham, visible from many miles away and commanding breathtaking views of most of Dorset.

Months later I would ask myself why, on that particular day, I had chosen this area but at the time I was simply enjoying a break in the weather, driving along country lanes that twisted and turned through the beautiful Dorset downland.

It was a crystal clear day and a wintry sun was at its zenith when I arrived at the monument. I parked the car alongside the only two other cars in the car park and grabbed my camera. I took several photos of the monument and the surrounding landscape before finding a grassy hillock a short distance away. Throwing my waxed jacket on the ground, I sat down upon it. The air was so fresh and clear up here and I breathed in great lungfuls, trying to rid myself of the strange mood that besieged me. I could see for miles and felt on top of the world.

The view from the western tip of Chesil Beach right the way along the coast to the Isle of Portland was breathtaking and I watched lazily as two tankers slowly worked their way along the horizon of a sparkling, mirror-like calm sea.

I had been sitting there for maybe fifteen minutes, allowing the scenery to work its magic and soothe my soul when, in the far distance way below, three dogs emerged from the edge of the woods. Casually, I focused on their rapid journey across the undulating landscape. They raced each other, stretching their limbs to the maximum and covering the ground with athletic ability, the terrier easily outrun by the two larger dogs.

As I followed their progress, on the periphery of my vision, I saw a man emerge from the trees and call to the dogs. With a start I recognised the figure—it was Nat. I sat very still, suddenly fully alert, my attention focused on the scene below. Nat called to the dogs again and the terrier halted its pursuit. It stood panting, looking back at the man as he strode across the landscape towards the exhausted dog. The two larger dogs were still racing each other, tearing up the hill towards the monument. As they drew closer I saw that they were a Weimeraner and Pointer and I recognised them immediately. My heart raced. Looking back down the hill I saw that the figure, too, had altered its course and was beginning the steep climb towards the Hardy Monument. Five minutes later the dogs came bounding over the ridge, now at a slower, more laboured pace and ran past me. They circled the monument twice before coming to a stop in front of me, panting heavily.

"Hello Baron and Casper!"

They cocked their heads, observing me. The Pointer approached, sniffed me and then lay down at my side. I smiled. Baron watched but, being the one-person dog that he was, kept his distance, waiting for his master. Maybe ten minutes later Nick appeared, breathing heavily; his lovely face flushed and energised. He stopped in surprise when he saw me.

"Maddie!" he said, in such a delightfully animated tone that it sent a tingle right through me.

"Hello." I smiled at him.

He bent double in an attempt to catch his breath and looked up, surveying me through narrowed eyes. "Hang on. I'll be with you in a minute!" he gasped.

Baron moved towards him and nudged him. Lovingly, Nick stroked the dog's head.

Again, I noticed his strong, capable hands and suddenly had an overwhelming desire to feel those fingers gently stroking my skin.

With breathing now less laboured, Nick straightened up, clambered over the ridge and sat down beside me. Baron immediately stretched out beside him.

"What brings you out this way?"

"Nothing in particular. I just felt the need for some air so drove out here," I replied.

"Well, at two hundred and thirty seven metres above sea level it's certainly a good place to catch the air!" He looked across me at his other dog. "I see Casper's claimed you."

At the sound of his name the dog looked up, thumped his tail on the ground but remained lying at my side.

"I told you these two like the fairer sex. Sensible dogs."

I smiled. Well, at least I was a hit with his dogs!

"The views are absolutely stunning," I said appreciatively.

"Yes. It's the only place where you can see the entire length of the Jurassic coast." He looked along the coastline. "Look, the Needles are clearly visible today."

I looked eastwards in the direction he indicated and there, shimmering in the far distance, I could make out the Isle of Wight's distinctive landmarks.

"They're about fifty miles away," he said. "And this is the only spot in Dorset where you can see the entire county and all its neighbouring counties."

"How tall is the monument?" I asked, squinting up at the obelisk behind us.

"Seventy two feet and built of Portland Stone. Did you know that it represents the spyglass of a ship?"

I shook my head.

"It was built in honour of Sir Thomas Masterman Hardy, Flag Captain of HMS Victory. The story goes that Hardy sailed by in 1805 on his way to fight the Battle of Trafalgar."

It comforted me that Nick should know such things.

"Not Thomas Hardy the writer, then?"

"No, though lots of visitors assume that. Thomas Masterman Hardy lived in Portesham until he joined the navy." He pointed towards the village below us. "Now, what other facts can I conjure up to impress the Irish lass?" he continued, teasingly. "Ah yes, the monument receives such a battering from the weather that as soon as it was built, in 1844, the stone began to crumble."

His eyes looked deep into mine and I was totally disarmed.

Suddenly overcome with unaccustomed shyness I looked down the escarpment for a diversion. "That's one hell of a climb."

"Yes, and don't you believe anyone who tells you the more you do it the easier it gets!"

He laughed; that lovely mellow laugh which set me alight.

The quiet, trance-like, reflective mood was still upon me and I gazed out to sea. Neither of us spoke for several minutes but the silence was companionable and not at all awkward and, for once, I didn't feel I was about to break out into an embarrassing schoolgirl blush.

After a while Nick asked, "How's that friend of yours?"

"Dan?" I asked, still looking out to sea.

"Yes."

"Oh, he's OK. Girlfriend trouble. That's why he came to see me."

"Ah," Nick said. "We've all experienced that at sometime or other."

'Obviously very happy with Sarah at present, though,' my inner voice irritatingly pointed out, as if I wasn't only too well aware.

I sighed and decided that I didn't have the strength to do battle with my inner self today. Still in the grips of introspective humour, I turned slowly in Nick's direction and caught him studying my profile. Quickly he turned away.

The sun was no longer high in the sky and a cool breeze blew in from the sea. I shivered and got to my feet, picked up my jacket and threw it over my shoulders, cape-like. Baron and Casper, now rested, also got to their feet and started to chase each other around the monument. I bent to pick up the camera and remembered the terrier.

"Where's the other dog?" I asked, looking down the escarpment.

"What other dog?"

"The terrier."

"Didn't see one."

"Oh. It was running with your dogs."

Nick got to his feet and surveyed the hillside below. "It's not there now," he said. "Must have returned to its owner."

I scanned the slopes below but there was no sign of the dog. Somewhere, buried deep within my subconscious, I knew that there wouldn't be but I was yet to acknowledge the truth of the terrier being long dead.

Nick checked his watch.

'Just looking to see how much longer he's got before getting back to the girlfriend,' said my unhelpful inner voice.

"What are you doing now?" he asked.

"Going home, I guess."

"Why don't you come back to the barn? There's still enough light for you to take some more photos for the magazine."

"That's not such a bad idea," I replied, wondering what Sarah would make of me just turning up unannounced, especially as the subject of extra photos had caused her such consternation.

He called to the dogs and obediently they came to heel. As we walked back to the car park I looked around for his Nissan.

"Where's your pick-up?" I asked.

"At the garage. Break problems." He laughed and pointed to the mauve Ford Ka parked beside mine. "I'm driving Sarah's. It's a bit of a squash for these two rebels."

He opened the hatchback and Baron and Casper hopped in. They sat huddled together while Nick closed the tailgate and peered out, their noses pressed against the rear window.

"Do you remember where the barn is or do you want to follow me?" he asked.

I remembered all right—how could I not? All roads led to his barn; it was imprinted on my heart! But I said I was unsure and would follow him.

We turned left out of the car park and followed the road for a couple of miles heading west. After a while we neared the Ashton Chase turning and I began to feel nervous at the thought of meeting Sarah again. I knew she would think I had engineered this visit even though it had been a completely random event. Firmly, I told myself that I would maintain my composure and that I was more than capable of handling whatever she threw at me.

We drove past the main house belonging to Nick's friends, a glorious, mellow stone, Georgian mansion set in extensive mature grounds, and through the trees I glimpsed a tennis court and swimming pool. We continued along the lane leading up to the farm with its myriad of rambling outbuildings before turning the corner and skirting the hill that formed the backdrop to Nick's barn. Even though I had seen the view before and knew what to expect, I switched off the engine and sat for a moment, savouring the panoramic vista down the valley to the sea beyond. I knew that the view would be wonderful in all seasons. It was simply glorious.

By now the dogs were out of the car and gambolling around the lawn on the top terrace and I waited with baited breath for Sarah to appear at the front door, demanding to know why I was there. But the door remained firmly closed. I grabbed my camera, climbed out of the car and glanced over at Nick. He was shielding his eyes looking intently at the sky.

"See the buzzards, Maddie?"

I followed his gaze and saw two birds of prey wheeling slowly and majestically on the thermals high above the valley.

"How can you tell they're buzzards?"

"It's easy to spot a buzzard by the way it soars with its wings held in that distinctive shallow V-shape. There's often a white patch on the underside of the wings, too."

"We always seem to get that pair here," he said. "This valley is their special place."

I focused the camera and took several photographs of the birds and the view, and also managed to get Nick in a couple of shots without him noticing. We watched the raptors a while longer before Nick turned and walked towards the barn and, extracting a key from his back pocket, unlocked the porch door. As he entered I saw him toss the key into a wooden bowl on a small side table. He glanced back at me.

"Feel free to take whatever photos you think necessary."

"Thanks. I think I'll take a couple of shots of the barn from the top terrace and I definitely want to get the lake in the late afternoon sun."

"I'll follow you down. Just need to check the answer phone."

As I stood savouring the solitude I heard the machine replaying its messages. The seclusion was wonderful, it was so peaceful. If I lived here I knew I would never want to leave.

From the top terrace I took several photographs of the barn at varying angles. The dogs thought it was great fun that I was still around and came bounding up to me, charging around my legs. They accompanied me down the steps onto the middle terrace. As I stood on the edge photographing the lake below, they both leapt off and dashed across the lower lawn to the perimeter of the lake. Two moorhens, startled by the sudden intrusion, called in alarm and hurriedly paddled across the lake's flat surface before disappearing amongst the reeds.

"Casper!"

Nick stood on the top terrace and called to the dog as it waded into the lake. Leaping down the roughly hewn stone steps, Nick called again. The Pointer hesitated, remaining in the shallows.

"Just look at that dog. I know exactly what he's doing. He thinks if he stays at the edge I'll be hoodwinked into thinking he's obeying me but as soon as my back's turned he'll be after those moorhens."

I laughed.

"Casper, I'm watching you!" he said sternly.

"He's very handsome," I commented. "As is Baron."

"Yes, they're a good pair and good mates. Casper, come."

Again, I wondered where Sarah was. I felt on edge not knowing and expected her to appear at any moment. I took a deep breath. "Is Sarah at home?"

"No. She's gone to London for a few days. Needed a break."

My heart began to thump so loudly I thought he might hear.

"When Becky said she was going up to the smoke to visit her mum, Sarah jumped at the chance."

Why did she need a break? If I had a life with Nick I would be reluctant to leave for any reason.

"It's good to get away once in a while," I said, trying not to sound too ecstatic.

The light was diminishing fast and, with it, the temperature.

Sun's going down," Nick observed. "Let's go indoors and I'll fix us a drink . . ." He checked himself and added, almost shyly, "If you'd like one, that is."

I glanced at him, surprised by the uncertainty in his voice. He did not meet my gaze.

"That sounds an excellent idea," I answered warmly.

As he turned towards the barn I saw him smile.

Even though it was early, Nick poured me a gin and tonic and a beer for himself and while I sat on the sofa with Casper sprawling beside me, he lit the wood burner. I started to relax and the strange, brooding mood that had besieged me all day finally lifted. Baron briefly deigned to place his chin on my knee so that I could stroke his head but, as soon as Nick sat down, he left me to sit at his master's feet. Outside, dusk encircled the barn but inside it felt cosy and safe. Warmed by the heat of the fire I closed my eyes and breathed out slowly, the tension leaving my body for the first time that day. When I opened them again I noticed Nick studying me.

"You look the picture of contentment," he commented.

"I do feel very comfortable." Absently, I fondled the Pointer's ears.

"That's good," Nick said. He took a slug of beer. "Do you miss your former life, Maddie?"

I thought for a while. "No, I don't," I replied truthfully. "I thought I might miss the wine bars and the constant partying that surrounds the film industry, but I've obviously outgrown that."

I sipped my drink.

"I really enjoy working at the Blacksmith's and Brian is a great boss," I continued. "Maybe that's filled that particular need."

"Yeah, Brian's OK," Nick said. "He and Vera have certainly turned that pub around. It was dire a few years back. When they first took it over we all thought its previous reputation might prevent them from making a go of it."

"Obviously bad reputation doesn't stand a chance against sheer personality," I suggested.

Nick laughed. "He's certainly no shrinking violet."

"I suspect Brian could get a party going at the frostiest of gatherings!"

Nick raised his eyebrows and nodded.

I remembered he'd said his family spanned generations in Dorset and I asked if there were still any in the area. He told me that Helen and Peter lived in a village just outside Poole and that his mother still resided at the family home in Melcombe Bingham.

"Dad passed away five years ago and, as you know, my brother flew the nest for a warmer climate many years back. There are still plenty of cousins around, though. We get together from time to time. Mostly family gatherings."

"How far back can you trace your family?" I asked.

"About three or four hundred years, I think. When dad died his brother felt the need to look into the family history. Said he'd managed to trace us back to the 17th Century."

"My sister, Martha, did our family tree for a school project once but she was unable to get further back than mid 19th Century," I said. "We put it down to the O'Briens having a murky past and not wanting to be traced!"

The Forgotten Promise

He laughed.

Dusk had now turned to night and, leaning across the sofa, Nick switched on a side lamp, its yellow light casting a warm glow across the room.

"The other week when I was fitting your bread oven door, do you remember you asked me what I'd seen?" he asked quietly.

I nodded, though he was not looking at me.

"Well . . ." he paused, his eyes slowly meeting mine. "I saw you and two children dancing in a circle."

I felt as if a bolt of electricity had shot right through me. "You saw it too!"

He nodded slowly. "I did, although I couldn't believe it. It was only when I was at the workshop the following day and saw the sculpture in the courtyard that I realised what I'd seen." He looked troubled. "It's an odd thing but when I first started working on that piece I had no idea what I was creating. When it finally evolved into the mother and children it seemed to me that the sculpture had a life of its own."

I had never felt so alive. There *had* to be some connection between Nick and me; I felt it in my bones. Dan had not witnessed any happenings in the cottage, he simply thought I was unwell and hallucinating when I experienced the visions. I was sure this feeling of complete familiarity I had with Nick was not just down to wishful thinking.

"My sister, Mo, is very sensitive and views life on a different plane," I said. "We always tease her that she's psychic. Well, when she was staying with me she said she saw a figure on the stairs—a man dressed in rough work clothes."

He looked at me and there was something in his eyes I didn't quite understand.

"I've also seen a man in the cottage on several occasions and at a graveside in the church at Shipton Gorge," I continued. "And I saw the same man today below the Hardy Monument. I don't know what it all means but Mrs McKendrick, the previous owner of The Olde Smithy, well . . . I think she witnessed things too."

I paused and looked across the table at Nick. He was listening closely.

"She told me that during the thirty odd years she lived there she was only ever looking after the cottage for *me*!"

The look in his eyes seemed to be one of recollection.

"That's an unusual thing to say," he said in a careful voice.

"It is, isn't it? And she always called me Mary, though her daughter dismissed this as senility."

He looked shaken.

Suddenly he asked, "Did you get the jewellery checked out?"

I told him how I had taken the pieces to Professor Stephens who had verified that they were very old, possibly dating back to the 1600s, and that he was carrying out further tests.

"It seems to me there's a story to your cottage, Maddie. You should write about it. It might begin to make sense."

"I have been keeping a diary of events."

He was thoughtful for a while and then said, "It may be that whoever is bound to your cottage needs to be given the opportunity to move on."

The temperature in the room seemed to turn to ice and I started to shiver uncontrollably.

The Forgotten Promise

"Are you OK Maddie?"

"Yes, it's just what you said." I hesitated before continuing. "Do you believe in ghosts then, Nick?"

"Not the 'white sheet and two eye holes' kind but I think there's a lot in this world that can't be explained rationally. I like to keep an open mind on the subject."

"But I wonder why I'm experiencing these things?" I said in bewilderment. "What am I to the story?"

He shook his head. "I'm sure it will become clear in time. Maybe you are the catalyst for this spirit to settle whatever is still unresolved."

I considered this, surprised and pleased that I could discuss it so openly with Nick.

"Do you think the cottage needs to be exorcised?" he continued.

"No, it's not an evil presence at all. It's benign and so full of love, it takes my breath away. But, I do seem to tap into very deep levels of emotion that have nothing to do with my own life." I hesitated, hoping that he wouldn't think I was completely mad. "I know this sounds really far-fetched but I think, somehow, a past life is living again through me."

I knew how that sounded, but Nick didn't make light of it.

"Promise me, Maddie, if you ever feel frightened you will phone me."

I was overwhelmed by his concern and felt a lump form in my throat.

"It doesn't matter what time of day or night it is."

'So near and yet so far,' my inner voice taunted.

I swallowed hard and thanked him, thinking all the while that Sarah would be really chuffed if I phoned at two in the morning.

"I mean it," he said. "If you ever feel threatened by anything in that property, phone me."

"I won't ever be threatened by anything there, Nick. It's my home."

'And a home where I knew a love like no other.'

The words popped into my head and took me by surprise.

"I know, Maddie, but you never know where these things can lead." He got to his feet. "Here, let me top you up."

I held out my empty glass to him.

"And you'll stay for supper?"

Oh yes, you bet! I wanted to shout. But I simply smiled politely and said I would like that very much.

It was a wonderful evening. Together we prepared a lasagne, found some part-baked rolls in the freezer and heated them up in the oven. Nick threw more logs into the wood burner and opened a bottle of red wine while I set knives and forks on the beautiful walnut dining table. It felt surprisingly comfortable and natural for us to be doing domestic things together. Over supper he brought up the subject of Dan again.

"How long were you and Dan together?" he asked casually.

Damn Dan, I thought. What's he got to do with anything?

"Eight years, or thereabouts."

He raised an eyebrow.

"On and off," I added swiftly.

"You must know each other very well then."

The Forgotten Promise

"Through and through!" I laughed. "In fact, I definitely know him better than he knows himself though I can't believe he fell for Lucy the way he did."

"Are you jealous?" Nick asked.

I was aware that Nick was under the false impression that Dan wanted to rekindle our relationship but wondered why he had asked that particular question.

"No, not exactly jealous. You see, I never thought Dan would make her a permanent fixture. We had a very open relationship and it's not the first time there have been others."

"Has he gone back to her?" he asked in surprise.

"I don't think so, and if he has any sense he won't."

He hesitated before asking quietly, "So why hasn't he taken up with you again?"

"She seems to have cast a spell over him," I replied. "He's completely transfixed."

I didn't want to talk about Dan. I didn't want him to be any part of the evening.

"He's a fool," Nick declared.

He looked directly at me for the first time during the course of this conversation and I felt myself blush.

"So his sister tells him," I said hurriedly to cover my confusion. "She thinks he should have put our relationship on a more permanent footing. But enough of me, Nick. What about you? How long have you been with Sarah?"

I didn't really want to talk about her either but I wanted to get the conversation off Dan.

"Ten years. I met her on her eighteenth."

What a great birthday present, I thought despairingly.

"And you've been together ever since?"

"More or less." He seemed as uncomfortable answering my questions as I had been talking about Dan.

It must have been the drink making me feel less inhibited but, having now started this topic of conversation, I thought that if I wanted to find out more about their relationship I had better ask now or not at all.

"A friend of Sarah's was at the pub on New Year's Eve," I spoke evenly, not giving away my feelings. "She said she thought you might have got engaged while you were in Australia."

A small frown creased his forehead and there followed a long pause. "Sarah wants to get married," he answered eventually.

"I guess it's not unreasonable seeing you've been together so long." I couldn't believe I was suggesting this. God, Maddie, please don't go persuading him it's a good thing to do!

"I know." He was truly ill at ease. "It's not unreasonable."

"So what's the problem?"

Who was this person asking all these direct questions, I wondered?

He hesitated and I could see that he was grappling with some inner turmoil. "I don't want to be disloyal to Sarah," he said. "She's a good girl. But that's just it!" His voice rose in frustration. "She can be so naïve, which I found charming . . . when I first met her."

He looked guilty for uttering these thoughts and my heart went out to him, but I was also consumed with jealousy that he should have such fierce loyalty to his girlfriend.

"It's OK to talk like this Nick," I said. "But we don't have to if you don't want to."

"I'd rather not." He smiled apologetically, picked up the wine bottle and leant across the table. "Top up?"

We polished off that bottle of red and then finished another. I knew there was no way I could drive that night and when Nick suggested I should stay and go back in the morning, I did not object.

"If you don't have to be anywhere early tomorrow we can have a leisurely morning," he suggested.

We stayed chatting in the warmth of the living room until I could no longer keep my eyes open.

"Well, I guess it's time to hit the sack. You have the bed, Maddie, I'll sleep on the couch," he announced.

I protested, saying that I was more than happy to take the sofa but he wasn't having any of it. Getting to his feet he headed towards the spiral staircase while I cleared the table and stacked the dishwasher. I was surprised at how unsteady I was. Normally, I could hold my drink. In a befuddled haze I realised that Storm would have to fend for himself and remembered that the original nest of sacks was still in the outhouse. I hoped he would use his old bed.

Carefully, I climbed the stairs and found Nick pulling a sleeping bag out of a cupboard.

He opened a drawer, selected a T-shirt and handed it to me. "You can wear this if you want. It's an old rugby 'T' of mine. It is clean."

I took it gratefully, wondering how I was going to get any sleep knowing that he was in the room below.

He smiled at me and said in such a gentle voice that I hardly heard, "You know, Maddie, you're very beautiful."

Shaken out of my drunkenness I looked at him in amazement, not believing what he had just said. "What . . . ?"

The look in his eyes was soft and his voice tender as he repeated, "You're very beautiful. I can totally understand why Dan hot-footed it down to Dorset to be with you. If the man had any sense he'd have stayed."

I started to blush furiously but not from embarrassment.

Nick moved towards me and, taking my face in his hands, kissed me softly. The deep emotion I experienced was so powerful I could hardly breathe. I pulled back and gasped.

"I've wanted to do that from the moment I first set eyes on you," he said in a husky voice.

Was I dreaming?

And then he kissed me again and this time I felt myself respond.

Suddenly he pulled away. "I'm sorry. I shouldn't have done that."

It's OK, I wanted to say. It's really OK! But my brains had turned to mush and my knees to jelly and it was all I could do to remain standing.

He looked guilty and remorseful. Sadly, I watched as loyalty and commitment returned to his demeanour. Sarah was one hell of a lucky girl. He picked up the sleeping bag, turned and walked down the spiral staircase to the room below.

I managed to make it to the shower room and, holding firmly onto the basin, met my gaze in the mirror.

'So near and yet so very far . . . '

I was flushed and there was a wild look in my eyes—was it despair? I splashed cold water on my face, squeezed toothpaste onto a finger and cleaned my teeth as best I could. I undressed, put on Nick's T-shirt, sniffing it deeply before pulling it over my head, and hugged it closely to my body. I staggered over to the bed, the room spinning madly, and lay there listening to the unfamiliar noises coming from the room below. I heard the porch door open and Nick call quietly to the dogs that he had let out to do their business. My respect for Nick was already huge but it went up a notch knowing that even when well-oiled he still acted responsibly.

Lucky Baron, lucky Casper and lucky, lucky Sarah, I thought miserably.

In a low voice I heard him telling the dogs to settle followed by the sounds of him making himself comfortable on the couch. Then it went quiet.

I lay there for what seemed like an eternity, listening to the sounds of breathing from the room below. I looked up through the glass roof panels at the inky, night sky and thousands of stars winked at me, as if they were all sharing some huge joke. I gulped back a sob and thought I had never felt so wretched and alone. I squeezed my eyes tight to stop the tears flowing and the bed spun ever faster. Eventually I fell asleep.

I came to, momentarily disorientated, wondering where I was and then it all came flooding back to me. Through the glass roof, the sky had the tinge of early morning and dense cloud cover now hid the stars from view. I peered at my watch—6.15am. So I had slept! Sitting up carefully, a raging headache instantly took hold. Gingerly, I got out of bed and walked unsteadily to the en-suite. Peering dejectedly at my reflection in the mirror I noticed how pale and sallow I looked, as if all the life had been sucked out of me. A thousand unanswerable questions filled my head.

Before returning to bed, I tiptoed over to the gallery and looked over. The barn was still and peaceful and filled with the grey light of dawn. Both dogs lay sprawled on one of the couches and Casper looked up at me eagerly; Baron did not stir. On the other couch lay Nick, flat on his back, the sleeping bag half off his body. He was sound asleep with one hand on his chest; his head nestled in the crook of his other arm. In sleep, he looked younger and there was a half-smile on his face. I wondered what happy dreams he was enjoying.

I stood gazing at him for a long while, committing to memory every little aspect of the scene below. He was gorgeous and I knew that I was lost.

Eventually the cold got to me and I climbed back into bed and snuggled deep beneath the duvet. Soon, the blessed oblivion of sleep claimed me.

A few hours later, the smell of frying bacon woke me and suddenly I felt ravenous. I stretched, sat up and looked around. Even though the barn was still a work in progress it struck me that there was very little of Sarah's on show. There was make-up and lotions in the bathroom but, apart from that, there were very few girlie things around. Beside the bed stood a chunky, abstract, wooden root of a table and in a simple slate frame was a photograph of Sarah and Nick with their arms around each other, both smiling happily into the camera. But, apart from this, there were no other displays of togetherness that I had seen; it seemed that this was very much Nick's place.

Footsteps on the stairs and Nick appeared, holding a mug.

"Ah, you're awake! Thought I'd let you sleep in."

"What's the time?" I asked blearily, hangover threatening.

The Forgotten Promise

"About ten thirty," he replied. "I've made you tea. You don't take sugar do you?"

I shook my head and thanked him as I took the mug from him. He crossed the room to the chest of drawers and selected a clean sweatshirt from the top drawer before turning back to me.

"Bacon and eggs?" he asked.

We had a companionable breakfast and I was relieved to find that conversation was easy and there was no tension between us. What had happened the previous night did not appear to stand in the way. I left around noon.

As Nick walked with me to the car I saw the two buzzards still circling on thermals high above the valley. I opened the car door and climbed in. I was about to close the door when he prevented me.

"I'm sorry about what happened last night," he said. Concentrating hard on the ground, he scuffed the gravel with the toe of his boot.

"Nothing to apologise for Nick," I said quietly.

"That's very magnanimous of you, Maddie." A small smile settled on his lips but when his eyes met mine they were far from happy. Softly he said, "It won't happen again."

I smiled sadly as he closed the door. I put the car into gear and drove away with a heavy heart, watching him all the while in the rear view mirror until he was out of sight. As I rounded the corner of the drive, he raised his hand in farewell and I felt my heart fracture; shards of glass piercing my very soul.

Last week in February

I was encouraged by the number of magazines that accepted my freelance articles and slowly the writing money—or at least the promise of some—began to trickle in. I was still working for Brian and Vera on Friday and Saturday nights, which suited me, and we had agreed that if they needed extra staff for special events then I would work additional shifts.

Towards the end of February I received a text from Mo.
Hi sis, check email.

I switched on the computer, connected to the internet and opened her email as instructed.

Hi Mads, Sorry to have been so long getting back with photos. Only just got home from whirlwind photo shoot across Europe! Interesting photo No. 11. I've sent it through full size for definition. Tell me what you think? Mo xx

I opened the photos and smiled at the ones of my French Lieutenant's Woman impersonation on the Cobb and marvelled at the way she had captured The Olde Smithy. Her photographer's 'eye' was unique and I totally understood why she was so in demand in her chosen career. And then I reached the eleventh photograph and I felt the hairs stand up on the back of my neck.

She had taken a picture of the sitting room from the far side of the dining room, the inglenook fireplace being the focal point. She had captured part of the old glass divide between the rooms and the bread oven was plain

The Forgotten Promise

to see. However, in front of the bread oven stood a figure, a fog-like apparition which, as I re-sized the photo, took shape. As the image became more defined, I focused on the face peering back at me from the screen and found myself gulping back sobs. I was a bundle of confused emotions; despair, grief, joy, elation, love. It was Nat, whose spirit I believed shared this cottage with me and who offered me such unconditional love. As the tears flowed unchecked down my cheeks, my fingers stroked the face on the screen. The eyes that looked back at me were full of wonder and tenderness and with a jolt, which momentarily stemmed my tears, I realised that I had seen that very look only the other week when Nick had gently taken me in his arms.

Grabbing a tissue from the bathroom, I blew my nose and firmly told myself to get a grip. But I couldn't get those eyes out of my head and as I returned to the screen they seemed to follow me wherever I moved in the room. I found my mobile and texted Mo.

Photo 11! Is this the man u saw on stairs?

After a few minutes she texted her reply: *Didn't c him clearly but wld say yes!*

I texted back: *He's man at grave!*

Soon came her reply: *Kurt busy but will decipher epitaph soon. Have you a story yet?*

Still working on it, I responded.

Good luck! Keep me informed. How's the gorgeous man?
Don't ask . . . Mads xx

She texted in capitals: *KEEP THE FAITH! xx*

I saved her photos under The Olde Smithy file, but kept Nat's face on the screen.

"Tell me what you want from me," I whispered to the empty room.

Stillness.

"What do you need me to do?" I asked a little louder.

Deep silence.

I sighed and sat staring at the dear, familiar face on the screen before me. How long I was there, I don't know. It was only the phone ringing that shook me out of my trance-like state. It was Caro, Dan's sister.

"Hi Maddie. How are you keeping?"

"Oh Caro. Well thanks!" I lied. "How about you?"

"Good, I think," she said. "John's just heard his company's relocating and he's been given the responsibility of overseeing the move."

"Oh! Where's it going?"

"Newcastle. All the departments are moving up in instalments but we're to relocate at the end of April. Seems a long way from London, but I've already checked and there are flights from both Exeter and Southampton airports so you can come and visit any time."

I agreed that sounded like a great idea.

"I hear Dan saw you recently," she said suddenly.

"Yes," I answered. "I was really surprised. Hadn't heard from him for weeks and then he just turned up out of the blue! Mind you, I haven't heard a peep from him since!"

"No you won't," she said. "The silly fool's taken up with Lucy again."

I groaned. Had he lost all sense? And after everything he'd said! What was it about that girl?

"I can't say too much to him," she said sadly. "He's very touchy about her but as he is my only family now I don't want to lose him. I make sure we see them, when they're in a socialising mood that is, which I must say isn't very often. They seem to be content holed up in that flat

The Forgotten Promise

of his. I have to remind him there's a bigger world out there."

I looked out of the kitchen window and watched Storm amusing himself chasing swirling leaves around the courtyard.

"He's lucky to have you as a sister," I said.

"Oh, he's a good soul," she sprang to his defence. "I just think he's lost his way a little. He's totally smitten. But I am worried about him, especially now that I won't be in London any longer. He doesn't look at all well."

"It's his life, Caro. Only he can make changes if it doesn't suit him." I didn't really know what to say. I had witnessed the hold Lucy seemed to have on him.

"I know," she said sadly. "But she's such a predator and he's so malleable. I can't help feeling protective."

"He'll be OK." I said confidently, though privately I wondered if he would be all right. Changing the subject I asked, "Do you think you'll be able to visit me before you leave for the north?"

"Sorry Maddie. Don't think so. I've got a huge PR launch at work to organise before I go and I've got to get the house sorted for letting. We're going to keep it but we need to get some income from it. You could always come up to London and stay with us before we leave."

"Good idea," I agreed. "Suggest some dates."

We checked our diaries, agreed on the first weekend in April and I marked it on the calendar. We chatted a while longer before saying goodbye.

I opened the back door and called to Storm. He looked up but didn't want to come in. It was a sunny, gusty day and he had the wind in his tail. He shot up the garden on some private mission. I followed him up the path, fighting my way through the unkempt garden and made a mental note to buy a lawnmower on my next visit into Bridport. As I approached the pond, Storm dashed through the fence into next door's garden. As it happened, Mrs Tomkins was in her garden and so I called 'hello' over the fence. She came over and told me that Rex, her aged ginger tom, had been taken ill over the winter and that the vet had put him to sleep the previous week.

"Oh I'm so sorry to hear that," I said gently. "What a horrible decision to have to make. I expect he gave you years of companionship, though."

"Oh yes, dear. He was nineteen-years-old and my Bert gave him to me as a twelve-week-old kitten."

I told her that I'd just seen Storm shoot through the fence into her garden.

"Your cat's often over here," she said. "He and Rex were good friends. They used to curl up together in his basket."

"He kept that one a secret!" I said.

"If you ever go away, dear, just let me know and I'll be more than happy to look after him for you."

I thanked her and thought what good timing, having just arranged with Caro to visit her in London. We chatted about my plans for the garden and my vegetable plot and she offered to give me some seedlings from her greenhouse to get started.

"Thank you, Mrs Tomkins. I feel guilty that you're offering so much to me. Is there anything I can do for you?"

"Well, I don't know, dear." She turned and looked back at her house. "I am having trouble with my back door. I think it's become swollen over the winter months and I find it difficult to open, what with my arthritis. Do you know someone trustworthy who could have a look at it for me? I don't like to use tradesmen without recommendation."

"As it happens I know someone who is very trustworthy," I said. "I'll go and get his number for you this minute."

I ran to the cottage and jotted down Nick's mobile on a post-it note. By the time I got back to the garden fence Storm was in my neighbour's arms with a smug look on his face.

"You don't mind, do you?" Mrs Tomkins asked indicating Storm, her eyes shining brightly.

"No, not at all. It's good to know he has so many friends!"

I realised she must be feeling very raw at the loss of Rex.

"I do wonder where Storm came from, though. Nobody's ever claimed him and he's such a handsome cat. It seems unlikely he hasn't a home of his own."

She agreed and Storm, purring on cue, nestled more deeply into her neck. I left them to it and walked back to the kitchen, made myself a sandwich and was halfway through eating it when the phone rang.

"Professor Stephens here. I've got some interesting news for you."

I held my breath, nerves jangling.

"Your treasure has proven very exciting indeed!"

"Oh," I said stupidly.

"Philip has confirmed my earlier findings and has emailed over a report. If you'd care to furnish me with your email address I will forward it to you."

I gave him the address and he said he would email it immediately.

"You can pick up the jewellery at any time but I would be most intrigued to see where you found it."

"Of course," I said. "When would you like to come over?"

"I'm free this Thursday morning, if that suits?"

I checked the calendar and confirmed that it was convenient. "Come in time for coffee," I suggested, smiling at the gossip it would create when he rolled up in his Porsche.

As I opened the laptop and logged on, I finished the remainder of my sandwich. Within a couple of minutes the email arrived. It read:

Observations on Jewellery for Ms Madeleine O'Brien:

Pendant—Maker unknown.
Charming 3D Heart ornament of interwoven polished cut steel.
Fashioned by a skilled craftsman (not professional jeweller).
Dimensions: 3 cms x 4.5cms.
During the 17th Century and up to circa 1940, brightly polished steel studs fastened to a steel backplate were fashioned into all sorts of jewellery. The studs were riveted or screwed into place. Highly polished cut steel gave the impression of diamonds. Silver later replaced cut steel as the preferred metal in jewellery making.
From 1620 to 1640 fashionable women in western Europe wore a single large jewel on their bodice, simply stitched to the fabric of the gown. This particular pendant has been cleverly crafted to either

be worn as such or to accommodate a ribbon necklace, which would originally have been of silk.

Note: Hearts were popular in jewellery design during the 1600s and the heart motif continued to evolve throughout the century and into the next.

Ring—Maker unknown.
Copy based on a German Gimmel Ring.
Circa 1600-1650.
Enamelled gold set with a ruby.
Diameter: 2 cms.

A Gimmel ring is made of three interlocking hoops. When worn, the ruby heart at the front of the ring is encircled by a pair of clasped hands. This intricate wedding ring is decorated with symbols of love and quotations from the marriage ceremony. The central motif comes from the Italian 'mani in fede' (hands clasped in faith), which was a popular symbol of love. The three connecting hoops, each with an attached hand or heart, fit together and appear as one band when worn. In this Gimmel ring, the ruby symbolises love and the clasped hands fidelity.

The inscriptions can only be read when the hoops of the ring are opened out.

Inscribed: *My beginning and my end; What God has joined together let no man put asunder; NC & MO, 8 August 1635.*

Note: Hearts were popular motifs for engagement and wedding rings during the 17th and 18th Centuries. Such rings often combined rubies (signifying love) and/or diamonds (signifying eternity).

I sat staring at the screen, my gut instinct telling me that this was an important clue; a waymarker to solving the riddle. I re-read the report half-a-dozen times. So, Professor Stephens had been correct. The jewellery did date back to the mid-1600s. But I wasn't any closer to finding out who the pieces belonged to or why they had been placed in the bread oven.

The following day I drove into Bridport and bought a lawnmower. I was eager to get started on the garden and wanted to be well prepared for the spring. I parked alongside the village green, as close to the cottage as possible, and was grappling with the lawnmower in the back of the car when I heard a familiar voice.

"Do you want some help with that, Maddie?"

Butterflies fluttered in my stomach and a dull ache settled on my heart. I glanced over my shoulder and saw Nick with an amused expression on his face. I swallowed hard.

"It went in OK so it *must* come out!"

He smiled. "Here, let me."

I stood back and watched as he picked up the lawnmower and easily manoeuvred it out of the car.

"Where do you want it? Round the back?" he asked.

I nodded and closed the car door.

Following him up the path, I noticed the ease with which he carried the lawnmower though his straining biceps confirmed its weight. We walked around the side of the cottage to the courtyard where he set it down outside the potting shed.

"Why are you here?" I asked.

He was about to say something but then stopped himself.

The Forgotten Promise

"I've come to look at your neighbour's door. Thanks for suggesting me, by the way."

He looked at me with such compassion that I felt my fragile heart crack a little further.

"No trouble," I mumbled, the lump in my throat causing my voice to distort.

"So, you're going to start clearing the garden then?" he said, looking up the pathway that led to the wilderness beyond.

The lawn about a foot high.

"Can't put it off much longer," I responded. "I've got to get that grass down before the growing season starts."

He laughed. "Like cleaning the house before the cleaner arrives?"

I acknowledged my irrational logic.

"It's probably a good idea to tackle it with a strimmer first," he said. "Don't want to knacker the mower before it's had a chance to show what it can do!"

I agreed. It felt so right being with Nick that I found myself smiling, despite the ache in my heart.

Turning towards the collection of outbuildings that created the courtyard, he peered through the window of the building attached to the cottage and then stood back, squinting up at the roofline.

"These look interesting," he slapped the wall of the outhouse. "The outside privy is a later addition but I would say that this building is probably the same age as the cottage."

I held my breath, instinctively knowing that this was important.

"Would it have been a dwelling?" I asked.

He shook his head. "More likely animal housing."

"Do you think there would have been a doorway connecting it to the cottage?"

"Possibly. Is there any evidence of one inside?" he asked.

I said I wasn't sure. He opened the door and walked into the outhouse. It was well-built with thick stone walls and ancient, gnarled A-frame roof timbers that had seen better days. I watched as Nick examined the building and he pointed out various features which I hadn't noticed before.

"That doorway is relatively new." He pointed to the door we had just entered through. "But look at the arch above it, Maddie, it extends virtually half the length of the building. I'd say that this was originally a cart shed or the forge."

He walked to the wall adjoining the cottage and peered closely at the wall, roughly brushing away cobwebs; the flaking render coming away easily at his touch. "Well, I think this answers your question. Look, this area's been filled in. Someone's bricked it up at some point."

Standing closer, I could see the outline of a doorway and my heart began to race.

"This would lead straight into the kitchen," I said excitedly, remembering how I had watched Nat disappear through an invisible doorway.

"And I think you'll find that the original front door would have been bang opposite," Nick said.

As I visualised this, I realised that each time I had witnessed Nat walking from the front to the rear of the cottage he was on that very route.

"Oh Nick!" In the excitement of this discovery I forgot what had transpired between us and I hugged him. His arms instantly held me and I melted, briefly, before remembering. Quickly I turned away before he could see my despair. "I'm going to check it out."

I rushed from the building and across the courtyard to the back door and was about to enter the kitchen when a voice halted me in my tracks.

"Mary!" the voice called urgently.

I turned slowly.

"Mary, I need to speak with you."

There was a thick stillness in the air and the scene before me had changed. He stood in an open archway and where the outside privy and potting shed should have been there was now a stone water trough. Behind him, in the far corner, I could see a blacksmith's furnace alight with horseshoes lying on the red hot embers and there was an acrid smell in the air. A chestnut horse stood patiently tied to the outside wall and Nick, though I could now see that it was Nat, stood looking at me. He wore a dirty leather apron over his rough work clothes and he was sweating from the heat of the furnace. His hair was tied back in a ponytail and as he wiped his brow, his long fringe stuck to his forehead.

I walked towards him.

"Mary, you and Elisabeth must go to the Hall," he insisted. "It's not safe for you here."

"But I don't want to leave you," I pleaded.

"Do as I say. For our daughter's sake."

He stroked my cheek gently and I closed my eyes, savouring his touch.

"When?" I asked.

"Tonight. I've heard word that Cromwell's men will be back before daybreak."

"Will you come with us?" I asked, my heart heavy, already knowing the answer.

"I will accompany you as far as your family but I must return."

"Nat, what's to become of us?" I was suddenly filled with the dread of premonition.

He shook his head, sadness clouding his eyes. "Make haste your preparations, Mary. Make haste!"

As I turned and walked towards the cottage I heard him whisper, "My love, my life."

I looked back wanting one last look at him and saw Nick staring at me from the outhouse door. The look on his face was the same as on the day we had discovered the jewellery; disbelief and wonder.

"Maddie?"

"Yes?"

"What just happened?"

"Did you see them, Nick?" I asked quietly.

Slowly, incredulously, he said, "The horse was here." He indicated the wall beside him.

Quickly he covered the distance between us and, taking my hands in his, looked searchingly into my eyes; his forehead creased in a frown. "Does this happen often?"

I nodded.

"Not as vivid as this. Normally I only see the man in dreams."

I was aware that he was stroking my hands, his touch so familiar.

"But do you remember when we found the jewellery?" I continued. "The children were there and you saw them too!"

"Cromwell . . . The English Civil War," he said quietly, as if to himself.

"And this cottage is 17th Century," I added.

He observed me through narrowed eyes. "Something happened here or to the people who lived here. That's what all this is about."

He checked his watch. "I must go next door, your neighbour is expecting me. But, Maddie, I mean it. If you're ever frightened by anything that happens here, phone me . . . day or night."

"Well, thanks Nick but I'm sure Sarah wouldn't be best pleased if I rang in the wee small hours!" I said, amused.

He looked at me in confusion and slowly his eyes cleared, as if he'd only just remembered who Sarah was.

"This is important," he said in a serious voice. "She would have to accept it."

He was still stroking my hands.

I smiled up at him and he bent towards me. For one glorious moment I thought he was going to kiss me but, quickly, the stroking stopped. With a troubled expression he let go of my hands.

"I mean it Maddie," he said as he walked away.

On the Thursday, Professor Stephens roared up in his Porsche. I had added the most recent visitation to the 'Happenings' file and on re-reading my diary of events, realised that a story was indeed taking shape.

Professor Stephens entered the cottage looking windswept and wild, carrying a large leather and tapestry holdall. I noticed that he was even taller than Dan and was on the point of warning him about the lowness of the beams in the dining room when he cracked his head. He sat down at the table rubbing his skull ferociously while cursing in his plummy, cut-glass voice. It sounded so much more effective than when I swore.

"Are you OK?" I asked. "That was one hell of a crack!"

He grimaced and said, "Silly old fool! I've probably shaken the very foundations of the building."

I wondered what else he might have shaken up in the process.

"Now, here's your jewellery young lady," he said, still rubbing his head. He produced the wooden box from the depths of his holdall. "By the way, had you noticed the initials carved in the lid?"

I shook my head as I reclaimed the box from him.

"They're very worn but if you look closely you can just make out the initials 'M' and 'C'."

I looked down at the lid and felt the letters with the tips of my fingers and knew that I had done this a thousand times before. I opened the box and saw the heart pendant and the wedding ring. The jewellery had been magnificently restored and the pendant shimmered at me like diamonds. I breathed a sigh of relief; they were in my possession once again.

"Let me demonstrate how the ring works," Professor Stephens said.

He reached into the casket and in one swift movement showed me how the ring untwisted into three separate hoops, each bearing an inscription. He held the ring out to me in the palm of his hand.

Carefully, I picked it up and read aloud each hoop. "'*My beginning and my end; What God has joined together let no man put asunder; NC & MO, 8 August 1635'.*"

A shiver ran up the full length of my spine as I spoke the words and when I closed the three interlocking hoops to make the complete band, I automatically slipped it on my wedding finger. It was a perfect fit.

"Well would you credit it," the professor said. "Obviously made for you!"

I had the strongest sense of déjà vu as I admired the ring on my hand. NC and MO—I knew who I'd have liked that to be. But who was the man that had originally given this ring, and who was MO? Reluctantly, I took the ring off and carefully placed it back in the box.

"Let me get some coffee on the go," I said, rising to my feet.

While I filled the kettle and spooned ground coffee into the cafetiere, the professor told me how Philp Harcourt-Jones had informed him that a German Gimmel ring, not dissimilar to the one in my possession, was on display at the Victoria & Albert Museum. I poured boiling water onto the coffee and placed the cafetiere on a tray together with two mugs and a jug of milk. Adding a plate of biscuits, I took the tray through to the sitting room. The professor was sitting on my IKEA sofa and, randomly, it occurred to me that he had probably never visited the store. I placed the tray on the coffee table and sat down opposite him and invited him to help himself to a biscuit.

"So, you found the jewels in the inglenook," he said. "Unusual place for them to be stored."

He selected a chocolate Hobnob and popped the whole biscuit into his ample mouth. I depressed the plunger and poured coffee into the mugs.

"When I first moved in, the bread oven was completely walled up," I explained. "I wondered if the jewellery had been placed there for safekeeping."

He took a gulp of coffee, helped himself to another biscuit and chewed, deep in thought.

"Safekeeping, possibly, but to brick up the oven afterwards? That's more like a hiding place or locking away a memory."

Locking away a memory . . .

The words seemed to hang in the air. But what memory and who had locked them away? And why?

"Well, this is a mystery," the professor said, eyeing the plate of biscuits again.

How could he be so angular? I wondered.

"Try the flapjacks," I suggested. "I bought them at Bridport Farmers' Market. They're very good."

I held the plate out to him.

"Well, if you insist!"

He selected a fat, moist flapjack and bit it into it with relish. Eventually he swallowed and then loudly cleared his throat. "How's that dear boy who accompanied you the other day?"

It hadn't taken him long to mention him, I thought, smiling to myself.

"Dan's OK but I haven't seen him since. He lives in London."

"He seemed very appreciative and had enthusiasm. I like that in a young man, yes I do. Tell him he's welcome to visit any time. I would love to take him for a spin."

There was no denying this man's gender preference.

I didn't want to disappoint the professor but I knew that his message would send Dan bolting for the hills. I also wondered how Lucy would react to a rival for her man being male!

My concentration returned to the jewellery once more. "I wonder how I can find out more?" I said, half to myself.

The Forgotten Promise

"Have you tried Bridport museum?" Professor Stephens asked.

I said I had and explained that although I had uncovered some interesting facts about Walditch over the centuries, there had been nothing specific about The Olde Smithy.

"What about a visit to the local graveyard?" he suggested.

"I've already been to St. Martin's," I said, thinking of the day I saw Nat distraught at the graveside.

"No, not Shipton Gorge. Here in Walditch!" he said.

"The village doesn't have a church," I replied.

"Oh yes it does," he countered.

"Where?"

"Formerly St. Mary's. I believe it's been deconsecrated and is now a comfortable family home." He drained his mug. "You can learn a lot from graveyards and you may find that there are still some headstones in the grounds."

St Mary's Lodge. I had seen the house at the top of the village with its unusual half-spire and clock tower but it had never occurred to me that it may have once been a church. I realised that I had passed the old church many times without giving it a second's thought.

"I don't suppose you know who lives there?" I asked.

He shook his head and looked at me, a wicked glint in his eye. "Most people are happy to open up their homes when they know that an eminent archeologist is interested in what their property may, or may not, have hidden within its boundaries."

I wasn't sure if I understood him correctly. Was he being less than ethical and playing the 'professional' card? He watched me closely as I grappled with the idea.

"Professor . . . ?"

He winked at me. "Young lady, you don't think I have worked hard all these many years to secure a place of standing in the world of archeology without being able to flex my professonial muscles from time to time? Yes, I live for my work but I do pull strings occasionally."

Well, the old rogue! Now I understood why he drove a Porsche and not some battered 'old faithful'.

And so it was that half-an-hour later, having witnessed Professor Stephens' silvery tongue in full flow, we were welcomed into the home of Mr and Mrs Rogers. The professor had insisted on taking the Porsche, 'to give the right impression, my dear'. As he held open the passenger door for me I noticed Janet cleaning the front windows of the pub. I waved at her and saw her jaw drop as she watched me climb into the car. In slow motion she returned my wave. I smiled as I slid into the soft leather seat, determined to savour the three-minute drive up the street to St Mary's Lodge.

It transpired that Mr and Mrs Rogers had bought St Mary's from the church four years previously and had spent the intervening years and a huge amount of money renovating the property. It was now in pristine order and full of ecclesiastical features; a stunning stained-glass window here, an original pulpit there, and there were a number of Gothic mullioned archways and, of course, the unusual, ornate half-spire rising from the centre of the roof. The Rogers explained that the upper part of the spire had been in a dangerous state and, rather than repair it fully, they had simply had the top half removed and capped with a low clock tower.

Professor Stephens enthused over the clever ways they had incorporated a home within the four walls of the church and then explained that his main interest

The Forgotten Promise

was in the grounds, particularly the graveyard. Opening the French doors, Mr Rogers beckoned us to follow him down a stone path, flanked either side by well-tended flowerbeds. We passed under a rose-covered arch into a less formal area of the garden and there, in the quiet solitude of a hidden, tree-lined clearing, we found the original cemetery. There were, maybe, thirty headstones. At once, I was overcome with a terrible sense of despair.

I heard Mr Rogers telling the professor that the headstones were mainly 17th and early 18th Century and that later village burials could be found at the church in Shipton Gorge.

"We are interested to see if there are any graves here belonging to former occupants of Madeleine's cottage in the village," the professor explained.

"You may be lucky," said Mr Rogers. "The graveyard is somewhat protected from the elements and most of the headstones are still legible. I'll leave you to look around." Turning on his heels, he walked swiftly up the garden path towards the house.

Professor Stephens surveyed the scene before us. "I suggest we work our way along each row in a methodical manner."

Turning away from me, he started to walk along the lines of headstones but I did not join him. I knew that he was heading in the wrong direction.

It was very peaceful in this garden of rest. There wasn't a sound to be heard except for the occasional burst of birdsong. I breathed in the solitude and serenity, trying to dispel the utter wretchedness I felt.

Remaining at the entrance, I looked across the clearing. On the far side stood a headstone larger than the others and some older instinct told me that this was what

I was seeking. I had an overwhelming urge to lie down at the foot of that headstone and stay there forever.

As I walked across the glade, a robin flitted from stone to stone, eyeing me inquisitively. A deep sense of sadness and grief engulfed me and the closer I drew to the grave, the stronger my emotions became. It was a very old gravestone and as I read the epitaph, a huge sob escaped me. Through my tears I read the words carved into the stone.

Here Lyeth
Nathaniel Carbayne
Farrier of this Village
2nd March 1612—18th December 1664
and Cherished Son
Francis
7th September 1639—15th October 1643
Rest in Peace

I began to choke and, gasping for air, pulled frantically at my collar. Suddenly a pair of strong hands gripped my shoulders.

"There, there . . ." Professor Stephens hugged me awkwardly.

Despite my distress, I was aware that this was a momentous act on his part. The bachelor had probably not shown such compassion to a woman for many a year, if ever. Looking over my shoulder, he read the epitaph.

"I believe we may have found an important piece of the jigsaw."

His large bony fingers gently rubbed my back and I began to breathe more easily. Soon I was able to extricate myself from his embrace. Sobbing quietly, I wiped away my tears with the back of my hand.

"Better now?" the kindly man peered into my face with concern.

I nodded, still unable to speak. Here lay my husband and son.

"I think we may have found a previous inhabitant of your cottage, Nathaniel Carbayne," he said.

He looked at me with compassion, without understanding.

"Farriers were very well respected in the 17th Century, you know. Their skills were more akin to those of our equine vets today. People would ask for their advice on all manner of ailments."

My aching heart swelled with pride.

"Now, his young son, Francis . . ."

Unchecked, the tears rolled down my face. I wondered what the professor must think of me but, although he shot me a quizzical look, he didn't say anything.

"Only four years old. Hmm . . ." He stroked his chin, deep in thought. "Well, let's see. He could have succumbed to the plague or smallpox. There was a lot of disease around in that century and there wouldn't have been much effective medication. Mortality rates, especially amongst children, were high and sanitation was not at its best. It became more so later in the century but mid-1600s . . ." he trailed off.

It was smallpox. The red face, the hot sweats, the rash. We had been unable to save Francis.

As the professor walked away down the line of headstones looking for proof of further inhabitants, I remembered how distraught Nat had seemed at St Martin's and I wondered why he had been at the church in Shipton Gorge. I looked around for something to place at this grave but there was nothing suitable, so I removed the blue glass bead necklace I was wearing and hung it from the top of the stone.

"God be with you," I whispered. Immediately, the greatest sense of pure joy and total forgiveness descended upon me and the lump in my throat abated. From out of nowhere, a warm breeze brushed my face like the gentlest of kisses.

"There's nothing else here that relates to your cottage that I can see," announced the professor walking back towards me. He stood beside me and acknowledged my necklace hanging from the headstone. "That's a nice touch, young lady. I'm sure that Nathaniel and young Francis are more than happy that you are living in their home."

'Once more,' spoke a voice inside my head.

That evening, as I entered the latest piece of the unravelling mystery into my laptop, I carefully considered all that had happened to me that day. I felt exhausted and it seemed to me that the visitations and experiences were drawing ever more urgently upon me. It felt as if something was coming to a close and I had a great sense of dread hanging over me, which I could not shake off. I thought of Nathaniel Carbayne and realised that he was the NC inscribed on the wedding ring and I assumed that the other initials where those of Mary. But who was she?

I was deep in thought when the phone rang. It made me jump and I answered it, feeling jittery.

"Maddie?" enquired a warm, female voice.

"Yes?"

"It's Helen Moore, Nick's sister."

I smiled. "Hello Helen, how are you?"

"Oh very well, thank you. And you?"

I said I was fine, ignoring the disquiet of my soul.

She explained that Peter had spoken to his partner concerning the potential article about his organic smallholding and that Charles had said he would be delighted for me to pay him a visit. I wrote his number down on the notepad by the phone.

"I have to warn you, however, Charles is a lovable rogue. He is very charming and he will love you!"

"You're painting a very interesting picture of this man, Helen," I said. "Didn't you say that if he hadn't been forced into becoming a solicitor he would probably be on the wrong side of the law by now?"

She laughed. "A slight exaggeration, maybe, but his family, like ours, is a Dorset family going back many generations. There have always been rumours over the centuries about members of the Bosworth family—mainly about their involvement with smuggling."

"Nick mentioned your uncle did your family tree," I said, only too happy to be talking about him with someone who knew him so well.

"Yes, that's right. When our father died, Uncle Robert researched the family history. I believe he managed to trace us back to the 1600s but we weren't Corbin then, the name has changed over the centuries. We were Carbayne."

Blood pumped through my body at an alarming speed and there was a loud whooshing sound in my head.

"Maddie? Are you still there?" she asked.

"Yes, yes. I'm still here. I need to tell you something. I've had a very unusual experience today."

I took the phone through to the sitting room and sat downs on the sofa. I told her about my visit to the graveside at St Mary's and how I believed that Nat Carbayne had once lived in The Olde Smithy. She listened quietly throughout, only speaking when I had finished.

Calmly, she said, "That would figure, Maddie. We come from this part of Dorset and all the men folk in my family have been skilled craftsmen. I've got a copy of the family tree somewhere. I'll look it out for you if you'd like. Nick said you were writing a book about your cottage. It might help your research."

I smiled, happy in the knowledge that he had discussed me with her. But a book? I hadn't thought of that.

I thanked her and said I would be in contact with Charles Bosworth.

Before she rang off she said, "Peter and I are off to Kenya for a month but when we get back we'd love you to come over and have supper with us one evening."

I wished her a good trip and said that I looked forward to visiting them on their return.

Early March

Two things happened during the first week of March. I received my first payment for the article in EcoWorld, which, although nothing like the salary I had been used to with Hawkstone Media, was all the sweeter for being the first of the freelance money coming into my account. The second was a letter from Nick; a letter I shall keep to my dying day.

I had not slept particularly well and had eventually surrendered to the bright daylight creeping through the crack in the curtains and risen early. I didn't bother to get dressed and was padding around the cottage in my dressing gown, trying to decide what to do with the day. Drinking a cup of coffee in the kitchen and looking out at the early spring day, I heard a noise at the front door as half-a-dozen envelopes dropped through the letterbox onto the mat. I wandered over, placed the coffee mug on the table and picked up the correspondence, shuffling the post onto the dining table in order of priority.

Bill, no thanks; another bill, no thanks; credit card statement, no thanks. What's this? My heart skipped a beat as I recognised the stylised writing on the blue envelope. I sat down and turned the letter over in my hands, not wanting to open it. Some sixth sense warned me of its content. Procrastinating, I examined the two other letters. One was from the local Cats Protection League asking me to volunteer my services and the other was a cheap car insurance flyer. Slowly, I returned to Nick's letter. Fingers of ice reached up from the pit of my stomach and held me firmly in their grasp. I was sick with premonition. Carefully sliding a finger beneath the flap, I opened the envelope.

The silence in the room was palpable. I heard Storm eating from his bowl but that was all. No sounds penetrated the cottage from the outside world. I was suspended in time, and time was waiting for something to happen. I read the letter and wanted to weep.

Ashton Chase Barn
6 March

Dear Maddie,

I have to write this letter. Though I have a skip full of mail that demands answers; though my day sheet is crammed with a mass of urgent chores and obligations that I have no hope of fulfilling, I have to write this letter. I have a very stern and hard-working conscience which is giving me no peace at the moment. This letter may quieten its angry clamouring.

It is to be a plea for my defence, a token of gratitude and hope for future friendship.

First, my defence. I am not one of life's great planners. I do not chart courses or control events. It cannot be said on my epitaph that he knew what he wanted and went out and got it. Whilst my successful friends bore across life's oceans in pursuit of lofty goals, I bob in their wake, drifting on the tide of circumstance, admiring the scenery that chance presents. Through such aimless navigation I arrive in situations by accident. I know enchanted creeks and peaceful backwaters that the captains of their own destiny will never see. But there are perils that await the drifter, rocky shoals and whirlpools that responsible people steer clear of.

In the same way that I don't control my life, I cannot control my feelings. I cannot be blamed for admiring attractive scenery. That a client happens to be both charming and beautiful should simply sweeten the working day. Where I am guilty is in not heeding the signs that something was happening within. I should have corrected things and started paddling away at the start when I found myself thinking of you too often and too fondly. That I didn't take evasive action was due to a naïve belief in some Enid Blyton Utopia where everyone exists as 'jolly good chums'—a world uncomplicated by the tangle of feelings, relationships, sexuality, envy and jealousy. The outcome is painful. And now I am dangerously close to being in love, if not already.

This is where the gratitude comes in. For the enchantment that your company has brought to my life. It is a nice feeling knowing there is someone around that you really like. Dorchester, Walditch and the Blacksmith's Arms are places that have grown a new attraction for me—that I might glimpse you. I enjoyed dusting off my peacock feathers (though I hope it wasn't too obvious). I did not make a play for you, rather I fell for you. Thank you for briefly and unwittingly making me very happy.

A grey dawn now fills the barn where I am writing this. It heralds a full day. I have used up all the paper trying to write this and there is no more left, and I have not said anything that I really wanted to say.

Maddie, I wish you the greatest fortune in your life. May the gods smile upon you and bless you with happiness—and may your friendship be mine.

Love, Nick.

That night, I was restless. I couldn't get comfortable however hard I tried and sleep evaded me. Eventually I went downstairs, heated up a mug of milk and settled on the couch with a fleece rug over me. A delighted Storm immediately jumped onto my lap and curled up, purring contentedly. I opened the book that Mrs McKendrick had sent me and started to read. I had already read it through once, though only skimming, but now I believed I owed it a more thorough reading. Francis had died in 1643 and Oliver Cromwell had been mentioned during the vision in the courtyard that Nick had witnessed, so the era was correct. Mrs McKendrick had definitely been trying to tell me something.

During the English Civil War, Dorset was mostly Royalist. Everyone from nobility to labourers joined the 17th Century fight between Royalists and Parliamentarians, with villages often split dangerously down the middle. While Dorset had a number of Royalist strongholds, such as Sherborne Castle and Corfe Castle (both of which were devastated by fighting), many towns, such as Weymouth, were under the control of the Parliamentarians.

By 1644 the Parliamentarians had virtual control of the entire county. The men of Dorset were noted at this time for their lack of enthusiasm for war, and Clubmen—groups of what would now be called conscientious objectors—were formed in substantial numbers.

The hours passed but I didn't notice the time. My eyelids grew heavy from reading and I drifted into a fitful sleep. Storm disturbed me once when he got up and turned around on my lap. I snuggled deeper into the cushions, pulling the rug up around my neck and soon I was visited by a dream so vivid that, when I thought about

The Forgotten Promise

it later, I wondered if I had somehow been transported back to that harsh, unforgiving time.

It was cold, so cold, and not just in the air; my heart was leaden. I sat astride the bay mare with Elisabeth sitting in front of me holding on tightly to the mare's coarse, black mane. I held a bundle of clothes in one hand and cradled my precious daughter with the other. Nat stood at Bess' head, talking softly to her while he looked anxiously over his shoulder in the direction of the sound of the approaching army. Bess was a cob of solid disposition but she, too, had caught something of the electrified atmosphere and stamped nervously. We could hear the marching soldiers drawing ever closer with an occasional whinny from the approaching horses caught on the wind.

"No time to waste," Nat urgently whispered. "We must away."

I urged Bess on and we rode across the village green towards the track leading to Shipton Gorge. Nat led the horse, keeping pace with her as we climbed steadily upwards. We did not speak. I was sick with worry. The afternoon was quickly turning to dusk and the chill in the air—a chill of impending disaster—seemed to penetrate through to the very bone. My daughter huddled more closely into me and I pulled my cloak around us both.

The journey was difficult in the deepening gloom but Bess was sure-footed and, despite her uneasiness, did not trip on the rutted path. The trees on either side swayed eerily in a silent wind; it seemed the world was quietly alert, straining to hear the slightest noise. I imagined eyes amongst the dense foliage watching our every move and felt Elisabeth catch her breath. She was a spirited child and gutsy, too, but I knew that she possessed a vivid imagination and that in this half-light it would be playing tricks on her.

"It's all right child," I whispered. "There's nothing to fear."

Fit though they were, Nat and the horse were blowing hard by the time we passed the old fort. Eventually, we emerged from the wooded hillside onto the level approaches to the village of Shipton Gorge but suddenly Nat stopped, holding up his hand, alerting us to remain silent. Listening intently, he stared into the darkness ahead. Was that a muffled cough? I felt Elisabeth stiffen. Bess, ears pricked, fidgeted against Nat's restraining hand on the reins. And then a figure emerged out of the gloom. It stood firm, with feet apart, a stick in its right hand.

"Who's there?" a boy's voice called out in panic.

"Nat Carbayne."

"Oh thank the Lord, Nat."

The figure ran towards us. It was Jacob, one of my father's stable boys. He stopped when he saw Elisabeth and me.

"Mistress Okeford!" he exclaimed. "I, I mean Carbayne."

He was overcome with embarrassment and Nat put a comforting hand on the boy's arm.

"It's all right lad. Where are you away to?"

"Waldyke. The King is at Maiden Newton and the master has been despatched to oversee the royal visit. We had word the Roundhead army was closing and the mistress instructed me to watch their movements carefully. I'm to report back."

"Then Sir Richard is not at home . . ." Nat sounded worried.

"Nay," confirmed the boy.

Glancing at Elisabeth, Nat spoke in a lighter tone. "We are away to the Hall now. Mary and Elisabeth will be staying awhile."

I thought I was going to be sick, so deep was my dread.

In low voices they muttered an urgent exchange, which I did not catch, and then Jacob bade us farewell and carried on past us down the track. I knew that Nat was trying hard not to frighten our daughter, but when he looked up at me his face was etched with concern.

"Father, how long will we be staying with grandmother?" asked Elisabeth.

"A short while," he replied, squeezing her knee. "But you must be strong, Elisabeth, and look after your mother for me until I return for you both."

She nodded and I saw her smile proudly down at Nat, feeling important to have been given such responsibility.

"Yes father."

My throat was tight. I prevented a sob from escaping knowing that I, too, had to be strong—for my last remaining child.

We continued through the village, which was eerily quiet, the occupants holed up behind closed doors. Dogs wandered the streets, scavenging amongst the dwellings, as we made our way silently past the church and down into the valley beyond. After a while, we turned up a track and presently came to the great iron gates and stone pillars that announced Hammiton Hall. As we passed through the gateway and made our way up the drive towards the Hall, some premonition told me that I would never leave this place again. Each step that Bess took brought us closer to our destiny and I had the strongest urge to gather up what was left of my family and flee in the opposite direction.

We approached the front entrance and I saw Duncan, my parent's faithful man servant, standing loyally beside my mother, who was dressed in her finery, awaiting the arrival of her daughter and grand-daughter. She looked older, I thought, though still handsome, but without the gaiety of spirit she had once possessed. This war had made old maids of us all.

"Mary, Elisabeth," she called.

Elisabeth immediately slithered from Bess and ran to her. Nat took my bundle and put it to one side on the ground. Looking up into my face, he held his hands up to me and I slid from the mare's back into his arms. With my back pressed against Bess' warm flanks, Nat hugged me hard. I breathed in his masculine aroma, trying to gain some slight comfort, but the story was unfolding and there was little reassurance to be found.

"Won't you stay?" I asked, knowing the answer already.

"Nay Mary. Your parents have never accepted me. They know there could have been a better marriage for you."

I looked deep into his eyes and proclaimed, "You know that's not true! I loved you before I ever knew your name." Tears slid down my face, my heart heavy with foreboding. "As soon as I saw you, you had my heart," I said in a small voice.

"Hush, my love." He wiped away my tears. "It's not safe at the forge, you know that."

I nodded.

"You are better protected here at the Hall, for the girl too."

He kissed me tenderly, holding me close. Bess shook her head and stamped a foot, impatient to be on the move.

I tried one more time, in vain. "But, Nat, I need you. We need you! If I pleaded with you not to go would you stay?"

"Cromwell's men need a farrier. They know where I am and will expect me to be with them."

"You know I will always love you," I said, my heart breaking.

He kissed me again, his hand lingering gently on my face. "Mary," he spoke the name like a prayer. "You are the most beautiful woman I have ever known. Should we find ourselves parted I promise to come for you."

Again, he hugged me hard and I clung to him as if I was drowning. Then he tore himself away. With agility the envy of younger men, in one leap he was on Bess' back, the mare's head coming up sharply as he gathered the reins.

Softly he said, "I will love you for eternity, Mary. For eternity . . ."

And with that he kicked Bess into a canter, away up the drive and into the fog.

"Please stay, don't go!" I called out into the cool night air. But there was no reply.

I awoke to a sharp knocking at the front door. Storm was no longer on my lap and through the curtains I could see daylight. I unlocked the door and opened the top half.

The postman looked up in surprise. "Oh, thought you weren't in what with the curtains all closed. I was going to leave this over at the pub."

He screwed up the card he had been writing and handed me a large brown paper package. He looked at me inquisitively standing there dishevelled in my dressing gown and I knew he was just itching to ask what I was doing.

"Hangover," I answered the enquiring look. "What time is it?"

"Gone eleven," he replied, a smirk on his face.

I took the parcel and placed it on the dining room table. I saw a Dublin postmark and immediately recognised Mo's writing. I opened it carefully to reveal a large box canvas picture. It was one of the photographs she had taken of me posing as the French Lieutenant's Woman. The composition was stunning. The Cobb took up most of the width of the canvas, diminishing into the horizon, with my lone figure standing at the end looking back furtively over one shoulder. The photo, itself, had wonderful depth but being printed on canvas it had an added texture. I picked up the note that accompanied it.

Dear Maddie,

Thought you might like to hang this in your charming cottage—a bit of contemporary to compliment the old.
Off to New York to see how they do St Patrick's Day celebrations over there!
Keep well.

Your loving sister, Mo xx

I walked around the cottage, trying the canvas in various locations and eventually decided on the rear wall of the dining room. Having found a hammer and picture hooks, I hung the canvas and stood back to admire my sister's work. Mo was right. Although obviously modern, the colours of that gloriously bright January day and the subject matter captured in the photograph looked perfect in the room.

The Forgotten Promise

Realising that the day was marching on, I decided to get dressed and was just about to run a bath when the phone rang.

A rich, chocolate-smooth, masculine voice asked, "Is that the delectable Irish lass?"

"Depends who's asking," I said. I hoped I hadn't sounded too rude.

The man chuckled. "Charles Bosworth at your service!"

I was taken aback as I had planned to phone him that very day.

"Helen said you were going to phone me," he explained. "But I got fed up waiting so thought I'd get things moving."

"This is strange, I was just about to phone you!"

"Well there you are. I pre-empted you. Now, I hear you are a writer 'extraordinaire' and that you wish to do a piece on my little patch of organic heaven."

"Yes, that was the idea."

"Well, I'm a busy man but I'm sure I can find a slot for you in my hectic calendar," he said, and I was unsure whether he was being serious or teasing.

"My time is currently flexible," I said. "You tell me when you'd like me to come over."

I could hear him flicking through a diary. "What about this Sunday afternoon, say around 3pm?"

I wrote it on the calendar and jotted down directions to his house. I said goodbye, thinking that if I ever had the need for a lawyer to represent me in court then someone with a voice like his would be the one to choose; that voice could charm the birds from the trees.

I ran a bath and added a good measure of bubble bath. Soon I was luxuriating in the silky, warm water doing nothing more taxing than amusing myself making mountains out of the bubbles and blowing them across the surface. In that somewhat meditative state of mind, I returned to my dream.

Hammiton Hall. I couldn't have made the name up, could I? I needed to look at a map of the area and see if there was such a property in the valley beyond Shipton Gorge. My thoughts then turned to Nat and although Helen hadn't yet shown me the Corbin family tree, my gut instincts told me that he was her ancestor. But, there was something more. A thought was forming in my mind and, if true, then my current situation was as sad as the story that was unfolding for the original inhabitants of the cottage.

Later I sent a text to Mo and thanked her for her generous gift, telling her that the picture was already hanging in pride of place on the dining room wall.

She texted back: *Knew it would fit in! Any news on research? R u celebrating St Pats Day?*

I replied: *Story emerging. Have theory. If true v sad. Working pub on 17th.*

She texted: *All work no play! Come to New York! Mo xx*
No time. Writing a book! xx

I looked at my text message. Indeed, it would be a good idea to write a book about Nat Carbayne and Mary Okeford if only to keep everything that was happening to me in perspective, if that was at all possible. As I hit the send button I stopped in my tracks—Mary Okeford, the woman in my dream! The Gimmel ring was inscribed NC & MO. I was being so slow!

I rushed upstairs and brought out the precious box from the bedside cabinet drawer. I stared at the top carved with the letters M and C—Mary Carbayne.

The Forgotten Promise

"I have found you," I said.

Placing the box carefully on the bed, I lifted the lid and saw Nick's letter lying there with the other keepsakes. I took it out but didn't read it. I picked up the ring and carefully opened out the hoops. As I read the inscriptions on each ring, my eyes lingered on the wording *NC & MO, 8 August 1635*. Presently, I closed the hoops and slipped the ring on my wedding finger.

"Mary, show me what happened," I said out loud.

I imagined I heard an imperceptible sigh.

"Show me and Nat will have salvation," I whispered.

Was it an illusion or did a warm current of air caress my body?

I sat there for a long while not noticing the hours pass and the afternoon turn to dusk. I considered everything that the cottage had shown me since I had first moved in. I knew that I was linked to the cottage in some way and that I had been called there for a purpose. I now believed that this purpose was to help Nat's restless spirit find a way to finally be at rest. However, although I had travelled a long way, I still had some distance to go . . .

Pine Lodge

Charles Bosworth's smallholding was at Higher Bockhampton, the village that had been home to Thomas Hardy, the writer. Even though Helen had warned me, I was ill-prepared for Charles Bosworth's charm and was surprised at how easy it was to like him. In his early forties, he had a pleasant boyish face topped off with a mop of thick, dark brown hair and the clearest of brown eyes which twinkled at me as I stepped out of the car. As I had noted before, what was it about these Dorset guys?

"Maddie O'Brien, welcome!" he said in his chocolate-smooth voice with more than a hint of familiarity.

I shook the offered hand and experienced a warm, firm handshake.

"You found the little place OK then?"

I looked over his shoulder at the imposing, three-storey, Queen Anne property behind him surrounded by majestic oak trees.

"Your directions were impeccable," I answered.

He smiled and, immediately taking my arm, walked me around the side of the house.

"I will show you around the farm first and explain the set-up and what we are working towards," he announced. "And then, if you have nothing else planned, I propose to take you to dinner."

The Forgotten Promise

It was a question, though not; he was not expecting an answer.

I nodded and smiled, wondering if this was to be a dinner for two or whether I was being invited to dine with the family.

Charles Bosworth's smallholding extended to just under twenty acres and backed onto Puddletown Forest. A short distance away from the main house stood a stylish stone building, which I had at first mistaken for a substantial range of garages. On closer inspection I saw that the central clocktower stood proudly above a series of dormer windows and three front doors. This, Charles informed me, was staff accommodation. At the far end of the terrace of cottages stood a large solar array that supplied electricity to all the properties.

"There's a back-up diesel generator and we have mains electricity as an option if all else fails," he explained.

I looked at the terrace of cottages and thought that if I was employed by Charles Bosworth, I would be more than happy with the living arrangements.

"I purchased Pine Lodge eight years ago when I first went into practice with Peter Moore," he continued. "It was rather rundown when I bought it. A divorce settlement. Actually a client of mine," he smiled at some memory. "She had done very little to it during the previous five years—too busy having affairs!"

He laughed and it occurred to me that he could well have been one of those affairs.

"Anyway, the land had been left to do what it pleased but, fortunately, she was into horses and sheep, and the grazing was in good heart. No pesticides or chemical-based products had been used for a number of years so I had a good basis from which to start."

He held open a tall wooden gate set within a high stone wall and we entered a walled garden to the rear of the main house, laid out as a semi-formal flower garden. A stone terrace ran the full length of the property and I noticed a hot-tub situated at one end. Along the south facing wall was a large, traditional, wooden greenhouse and Charles proudly showed me the vines, fruit bushes, early vegetables and seedlings growing under protection of the glass.

"This greenhouse is heated by low-level, green energy, soil heating via the woodchip boiler situated at the end of the staff block," he explained. "The boiler also heats the hot-tub—a very popular distraction at dinner parties!"

I smiled. I could so easily imagine Charles Bosworth throwing dinner parties where the guests ended up in that hot-tub on the terrace. I dragged my mind back and concentrated on what he was saying.

"We all benefit from the smallholding's produce. Staff have the option of eating what we've grown, but it is by no means compulsory," he beamed at me. "It's all part of an effort to make the smallholding more self-sufficient and sustainable."

"Do you mind if I write as we go along and take photos?" I asked.

"Please do."

I rummaged in my bag for a pen and notepad. I was disconcerted by the positive energy emanating from Charles Bosworth. Perhaps this was what Helen had meant when she'd warned me that he was a lovable rogue.

I scribbled notes as Charles talked about his plans, the ultimate objective being to reduce his carbon footprint and work towards a more sustainable future. As he talked, we walked and, presently, we passed through another gate that led out onto a grassed walkway that ran adjacent to the walled garden. This overlooked a series of paddocks, all neatly fenced, the far ones bordering Puddletown Forest. The land was mainly level and in the paddock nearest to us stood a large open shelter and a couple of hen houses. Twenty alpacas of various colours and sizes grazed peacefully in the afternoon sun and a dozen or so rare breed chickens busily scratched the earth around them. Charles held open the field gate for me and at the sound of the latch, two young alpacas broke away from the herd and headed towards us.

"They're inquisitive by nature but harmless," he said.

I wondered exactly how harmless they were as the two young alpacas gambolled ever nearer.

"They're only eighteen months old—just testing out their masculine prowess. Don't run, you'll be fine," Charles said, as the young males circled us.

His words did nothing to reduce my dry mouth and heightened adrenalin level. He spoke to the animals in a mellow tone and the larger of the two, a white alpaca, cheekily picked up my camera strap in its teeth and pulled.

"Now Boris, put that down," Charles scolded.

The alpaca continued to pull and Charles firmly removed the strap from its mouth. The smaller of the alpacas, dark fawn in colour, came around to my elbow and nuzzled against me. I had not experienced these animals close-up before and as I stroked its long, flexible neck I was surprised at the softness and thickness of its fleece.

"Did you know that alpacas hate foxes?" Charles chatted on amiably.

I said I didn't.

"They make excellent guardians for other livestock. Those chickens have nothing to fear from Charlie Fox!"

"Maybe every farmer should have an alpaca or two," I suggested.

I took photos and tried not to be too distracted by the two youngsters. I had to jump out of the way of the white alpaca that, having had its game with the camera strap thwarted, was now rearing up at me and trying to eat my hair.

"These are third year offspring," Charles continued. "I decided to breed them having first started with just a pair of wethers to make the place look pretty."

"Wethers?"

"Castrated males," he explained. "Then I discovered just how easy they were to look after and became hooked. I bought a couple of breeding females and it just went from there. I hope we'll have three, if not four, crias this year."

Before I could ask, he said, "That's babies to the uninitiated!"

We crossed the paddock under the watchful gaze of the rest of the herd towards a series of poly tunnels sited on the far side of the fence. The two young alpacas still frolicked around us.

"Do you sell the offspring or just keep them for your own interest?" I asked, trying to keep apace with Charles.

"From time to time. A good quality male has a very high breeding potential and can be worth many thousands of pounds. There's also the opportunity of high income from stud services and females can be worth anything from a few thousand to ten thousand pounds or more. But I really do it for the fun. The law practice can be very stressful and this is my release."

We reached the far gate and, ever the gentleman, Charles held it open for me. Quickly, I slipped through. The young alpacas watched us as we moved into the next paddock, a soft humming emanating from the smaller of the two.

"Oh, that's so charming!" I exclaimed.

Charles smiled. "Yes, they're very gentle animals and highly intelligent, though spitting is perhaps their least endearing feature!"

"Why do they do that?"

"It's one of the few defence mechanisms an alpaca has and I can tell you it is quite an effective deterrent! It's rare for them to spit at people, though. Normally it's used to sort out the pecking order with other herd members."

We stood at the fence watching the two young alpacas that were now scampering around the paddock together.

"Once I happened to step between two squabbling youngsters and I received a faceful." Charles said. "I was throwing a dinner party at the time and I can tell you the old DJ did not come off too well!"

I laughed.

As we walked towards the first large poly tunnel we passed another paddock with a dozen or so Gloucester Old Spots and Tamworth pigs rooting amongst the grass and lying outside their pig arcs. Charles called over to them and one of the Gloucesters approached with a grunt.

"Very intelligent, these pigs, and kind too," he said, scratching behind its ear. "Great pets, though we do rear them for meat. I supply a couple of the local farm shops. The Gloucesters produce particularly fine bacon."

I tried very hard to ignore the wise look in the eyes of that pig.

As we entered the first poly tunnel, Charles explained that it was being used as a tree nursery. Through the open entrance at the rear I could see a distant paddock planted out with a large crop of maturing Christmas trees.

"You'd be surprised how many people demand organic Christmas trees these days," he said, noticing my gaze. "In the run-up to Christmas I open up the smallholding and customers can either buy direct from me here or I have a couple of young lads who sell them for me at Dorchester and Bridport markets. People seem to like buying their Christmas tree from the local solicitor!"

The next two poly tunnels were used for growing organic vegetables and the next two were filled with soft fruit bushes. A young couple were working in the furthest poly tunnel and Charles stopped and introduced me.

"Luke and Kerry came to work here one summer and never left. How long have you been here now?"

"Coming up four years," replied the young man.

"My helpers are very much a part of the whole process and we have regular meetings to make sure we're all singing from the same hymn sheet," Charles said. "I'm also open to new ideas and suggestions and all can contribute. Everyone has a voice."

"That's true," agreed the girl. "We've worked on several smallholdings since leaving uni and, well, really this place is like our own. Mr B. never plays the big boss." She smiled at him.

We chatted a while longer. Leaving them to their work, we said goodbye and I followed Charles out of the poly tunnel. Once we were some distance away he turned to me.

"I don't like playing the 'big boss'. I get enough of that through my work. As long as everyone here knows what everyone else is doing, I leave my workers alone."

We reached the woodland area at the furthest point of his land and he pointed out the crystal clear, babbling stream which wound its way out of Puddletown Forest. It fed a lake where a number of wildfowl dabbled amongst the reeds in the shallows.

"Water rates are minimal as this spring feeds a borehole and there's mains if necessary," Charles explained. "My woodland supplies all the wood we need for the woodchip boiler and for every tree we fell, we plant two."

He glanced at his watch. "Well, that's about it and it's nearing dinner time. You will grace me with your company a little longer?"

Again it was a question, but not. I said that I had nothing planned for the evening and that I would be delighted to have dinner with him.

Walking back to the house, I quickly jotted down an opening paragraph for my article.

Pine Lodge is a twenty acre, organically certified, biodynamic, eco-powered smallholding situated in secluded woodland with its own stream and spring water source. The property borders Puddletown Forest and enjoys complete seclusion and privacy where the unique, natural diversity of a practical and replicable lifestyle conserves, recycles and enriches.

As I followed Charles into the kitchen he asked if I would like to freshen up and showed me to a downstairs cloakroom. He was obviously wealthy and the house reflected this, but it was more homely than ostentatious. On my way back to rejoin him I stopped to admire the gallery of photographs that adorned the walls of the hallway. There was one of Charles, a teenage boy and girl; the girl with various ponies and dogs; the boy and Charles skiing and scuba diving; and pictures of a younger Charles with a blonde, aristocratic-looking lady of similar age.

"The family," he announced from the kitchen doorway.

"Oh, I wasn't prying," I said, overcome with embarrassment.

"Didn't think you were," he replied easily. He joined me and pointed to the children. "My finest achievements! Celeste, and this young ruffian is Oliver. And the woman is my wife . . . ex wife," he corrected. "Deborah."

"Oh, sorry to hear that," I said.

"Don't be. We tried marriage but it just wasn't for us. She's living in St Lucia now with her toy-boy hotelier boyfriend and good luck to her." He said it without a hint of bitterness.

"Where are your children?" I asked.

"Both at university. Oliver's at Oxford and Celeste, she's at Edinburgh. They come and visit their old man in the holidays when they're not gadding around the world!" He picked up a set of car keys from the hall stand. "Ready?"

I followed him out of the front door and around the side of the house. In a large, stone-built, detached garage sat a gleaming, midnight blue Audi TT. I waited as he reversed the car out onto the drive before getting into the passenger seat beside him.

Cheekily I asked, "And where does this fit in with your lesser carbon footprint?"

Intelligent eyes observed me, assessing my question. "Good question Madeleine O'Brien!" He put the car into first gear. "You see, I like the finer things in life and until 'they' manage to make petrol out of thin air I will continue to enjoy the fruits of my labours, even if it means putting petrol in its tank!"

I smiled, sat back and enjoyed the ride into Dorchester with Charles expertly navigating the country

The Forgotten Promise

lanes. His energy was infectious and I couldn't help but like the man.

The restaurant he had chosen was a charming French bistro in the centre of the market town. It wasn't far from his practice, and Charles informed me that he and Peter often frequented it entertaining clients. As he held open the restaurant door for me, the Maitre d' hurried towards us and greeted him.

"Monsieur Bosworth. Good evening," he said in a thick French accent.

"Bonsoir Jean-Pierre. And how are you this evening?"

"Being Sunday not so busy, sir."

I looked around in surprise. Despite his remark, the restaurant appeared to be full.

"A table for two?"

"Thank you, J-P. Perhaps the gallery?" Again it was a question, but not.

Jean-Pierre immediately found the exact table that Charles had requested. I was quickly learning that this was how life was with Charles; a charmed existence indeed. The Maitre d' took our jackets and then led us upstairs to the gallery area which overlooked the main restaurant. As we reached the upper floor I happened to glance across the room to a table at the back and my heart leapt straight into my mouth. There sat Nick and Sarah. Of all the nights and all the restaurants!

Charles pulled out a chair for me and I sat down, quickly accepting the menu Jean-Pierre handed me. Frantically, I wondered how I was going to handle the situation; my mind was in turmoil and my heart raced. Damn Nick! Why had I allowed him to get under my skin so deeply? Charles took his seat opposite me and ordered a bottle of champagne. As he opened his menu he casually looked around the restaurant, his eyes alighting on the far table.

"Nick, my man. How are you?" he asked in an enthusiastic voice.

I watched as Nick made eye contact with me. I smiled sadly and looked away.

"Good Charlie. And you?"

"Excellent. And Sarah, my dear, as lovely as ever."

I glanced at Sarah who was smiling flirtatiously at Charles, not a care in the world. Lucky girl. I was aware that Nick was still watching me and I couldn't help but look at him again before dragging my eyes back to the menu.

But Charles was in ebullient mood. "Nick, you never warned me how ravishing Maddie is!"

Charles winked at me and I blushed, embarrassed, but it was hard to be cross with someone who embraced life so fully. Shyly I glanced at Nick but he wasn't smiling.

"Thought I'd let it be a surprise," he said evenly.

"It certainly is and such a pleasant one at that!" Charles smiled broadly across the table at me before turning his attention back to the far table. "You must come over for dinner when Peter and Helen return from their travels."

"Oh yes!" exclaimed Sarah. "And go in your hot tub again, pleeease!"

So they had been to one of his outrageous dinner parties.

"Only if you promise to wear that teeny-weeny blue bikini," Charles teased.

Sarah said that she would do just that as she still had the remnants of her Australian tan. Nick was silent.

In an amused voice Charles replied, "Well, then, I'd better organise a party before your tan disappears!"

The Forgotten Promise

Turning his attention to me once again, he asked, "Have you decided what you'd like, Maddie? I can highly recommend the moules."

We placed our orders and the champagne arrived soon after. It would have been a great evening had I not been so aware of Nick sitting on the opposite side of the room. He and Sarah had obviously arrived just before us and so our meals were served almost simultaneously. Charles was the perfect host, toasting me with champagne, his eyes dancing wickedly at me all the while. His conversation was amusing and accomplished and he was interesting company. If it hadn't been for Nick, I could have fooled myself into thinking that I was on a date and relaxed into the evening. At one point during the meal Charles kissed my hand, his brown eyes looking deeply into mine. Flustered, I immediately—and guiltily—looked across at Nick who sat at his table very straight-faced. When my gaze returned to Charles he was looking inquisitively from me to Nick. He smiled warmly and squeezed my hand before letting it go.

"Tell me, Maddie. Is there a man in your life?"

He was not prying; he seemed genuinely interested.

I shook my head and said, vaguely, "It's a bit messy."

"What's a great looking girl like you doing on your own? How come you've slipped the net?"

I breathed in deeply and looked straight into those deep brown eyes. There wasn't a hint of duplicity in the look that met mine.

"I guess I've never met the right man," I replied, my heart breaking.

"Well, I've never met the right woman but despite that I've managed to beget a son and daughter!"

I smiled.

"I guess I could ask you the same question," I countered. "Why is a good looking guy like you on your own?"

"Twelve years with Deborah taught me that it's not everything to end up with the prerequisite wife, two children and a couple of Labradors, now deceased . . . the dogs, that is! But it hasn't stopped me from appreciating the opposite sex." He looked long and hard at me. "Oh well, Madeleine O'Brien. There's plenty of time for all that messy business to sort itself out."

He polished off his glass of champagne with a flourish, topped up my glass and poured himself another. "Plenty of fish in the sea and, personally, I like fishing!"

I laughed. You couldn't be sad around Charles for long.

About twenty minutes later, Nick and Sarah settled their bill and prepared to leave. On the way to the stairs they stopped at our table. Charles immediately leapt to his feet and started flirting with Sarah.

Nick softly asked, "You OK Maddie?"

"Yes."

"No more happenings?"

"Plenty," I replied quietly.

The look of concern on his face tore my heart apart.

Sarah, laughing at something Charles had said, glanced at us and a small frown settled on her face. Not a solicitor for nothing, Charles noticed everything and quickly smoothed over the situation, engaging us all in conversation.

"Well this has been fun," he said. "Even though I've been forced into organising another hot-tub party!"

He winked at Sarah who responded by giggling.

We said our goodbyes and I watched as they walked down the stairs, collected their coats and disappeared through the main entrance. It seemed to me that I was destined forever to watch Nick walk away from me. The champagne must have gone to my head as, to my consternation, a tear slid down my face. Angrily, I brushed it away and caught Charles thoughtfully observing me.

"Madeleine O'Brien, may I say something?" Again, it was a question, but not.

Despite my fragile state, I recognised that the man would be a force to be reckoned with in any courtroom.

"You're a lovely lady and I've had a thoroughly enjoyable time. I'd like to think that we can repeat it sometime, no strings attached."

He raised a confident eyebrow and I nodded. After all, life had to go on and he was good company.

"However, if, in the meantime, you and Nick get it together, well, then I will understand."

I opened my eyes in amazement and he laughed. "It's not really obvious!" he said, amused. "Poor bugger."

"What? Who me?" I asked.

"No, not you. Nick! There he is, good man that he is, been with Sarah donkey's years and doing the right thing by sticking with her. And then you come along to upset the apple cart!"

Once again, tears welled up and threatened to spill over.

"It's enough to turn any man's head."

It was the first time anyone had so openly acknowledged our situation. He handed me a serviette and I got the impression that he was well versed in coping with female emotions. I dabbed my eyes, thankful that I was wearing waterproof mascara.

"Listen, I understand if you don't want to talk about it but, if you do, my door is always open," he said generously. "And Maddie, if there's a bit of advice I can offer, have a little faith."

I looked at him askance. "That's what my sister says!"

"Your sister's right and if she's anything like you—and single—I'd like to meet her too." He laughed, and even his laugh was as smooth as chocolate. "In fact, she has an invite to the hot-tub party as well!"

The next morning, with the map open on the seat beside me, I drove towards Shipton Gorge. It was a dreary, damp morning and it suited my mood. Although I had enjoyed my meal with Charles the previous evening, unexpectedly seeing Nick and Sarah like that had only heightened the realisation of how desperate my situation was becoming. I wanted to live in Dorset and, particularly, The Olde Smithy. I had moved here in the belief that a new life awaited me and yet I was beginning to feel downhearted about my circumstances. My father's words rang soundly in my ears, *'Enjoy the adventure, Madeleine, but don't stay in the wilderness too long'*.

As I drove along the country lanes I considered my options. I didn't particularly want to go back to London. With Caro and John moving to Newcastle and Dan now being heavily involved once again with Lucy, there wasn't much to tempt me back. And, besides, I sternly reminded myself, I didn't believe in 'going back'.

I reached the inn at Shipton Gorge and followed the road around to the left, past St. Martin's Church. As in my dream, the road led down into the valley beyond and I followed the country lane looking out for a road leading off to the right, but a couple of miles later I reached the A35. This was wrong. I turned the car around, pulled over and studied the map. It was a general road map without any great detail and there were no roads depicted leading off to either side of the lane. I cursed myself for not having an Ordnance Survey map. Putting the car into first gear, I pulled away and drove back towards Shipton Gorge, keeping an eye out for any lanes leading off.

After a mile or so, I came upon a dirt track to my left. This was certainly no roadway leading to a significant house but there were no other turnings. I turned the car onto the track and saw an old wooden sign, half-hidden in the hedge, announcing Hammiton Farm. Well, at least the name was correct. With an increasing sense of excitement I drove towards the farm. The track skirted woodland to my left and, about half-a-mile further on, a ramshackle collection of farm buildings came into view. The lane appeared to lead directly into the farmyard where a sheepdog rose to its feet and barked noisily, running at the wheels of the car as I followed the track, turning right between the farm buildings and then around a sharp left hand bend. All at once, and for no apparent reason, my breathing became laboured, my vision blurred and I felt a sudden shooting pain across my forehead. Gripping the steering wheel firmly I carried on, manoeuvering the car around several large ruts as best I could.

After a mile or so, I began to breathe more easily and the headache started to abate. The lane took me through another series of farm buildings and eventually I arrived at a T-junction. Instinctively I wanted to turn right, but there was something wrong. In my dream the turning had been a lane, but this was a main road. If I turned left, I would come out on the A35 again but if I turned right, where would that lead me? I looked at the map. The road led to the village of Swyre and then eventually to Abbotsbury via the coast road. I turned towards the village, even though it didn't feel right. According to the map I was heading away from Hammiton Farm, but something made me want to head south. I got as far as Chilcombe village, a matter of half-a-mile, when the headache started again and I had to pull over. I was strangely fearful.

It had started to rain steadily but I got out of the car, pulled up the hood of my jacket and breathed in deeply, slowly turning around to survey the scenery. Interestingly, I noticed that when I faced south, east or north, the fear dissipated, however, when I looked in a westerly direction I felt decidedly nauseus. Why? Across the road stretched a series of fields and away in the distance, on a hill to the west, I could see the tower of St Martin's Church. I knew I was close, but not close enough. I must have missed the turning.

I jumped back as a passing car sped by, sending up a sheet of water from a deep puddle in the road. The occupants looked at me with open mouths and I realised that I must look decidedly strange standing out in the torrential rain. Getting back into the car, I backtracked and turned left down the rutted lane from which I had previously emerged. I passed the range of farm buildings and, after a mile or so, came to a bend in the lane. As I negotiated the bend, a rabbit shot across my path and I had to swerve to avoid it, stalling the car in the process and ending up in the hedge. I was just about to put the car into reverse when I noticed that the hedge seemed to be less thick at this point and, on studying it more closely, I could just make out an overgrown track leading off to the left. This had to be it. It was obvious that no-one had ventured down the track for a very long time and the rampant foliage grew unhindered. No wonder I had

The Forgotten Promise

missed it! I parked the car tightly against the hedge and stepped out once more into the rain.

Forcing my way through the bushes, on several occasions I had to disentangle myself from unforgiving brambles that grabbed at my legs and tore at my wax jacket. The track was deeply rutted and the pouring rain had turned the mud into a lethal, slippery surface. The going was hard and I scrambled along the path as best I could, my legs becoming increasingly leaden, as if I was being physically held back. I had to force one foot in front of the other to make any progress at all. After five hundred yards or so, the track petered out and I stood and stared at the open field before me, empty of stock and lying fallow.

With an ever-growing fear, I started to panic. I thought I was going to pass out and with hands on knees, breathed in deeply, oblivious to the rain. Feeling marginally better, I straightened up and looked around. Every fibre in my body told me that this was where Hammiton Hall had once stood but there was nothing to see apart from a curious mound to my right that seemed out of place with the surrounding landscape. I walked to the small hillock and started to pull at the grass, which came away in sodden clumps. With mounting feverishness I tore at the earth, mud forcing its way under my fingernails. Picking up a loose rock, I hacked at the ground, making deep depressions that filled with water as soon as they were formed.

After twenty minutes, or so, I broke through to rubble and removed this to one side and soon a square of stonework revealed itself. I walked a few yards in the opposite direction and stopped. The ground felt stony underfoot, unlike the soft grass and mud in the centre of the track and, falling to my knees, the cold rainwater soaked through my already saturated jeans. I was wet through but oblivious to my immediate environment. Frantically, I pulled at the grass. Some fifteen minutes later I had exposed another square of stonework, long buried under the earth. I knew that these were the remains of the pillars to Hammiton Hall, though the building itself was long gone. In my mind's eye I saw the great iron gates and huge pillars that I had seen in my dream.

Scrambling to my feet, I walked through the entrance and up what would have been the drive towards where the Hall had once stood. With an ever-increasing and inexplicable terror I began to shake uncontrollably and, suddenly, violently threw up. I stood in the rain feeling retched and very alone. Delving deep into my pockets, I found a tissue, wiped my mouth and realised that my face wasn't just wet from the rain; I was crying. Something terrible had happened here and, at once, I knew it was something concerning me.

I forced myself to look around the site, despite the panic which still had me in its hold, but there was nothing more to discover. The foundations of the house were nowhere to be seen. I made my way back to the car and, still shaking, managed to put the car into gear and drive down the lane through Hammiton Farm. As I passed by the farmhouse, a man stood and stared from the front porch and called sharply to the collie as it, once again, ran at my tyres.

I arrived back in Walditch, shaken by my experience, and parked alongside the village green. I was cold and wet but I couldn't face being on my own and needed some form of distraction, so I went to the pub.

Brian did a double-take as I walked in. "Maddie, you look terrible! Come here. I'll get you a drink."

I clambered onto the bar stool, my hands still shaking violently, my wet jeans clinging to my legs. Brian set a glass of whisky on the bar infront of me.

"What have you been up to? You look like you've seen a ghost!"

I looked at him wide-eyed and burst into tears. Immediately he came around the bar and wrapped me in a huge bear hug, despite my wet clothes.

"Hey, come on sweetheart. It can't be that bad!"

"I think it is," I sobbed.

"No Maddie. Nothing's that bad. Drink up."

I was shaking so much I had to hold the glass with both hands. I took a large slug and the whisky burned the back of my throat.

"You know I don't just give any old person my finest single malt!" he said kindly.

I managed a smile, of sorts.

"You just got cold and wet, didn't you?" he said, as if talking to a young child.

The shaking began to subside.

"I guess so."

I knew that Brian would never understand anything that was happening to me. He was a regular bloke without an ounce of 'other worldliness' about him.

"Good, well now you're here . . ." he said, grinning.

Now what was coming?

"Vera and I have decided on an emerald theme for the 17th, so wear anything green. I know you'll look smashing, what with that auburn hair of yours."

Trust Brian to bring me back into the moment.

"And I've risked my reputation once again," he added. "You'll be on waiting duties."

I finished my drink and said I was getting quite a dab hand at the waitressing thing and that I would dig something out of the dressing-up box for the evening.

I walked back to the cottage, closed the front door on the world and momentarily leant back against the door. With a deep sigh, I finally changed into some dry clothes, settled down at the dining room table and opened up the laptop to record the latest twist in the sad tale that was unfolding.

St Patrick's Day

The evening of the 17th was crisp and clear and, thankfully, earlier that afternoon it had stopped raining. I ran across the village green, careful not to slip on the wet grass, and fairly flew through the pub door. Vera, talking to Janet, looked up sharply at my noisy arrival and acknowledged me before returning to her conversation. Hanging my jacket on the coat hooks by the door, I noticed that someone had lit a fire and I glanced up at the picture hanging above it, as I always did.

"Hey, Maddie, like the skirt!" called over Janet.

I swung round to see her observing me over the top of her clipboard. In response to Brian's request for us to wear something green that evening I had chosen black leggings and a short pleated skirt in emerald-green tartan that had not seen the light of day since my London media days. With some satisfaction I had noticed it still fitted me, even though I wasn't as active now as I had been when I was constantly running around at the whim of the latest 'rising star'. My hair was tied back in a single plait with a green ribbon braided through it and on my black T-shirt I had pinned an an old Christmas cracker gift, an emerald-green enamelled brooch in the shape of a four-leaf clover.

"Thanks Janet. And you look great."

She wore black trousers and a striking green and white blouse over which she wore a wide, black patent belt that accentuated her slim waist.

"The band's already here," she said excitedly.

I could see the six-piece Irish folk group setting up their equipment at the far end of the restaurant. I knew she fancied the lead singer, Tony, and she had been ecstatic when Brian had suggested he hired them for the evening.

"How many have booked tonight?" I asked.

"Thirty six, but we're expecting more."

I had yet to see the list of diners and was nervous that there might be a table in the name of Corbin, as there had been on Valentine's Night. She handed me the clipboard and I quickly scanned the names, experiencing both relief and disappointment when I saw the surname not listed. However, I did notice that Janet had marked herself down to look after all the tables nearest the band and she charmingly blushed when I pointed this out to her.

The restaurant had been dressed with emerald streamers and each table sported a smart green tablecloth on which had been placed a small vase of perky daffodils. The Irish folk group had also entered into the spirit of the occasion and various shades of green tassels embellished their instruments. Each band member sported something green and the young, energetic, lead singer had somehow found a pair of shoes that were of a particularly lurid shade. I watched Janet chatting to him, enthusiastically comparing the colour of her blouse to his shoes. Trying not to think about my own obsession with a certain person, I hoped that something would come of Janet's infatuation with Tony. The group had played at the pub before—a mix of traditional Irish folk and rock—and were very popular and Brian was expecting a good turnout.

Soon customers began to arrive and I found myself busy behind the bar. Each time the door opened I held my breath, but Nick did not appear. It was ridiculous to be

The Forgotten Promise

so on edge and I kept reminding myself that I didn't want him to turn up in any case. At around 8pm Brian asked me to work the tables for the remainder of the evening. I was pleased to do so as the entrance doors were not visible from the restaurant and the lively atmosphere, what with the band playing at the far end, would more easily distract me.

Sometime around 9pm, Charles Bosworth appeared in the restaurant with Sarah. My heart did a double-flip expecting to see Nick, but it was Becky and Mark who followed in their wake. Charles approached and, with a playful glint in his eyes, planted a kiss on my cheek.

"Good evening lovely lady," he purred. "I've only just discovered that you can be found here and I may have to change my watering hole!"

I smiled at the compliment.

"Hello Charles. Have you booked?" I asked, thinking that I hadn't seen Bosworth on the list.

"No, last minute decision. Thought we'd come and surprise you."

I looked past him at Sarah whose mouth twitched into some form of a smile but her eyes coolly surveyed me.

"A table for four?" I asked.

"Please. Not too close to the band but preferably one with a good view."

I checked the restaurant bookings. There was a free table over by the window, half-way down the room and, as he had requested, not too close to the band but with a good view. His charmed life continued.

"Hope you don't mind the company I've brought?" he said, putting his hand on my waist. "I tried to persuade Nick to come too but he said he wasn't feeling well." He smiled at me and winked, then added, "Thought that was only ever a female complaint!"

So Nick had bowed out. Some friendship we were having, I thought miserably.

As they settled themselves at the table, I distributed menus and handed Charles the wine list. Sarah, sitting next to Charles, looked animated and excited. Becky merely glared at me.

"I'll leave you to make up your minds," I said.

I cleared plates from a nearby table and as I walked through the kitchen swing doors with crockery piled high, Janet came up behind me.

"That Becky Milner's got a face on her tonight," she said. "Probably had an argument with Mark. God knows why he puts up with her!"

Janet and I got on well. Coming from a family of four boys, she treated me like the sister she didn't have and often confided in me. She had lived in Walditch all her life and had been at school with both Sarah and Becky.

"Yes, seems to have a bit of attitude," I agreed.

"She's always been that way," Janet continued. "Mark must be really spineless to stay. You have to watch your back with her."

"Have Sarah and Becky always been friends?" I asked.

"Yeah, best mates. Always doing things together."

That would explain why she was so quick to rush to Sarah's defence over Nick, I thought. I set the dirty dishes on the work surface next to the sink.

Vera, plating up, handed Janet a couple of main meals to take through to the restaurant.

"How long have Becky and Mark been an item?" I asked.

Janet thought for a moment. "About five years I think. She was well pissed when Sarah first took up with Nick. Really jealous! Felt completely left out. We all knew Becky fancied Nick like mad. You should have seen her trying to get off with him at Sarah's eighteenth, she was all over him like a rash! But it was her best mate who hooked him. Ended up not only jealous of Sarah but Nick as well."

"No wonder she's got attitude," I commented, holding open the swing door for Janet.

She looked at me as she walked through into the restaurant. "Always had, even at primary school. Used to really bully me."

I walked back to the Bosworth table and took their orders, noticing how Sarah sat very close to Charles. She looked at him with big, round, innocent eyes, giggling and flirting and it was obvious she felt she was on a night off from Nick. Charles was being his usual charismatic self and seemed to display no particular favour towards Sarah, being as charming to Becky and me and even Mark, I noticed.

The evening went well and the band played on. At around 11.30pm, Charles and his party prepared to leave. On his way out to the bar, Charles approached and put his arm around my shoulder.

"Thank you, Madeleine O'Brien for a good evening made even more enjoyable by your presence," he said in an exaggeratedly courteous voice. "It could only have been eclipsed had you been seated at my table!"

I smiled, thinking that it was the last place I would have wanted to be, considering the company.

"I will phone you soon to arrange a dinner date."

He said it in such a way, as if it would never occur to him that my acceptance of his dinner proposal was anything other than a foregone conclusion. His confidence made me smile. In anyone else it would have been perceived as arrogance, but in Charles . . . Well, it was very easy to like him.

"I look forward to it," I replied.

He kissed me on the cheek, turned and walked through to the bar area to join Sarah and Mark who had just passed by. I was about to attend to another of my tables when Becky sidled up to me with venom in her eyes.

"Don't think you've got him yet," she hissed. "He's not that easily won over."

I was getting so fed up with the way she thought she could treat me. Who did she think she was?

"I have no idea what you're on about," I replied flippantly.

"Don't give me that shit! Sarah's so sweet she doesn't see it, but I know your game."

I regarded her coldly, thinking how right Janet was. Becky Milner did have a face on her; an ugly and unattractive one.

"Unlike you, Becky, I've grown up. I don't play games."

I thought she was going to hit me. She wasn't much taller than me but more heavily built. Pulling herself up to her full height she barged into me, causing me to stagger back and, before I knew it, she had me pinned against the wall. I could smell the drink on her breath.

"What makes you think he'd look at you anyway?" she spat out the words with contempt. "Leave Nick alone! He's not yours."

Like a spoilt child who couldn't get her own way she caught hold of my bare arm and viscously twisted it, digging her nails into my skin. I winced and tried to escape her hold, but she was surprisingly strong. She dug her nails in further.

As luck would have it, at that moment Brian walked through from the bar. He hesitated, assessing the situation, and looked enquiringly at me.

"What's going on here?"

"I think one of our customers has had one too many," I replied, keeping my voice steady. My arm hurt like mad.

Becky still had me pinned against the wall, her elbow now digging into my stomach and she glared down at me.

"Don't think you've won," she growled menacingly, her face very close to mine. "And you ain't gonna either."

Brian walked up to us and faced her.

"Becky Milner," he said loudly and slowly. "Whatever your problem is with my member of staff I will not have you behaving like this in my establishment, do you understand?"

Mark, having realised that Becky was no longer with their group, had come back into the restaurant looking for her. On seeing the situation he groaned.

"Come on Bex. Leave it." He grabbed her arm but she flinched away from him.

"Don't touch me!" she screamed aggressively.

Fortunately, the music from the band was loud and only a couple of nearby diners looked up startled, astonishment settling upon their faces when they saw what was going on.

"Right, that's it! I will not have you causing a scene in my restaurant."

Brian caught hold of her shoulders and she struggled, trying to break free. With a firm grip, he frog-marched her out towards the bar with Mark trotting behind. Before they disappeared through the archway, Becky looked back over her shoulder at me.

"I'm watching you!" she shouted threateningly.

I stood there in shock, fingers of ice reaching up from the pit of my stomach. Janet, having seen the tail-end of the skirmish, came over and asked if I was all right. I nodded, rubbing my arm; it smarted badly. A red wheel now encircled my wrist and there was the beginnings of a violent, purple-coloured bruise. And where her nails had dug into my arm Becky had drawn blood.

"You're right, Janet. She is a bully."

Early April

On the last Friday in March I handed Storm over to the care of Mrs Tomkins, packed a weekend bag and headed for London. I had not been back since moving west and was unsure how I felt. Would this visit make me yearn for a return to that way of life?

I left Walditch around mid-afternoon. It was an easy journey and the traffic wasn't too bad. The closer I got to London I noticed that most of the cars were heading in the opposite direction, escaping the city. I had arrived by early evening.

Caro and John welcomed me into their home, a handsome, three-storey Victorian house on the edge of Clapham Common. I had been to many a party there. They didn't have children and on every occasion I had visited their home it had appeared orderly and tidy; everything in its place.

"Oh God, Maddie, I've got so much clearing to do!" Caro exclaimed as she opened the front door and hugged me affectionately. "You'll have to excuse the mess."

"Looks fine to me," I said, noticing how neat everything was as I followed her down the hallway. A delicious smell wafted through from the kitchen.

"Paella," she said, over her shoulder. "Hope that's OK?"

"Fantastic!"

John was sitting at the marble-topped breakfast bar, an open bottle of wine and a half-filled glass before him. He jumped up and hugged me warmly.

"Hi, Maddie. You look well. Country air obviously agrees with you!"

I kissed him fondly on the cheek.

"Here, pull up a chair. White OK?" He held up the bottle.

"Very OK!"

He busied himself finding a glass and pouring the wine. Caro, standing in front of a huge stainless steel range cooker, checked the sizzling contents of a large frying pan.

"I asked Dan over to supper tonight but he said he was otherwise engaged." She gave the paella a stir. "However, he is coming with us tomorrow to the theatre."

"With Lucy?" I asked.

"No, she's gone up to Bristol for some reason. I guess that's why he feels he can be let out on a Saturday night."

"Caro, you make him sound like some puppy dog!" admonished John.

"Well, she's got him on such a short leash I think that's what he's become."

We had a quiet meal in, just the three of us, and they talked excitedly about their imminent move to Newcastle. John was already living there for part of the week in hotel accommodation and he had brought back a selection of property sales particulars to consider. We spent the evening discussing the various merits of each one, putting them into different piles; 'definites', 'possibles' and 'absolute nots'. Caro and John were charming, intelligent, easy company and with a sharp pang I realised that I did miss this aspect of my old London life.

The Forgotten Promise

After supper we withdrew to the sitting room and relaxed in fat, comfortable, oversized settees. It was a grand room with a high ceiling, the central ceiling rose and ornate cornicing still intact, and there was an original marble fireplace above which hung a large, gilt-framed mirror. The mantelpiece was crammed full of framed photos of various nieces, nephews and God children and in the centre stood a fancy carriage clock. The previous summer Caro had employed professional decorators to paint the house in neutral colours and interesting, original paintings adorned the walls. It was a stylish home reflecting its owners' good taste.

"So, Maddie, Caro tells me you're doing some freelance writing these days," John said as he handed me a brandy.

"Yes," I replied. "Regularly for a couple of mags, ad hoc for others. I can't tell you how excited I was when I received my first freelance payment!" I laughed, remembering how little it had been compared to my usual monthly salary from Hawkstone.

"Well good for you!" he said genuinely. He smiled at his wife and I had the strongest impression that he was trying to reassure her in some way. "I know it's not easy," he continued. "But do you think you'll be able to make a living from it?"

"Early days, John, but I hope so."

"Bet you meet some interesting people," commented Caro.

I told them about Charles Bosworth and how charming he was. I caught Caro's meaningful look in John's direction but he pretended not to notice.

I laughed out loud. "Caro!"

"Well, I'm just concerned that you're down there in the depths of the countryside all on your own," she said sincerely.

If only she knew, I thought.

"Well thanks for your concern but I'm happy on my own at the moment," I said, knowing that this was far from true.

"Better for Maddie to be on her own than to be with someone who won't let her out of their sight," said John. "I'd stick with the occasional, charming dinner date if I were you. Far healthier."

Caro sighed.

"Is it no better with Dan then?" I asked.

"If anything, it's worse," she said. "We never see him any more. He's only coming tomorrow because you're here and he wants to see you. Lucy doesn't know, by the way. He said if she did she'd cancel her trip to Bristol."

I wondered how he could stand living with such a jealous and controlling person.

"It will be nice to see him too," I said genuinely. "Now, Caro, tell me about this PR launch of yours."

The following day, Caro and I spent a girlie day together shopping in Covent Garden. We had lunch at a wine bar that I used to frequent when I worked at Hawkstone Media and bumped into some of the old crew. It was good to see them again and they eagerly told me how my replacement was not fitting in and that Ken Hawkstone constantly bemoaned the day I had handed in my notice. I wasn't sure if this was true, but it massaged my ego.

We joined them at their table, polished off a bottle of wine and caught up on the gossip. Around mid-afternoon, Caro and I made our way back to Clapham, heavily laden

The Forgotten Promise

with our purchases. Dan arrived sometime after 5pm. In all the years I had known him he had always been verging on the lean but I was staggered to see him looking so gaunt.

"Maddie," he hugged me hard. "So good to see you!"

"Likewise, Dan. But, you know, we do live in the 21st Century. There are such things as mobiles."

He looked sheepish. "I know, I know. Don't start!"

He didn't look at all well. His hair was long and lank and his skin had a grey tinge to it, as if he hadn't seen the light of day for sometime. Dark circles surrounded strained eyes.

We walked through to the living room where John was quietly reading a newspaper. Immediately he put it to one side and rose from his chair. "Dan, my man. Long time no see." Brusquely he hugged his brother-in-law, slapping him on the back.

"Yeah, too long." Dan quickly extricated himself from the male bonding. "Congrats on your promotion, by the way."

"Thanks. It's a good move up the old career ladder," said John.

There was a sudden, noisy commotion at the door and Caro rushed into the room. "Dan! Come here baby brother." Standing on tiptoes, she hugged him and gave him a huge kiss on the cheek.

"Hi big sis!" Dan's arm encircled her waist and he easily lifted her off her feet.

Not for the first time I thought how unlike brother and sister they were, one tall and often ungainly; the other so petite and self-contained. She smiled happily.

"Oh, it's so good us four being together again," she cried enthusiastically as her feet touched the ground.

A shadow moved across Dan's eyes as he looked at me.

"But you're so skinny!" she exclaimed. Standing back from him, Caro critically studied her brother and I watched him flinch under his sister's scrutiny.

"Your jeans are falling off, there's nothing of you any more! Doesn't she feed you?"

"We eat well, Caro. Don't fuss!"

There was irritation in his voice; the even-tempered Dan I knew had certainly departed.

John, sensing disquiet, glanced at the clock and announced that we had better get our skates on if we were to arrive in time for the performance. "You know what the Underground can be like on a Saturday night."

We found our coats and departed for the theatre. Dan stayed close to me throughout the journey and, as the minutes ticked by, the strain began to lift from his face.

Caro had, somehow, managed to obtain tickets for the latest musical which had opened to sell-out audiences and rave reviews. It was a great show; the cast were young and energetic and the songs memorable, and I savoured the theatrical environment once again. Afterwards, we ate at a restaurant not far from the theatre and it was good to be part of London's bustling nightlife. I felt as though I had been away on a long journey for many years and had returned to a comfortable, familiar environment. However, in my heart I knew I had moved on and this was but a fleeting return to an earlier, seemingly easier life.

The tube was packed on our return journey to Clapham Common and with only one vacant seat, I insisted Caro took it. We stood crushed together, Dan and John holding the overhead bar while I held onto Dan. At every sharp jolt of the train, Dan seemed to move closer to me and I noticed the small smile that settled on Caro's lips. But I felt swamped by his presence.

As we emerged from the tube station she commented on how cold it was and immediately linking arms with her husband, she smartly walked him up the road towards their house. It was cold but I knew she was deliberately putting some distance between us. I smiled wryly. There was no way that I was going to attempt to rekindle a relationship with her brother, but her heart was in the right place.

As we followed in their wake, Dan put his arm around me. "You know, it's good to see you Mads," he said. "I miss our times together."

With my arm around his waist I could feel how thin he had become.

"How is it with you?" I asked.

"Oh you know. Much as before."

I stopped and stepped away from him. "You don't mean Lucy's 'ex' is still on the scene?" I asked incredulously.

He shook his head. "I don't ask. It's easier that way."

Where was his self-esteem?

"Don't look at me like that Mads." He put his arm around me again and we started walking again.

"But Dan, if she was still seeing her 'ex' would you do anything about it?" I asked.

"Probably not, Mads. I'm trapped." He sounded so despondent.

"No-one is trapped, Dan. Only you can choose how you want to spend your life." I thought about my own situation and did not truly believe the words I had just uttered.

He grunted but said nothing and we walked on in silence for a while, Dan holding me close and only letting me go when we reached the house. Through the open front door I could see John busying himself in the kitchen.

"Anyone for tea or coffee?" he called lightly.

We hung our coats in the hallway and saying 'yes' to coffee, walked into the living room. Dan sat down on the nearest settee and, in order to distance myself from his attentions, I sat opposite him. It was quiet and peaceful in that room and I noticed how much more relaxed Dan now seemed compared to earlier in the evening. Here, before me, was some semblance of the man I had known and cared about for all those years.

Suddenly Caro appeared at the door, an innocent look on her face. "I'm bushed," she announced. "If you two don't mind, I'm going to bed."

She came into the room and gave Dan a hug.

"Please look after yourself Dan. Promise you will see us at least one more time before we depart for Newcastle?"

He said he would. She kissed him and wished me a comfortable night's sleep. As she left the room, I watched as she looked directly towards the kitchen and I knew that she and John were sharing a long and meaningful communication, as only husband and wife can. A few minutes later he came through with the coffee.

"I'm knackered so if you two don't mind I'll say goodnight. If you could switch the lights off when you come up to bed, Maddie?" He smiled at us both before following his wife upstairs.

Dan and I were alone in the living room. Looking across at him, I burst out laughing.

"Well, that wasn't very obvious!" I said. "Your sister!"

Dan smiled thinly. "We did have good times, didn't we Mads?"

The Forgotten Promise

"Yes we did," I agreed. I sipped my coffee, thinking back to the times we had shared and, before I knew it, Dan had crossed the room and sat down beside me.

"Do you ever think what might have been?" he asked.

Careful, I thought. Dangerous territory.

"I don't think like that," I said cautiously. "I like to look forward in life."

He nodded, took my mug and placed it on the coffee table. His large hands easily encompassed mine and he stared deeply into my eyes. "But if you did look back would you wonder?"

"No Dan," I said quietly. "We had plenty of time to sort things out and we didn't."

He looked so forlorn. "I'm not happy Mads."

"Then do something about it," I replied, not particularly gently.

"I can't. I don't know what to do. I need a way out."

And that's *not* going to be me, I thought harshly.

"Just tell her to go," I suggested, removing my hands from his.

He shook his head miserably. "Can't do that."

There was that awkward distance between us again, and then he asked, "Are you happy, Mads?"

Loaded question. Where do I start?

"Sort of, Dan," I replied.

We had known each other so well, it was hard not to be honest with him.

"What does that mean?" he asked.

"Well . . ." I hesitated, and then ploughed on. "I'm not sure I can stay in Dorset."

"Why?"

I sighed. It was a long story which had yet to play its course.

"I don't think there's a life for me there anymore," I said simply.

"But Mads, you gave up a bloody good career to move there!" he said rather angrily. "I distinctly remember you saying that you were 'going home', although I could never understand it."

"I was. Going home, I mean," I said. "But now that I'm there it's not that simple."

He didn't say anything and the silence between us hung heavily in the air.

"It is . . . was my home," I said quietly.

He looked at me uncomprehendingly.

"I have something to do, Dan," I continued. "Then I think I'll move on."

It was the first time I had formulated my thoughts out loud.

"Where will you go? Will you come back to London?"

I caught the hope in his voice, even though I had told him there was no going back.

"No, not London. I've done that. I might go to Dublin," I said, surprising myself.

"Back to the fold," he murmured.

"Well, yes, for a while. Perhaps reassess everything and then move on from there."

I hadn't considered returning to my city of birth until that moment but now I toyed with the thought and decided that it was not such a bad idea.

"Wherever you go, you will keep in touch won't you Mads?"

"Bloody hell, Daniel, I've tried!" I said, rather too loudly. "You never answer your damn phone!"

"I know, I know. But if you moved away for good I would die."

"Don't be daft, Dan."

"You know what I mean. It would be final. Knowing you're in Dorset doesn't seem final somehow. Promise me?"

He looked so defeated. Suddenly he leant forward and kissed me. It was a sad, lingering, goodbye of a kiss, full of the memories of happier times.

"Sorry Mads. Had to do that one last time. I miss you so."

The next morning dawned clear and blue, the spring sunshine surprisingly warm after the cold snap of the night before. Caro, John and I had a leisurely breakfast at one of the many cafés in the neighbourhood and then, amidst promises to visit them in Newcastle, I wished them a successful move north and headed west once more. As suburban roads gave way to open countryside, I felt tendrils of invisible ivy pulling me back to Dorset. I had enjoyed my visit to London, though it had tugged at the heartstrings but I knew, ultimately, it was not what I wanted anymore. I arrived back in Walditch with a renewed, unwavering determination to get to the bottom of whatever The Olde Smithy needed me to resolve.

7*th* April

It was late afternoon and I was driving home to Walditch having once again visited Strippers. I had found a wrought iron gate for the front garden amongst all the salvage and was pleased with my purchase. As I drew up alongside the village green, I glanced over at The Olde Smithy and thought I saw a young girl run around the corner of the cottage towards the courtyard. I liked children but it was certainly time to fit a gate; anyone could just wander in.

I got out of the car, crossed the green and walked up the garden path, preparing to ask the girl why she was in my garden, but when I rounded the corner of the courtyard I was stopped dead in my tracks. There was Nat with a very young Francis in his arms and Elisabeth, aged about five, running circles around them. They were all laughing and seemed so happy. Immediately, I thought of the statue at Nick's workshop and some deeper understanding told me what he had captured in that piece. I remembered his words, *'When I first started work on the yew I had no idea what I was sculpting; it seemed to me that the sculpture had a life of its own.'*

I delighted in the scene before me, all such dearly beloved people, but suddenly they began to fade from sight. Instantly, I felt bereft.

"Oh, please don't go!" I called.

The Forgotten Promise

Nat looked questioningly in my direction but didn't see me and the next minute the figures had vanished into thin air. The courtyard was quiet and empty.

Thinking of sand running through my fingers I walked sadly back to the car, deep in thought. With difficulty, I forced my mind back to the present and carried the gate to the front entrance, propping it against the hedge.

Storm called a greeting to me as he scampered across the village green having been on some secret mission. Together we walked up the path towards the cottage and from the depths of my bag I could hear my mobile alerting me to a missed message. Once inside, I checked to see who had texted me. It was Mo.

Hi sis, Great news—Kurt has cleaned headstone pic. Check email. Wot does it mean? Mo xx

As the laptop powered up, I made a cup of tea and then settled down in front of the screen. I had about twenty new emails but ignorned those and double-clicked on Mo's email.

Hi Maddie

Kurt says he loves a challenge, but this particular one has been quite spectacular! He says this is the best he can do. Does it make any sense to you? Let me know where it fits in with the story.
Love, Mo xx

P.S. Jeff has a friend with a holiday villa in Majorca and we are thinking of having two weeks there. Do you want to come? He can't wait to meet you!

Hmm . . . Maybe I needed a holiday. I would seriously consider that.

I clicked on the attachment and watched as the jpg opened. It was huge so I had to resize it and, as I did so, I froze. Mo's friend had managed to decipher the eroded lettering on the headstone in St Martin's churchyard. It simply read:

> *Here Lyeth*
> *My Love, My Lyfe,*
> *Mary*
> *born twelfth April 1619*
> *and beloved daughter*
> *Elisabeth*
> *born thyrd July 1636*
> *both cruelly tayken*
> *eyghth day April 1644*

I sat there staring at the screen as if stupefied. I re-read the epitaph half-a-dozen times. What had happened in 1644 on the 8th April to have taken both Mary and Elisabeth? With sickening dread, I realised that buried deep within my subconscious lay the answer. The question was really hypothetical; if I could only tap into my memories I would realise that I already knew.

I found Mrs McKendrick's book on the Civil War and frantically thumbed through the pages. I had previously read a section referring to skirmishes that had taken place in the area but their significance hadn't registered at the time. I read a couple of paragraphs but couldn't find what I was looking for. I checked the index to see if there was any direct reference. Was this what I had been searching for?

Abbotsbury—The Battle in the Pulpit: page 160.

I quickly flicked through to the page and devoured the following words.

During the Civil War years, the superb Dorset village of Abbotsbury was owned by Sir John Strangways, an ardent Royalist. The village was the site of one of the bloodiest 'misfortunes' of the conflict. In what became known as 'The Battle in the Pulpit', Cavaliers sniped at the Roundheads from the church tower of St. Nicholas in October 1644. The pulpit still bears the scars from shots fired by Cromwell's men. After a stubborn resistance in the church and manor house the garrison surrendered, but when the victorious Roundheads entered the house the magazine blew up, completely destroying the house and killing the plunderers.

No, that was in the October. But, instinctively, I knew it had something to do with what I was searching for. I fanned back through the book and found a previous chapter that looked more promising.

The neighbourhoods running along the coast of Dorset between Weymouth and Lyme Regis were much affected during the Civil War. In 1644, Sir Edward Walgrave was quartered with his regiment of horse at Bridport when he was surprised by Parliamentarian troops. However, he engaged them near Shipton Gorge, slew some and took forty horses and a cornet. This fighting may have accounted for the two lead musket balls recently extracted from the west door of St Martin's Church in the village.

An interesting epitaph on the south wall of the church suggests that the Roundheads may have pillaged the home of Sir Richard Okeford of Hammiton Hall, close by.

I stared at the last sentence in horror; I had skimmed over it when first reading the book and had not realised the enormity of it. There it was, as plain as plain could be—Sir Richard Okeford of Hammiton Hall. I continued

Kate Ryder

to read, every nerve in my body on high alert, dreading what I would learn.

In 1644, there was a fine manor house in the neighbourhood of Shipton Gorge owned by the staunchly Royalist Okeford family. During the first week of April 1644, a large Parliamentary force under Sir Anthony Ashley Cooper marched from Dorchester with the intention to rid Abbotsbury of its Royalist garrison which was then commanded by Colonel James Strangways. It would appear that on the way the Parliamentarian troops mounted regular raids and on the 8th April lay siege to the Okeford family home. Unfortunately for the Okefords, Sir Richard was away at the time overseeing the visit of King Charles I at Maiden Newton, and when his wife, Lady Catherine, refused to co-operate with the Parliamentarian troops, the house was ransacked.

The siege of the house itself began with Sir Cooper's men setting fire to the entrance porch whilst keeping up a constant fusillade of musket fire that forced the family and their servants to retreat upstairs. Inside, Lady Catherine bravely refused all offers of surrender and so the order was given that no prisoners were to be taken alive. With the lower half of the house now well alight, screams were soon heard as the flames climbed higher. A second Parliamentary force used grenades, fireballs and scaling ladders to reach the second floor windows at the rear and, wrenching open windows, threw in bundles of faggots, setting the entire house ablaze.

Lady Catherine's daughter and grand-daughter were fatally wounded by musket fire while attempting a daring escape and several of the servants perished before Lady Catherine begged for mercy for herself and those remaining. They were spared. As was common practice then, the victorious Parliamentarian soldiers rushed into the burning house to ransack it before it was fully destroyed. Today, nothing remains of the Hall.

I put the book down and covered my face with my hands and sobbed. Not only had Nat lost his son to smallpox in 1643 but also his wife and daughter during the course of one day the following year. No wonder his spirit was restless. He had made a promise to Mary that should they ever find themselves parted he would come for her and, true to his word, that was what he was doing to this very day.

After a while, as the intense emotions abated, I looked up to see Storm watching me curiously from the kitchen doorway.

"It's OK boy," I said softly. "It's all over."

He walked over to me and jumped onto my lap and I hugged him close.

That night I had nightmares. I was trapped and surrounded by fire. Elisabeth, brave girl though she was, whimpered quietly at my side, her eyes filled with terror. We were in the front room on the upper floor above the porch. Flames crackled around us and the sound of musket shot rang loudly in our ears. The noise was deafening. My mother was a fierce warrior, determined not to let the soldiers take our family home, but the servants quaked in fear and kept well back in the room, all except Duncan who stood loyally by my mother's side. I held Elisabeth close and told her it would be all right. How could I have lied so? She held tightly onto my skirt and I tried not to show the fear I felt in my heart.

Suddenly, above the sound of the fire, we heard windows being wrenched open followed by thuds which we did not fully understand until it was too late. The bundles of flaming faggots took hold and the evil fire licked its way up the curtains, setting light to anything flammable in its path. The roar of that fire is a sound I will never forget. Some of the servants started to scream and, if I could have found my voice, I would have joined them. Two maid servants ran forward from the fire which had spread quickly at the rear of the room and shots rang out; the women fell dead at our feet. Elisabeth screamed and I quickly turned her away from the horror unfolding before our eyes.

"Mary," my mother shouted at me. "You and Elisabeth go to the next room."

"It's alight, mistress," screamed Duncan.

"It will be safer than here above the porch," she said, and I heard the hysteria creeping into her voice. "Oh Richard, where art thou?"

Elisabeth stood rooted to the spot, but I managed to coax her into the next room. The glass in the windows cracked and shattered under the fierce heat and there was an acrid stench in the air; a stench of death. I huddled in the corner with Elisabeth and heard my mother bravely shouting down to the commanding officer that she would never surrender her home and that they would have to burn us all within it. I needed to escape, for the sake of my last remaining child and husband. Speaking urgently to Elisabeth, I told her that we would make our way down the stairs and slip out at the back of the house. She seemed paralysed with fear, but I grabbed her hand and she came with me as I hurried towards the doorway. The flames cruelly licked their way up the stairwell, the wood charred and glowing, but the far side of the stairs appeared relatively clear of fire. Carefully we made our way down the burning staircase.

The Forgotten Promise

Suddenly, an unearthly scream rent the air and I heard my mother calling, "Duncan, oh Duncan!"

I didn't turn around but carried on down the stairs, holding tightly onto my daughter's hand. It was dark, the air thick with smoke, and it was hot, oh so hot. Choking, I told Elisabeth to cover her nose and mouth with the hem of her skirt.

We managed to avoid the falling timbers and made our way along the burning hallway into the servants' quarters. I turned right through the kitchens and came to a side door, burnt through. This was our escape. Sobbing with relief, we spilled out into the stable yard and breathed in great lungfuls of fresh air, the night sky lit by the orange flame of fire all around. We had made it! But, as I felt the cobblestones beneath my feet, I heard two clear musket shots ring out and watched in disbelief as Elisabeth fell away from me with an astonished look on her face; her mouth open as if to say something. She hit the ground, her eyes open wide, unseeing, and a dark globule of blood spilled out of the corner of her mouth.

I staggered and clutched my chest. Through my fingers I felt the warm ooze of blood and I watched as my bodice turned red. I fell to the floor, a searing pain spreading through my body.

Clutching at my heart pendant, I whispered, "I'm sorry Nat. I tried."

A while later I heard men's voices.

"This one's still alive."

Opening my eyes, I saw the kindly faced soldier who had seen us at The Olde Smithy peering over me. Recognition registered in his eyes.

"Lie still," he said gruffly. "Don't move."

I fought for air, my throat filling with blood. With difficulty I held out the pendant towards him.

Drawing deeply on my last breath, I whispered, "Please . . ."

He knelt by my side and removed his helmet.

"What's that you say?"

The pain was unbearable; I could hardly breathe, let alone speak.

"Take this and my ring . . ." I managed to say.

He bent his ear close to my mouth.

With one final attempt, I croaked, "Farrier . . . Waldyke."

My vision blurred but not before I saw the soldier nod in understanding as the black tunnel closed in around me.

I awoke, hyperventilating. The room was pitch black and for a moment I thought I was still in the house of fire. I clutched at my chest. The pain was so intense that I thought I must have died. Sitting up, I fought for breath. I was confused, bewildered and alone. I didn't know what I was doing. I cried for Nat, I cried for Mary and Elisabeth, and I cried for that poor dear boy, Francis, who had never really had the chance to know life. I was distraught and the pain in my chest would not go away.

Reaching for my mobile phone, I punched in the number. After seven rings a sleepy voice answered and I glanced at the clock on the bedside table—3.15am. I tried to speak but could only manage a deep, racking, drawing of breath.

And then his voice, suddenly fully alert. "Maddie, is that you?"

Again I tried to speak, but still no sound.

"Maddie, breathe slowly."

I did as he suggested and, once I was able to catch my breath, started to cry.

"Nick," I sobbed. "I need you."

I heard a sharp intake of breath on the other end of the phone. "I'm coming over now," he answered urgently.

I breathed out with relief, the pain finally easing in my chest.

"Thank you, but not here. The churchyard at St Martin's. There's something I need to do."

8th *April*

The night sky had given way to a sullen greyness and a dense sea mist hung low over the valley. The earth was shrouded in a thick blanket; the silence impenetrable. There was no-one around at this ungodly hour, not even the birds, but as I drove into the church car park I saw Nick's silver Nissan. So he had come.

I parked and slowly got out of the car, still shaken by the night's revelations. I walked through the lych gate, up the path towards the church and looked around for him. As I rounded the corner of the West Tower, through the fog I could make out a figure standing at the far side of the graveyard, carefully placing flowers at the foot of Mary and Elisabeth's headstone. It was Nat, his head bowed in sorrow.

I watched for a few moments and then called out softly, "Nat."

He raised his head.

"Nat, I have come."

Slowly he turned towards me.

He was older, much older, and I wondered if he was approaching the end of his life; a life that had been long and hard. His hair was grey and his face deeply lined and etched in sadness. He looked at me in confusion and then disbelief. I smiled and slowly the despair begin to lift from his eyes and tentative hope take its place.

"Be at peace," I said and watched as his face filled with joy.

He took a step towards me.

"Mary's spirit lives on through me."

He hesitated, consternation settling on that dear familiar face, and I saw the bewilderment as he observed my modern day clothes.

"Do not fear, Nat," I gently called again.

His lovely, soft blue-grey eyes urgently sought mine for confirmation and suddenly I was filled with the purest of emotions. He smiled slowly, our love reaching out across the distance and years between us, and I fought back tears as that dearly beloved man faded from sight for the very last time. In a blink of an eye he was gone.

Nick stood by the gravestone looking at me through the same soft blue-grey eyes. The love I felt for this man was immense and yet I faltered, unsure of where I stood. He watched me hesitate and took a step towards me, opening his arms wide.

"Come to me, Maddie. I won't lose you again."

The tender look in his eyes told me everything I needed to know and, as if in a dream, I walked towards his loving embrace.

"It was always you," he murmured, as he took me in his arms.

We kissed with a passion we both knew we had experienced before and, once again, I became aware of a sense of well-being and a delicious peace settling upon my soul. Eventually, and reluctantly, I drew back for breath.

Away to the east, a pink glow warmed the horizon and burnished gold and silver rays from a rising sun streaked the sky. Filtering up from the valley below came the exuberant chords of an early dawn chorus and all at once there was an easing in the dense, sea mist that shrouded the earth. The fog rolled away from the high ground and slowly revealed the church. Suddenly the subtlest of warm air currents encircled our bodies, as if investigating us. I knew Nick felt it too. It seductively caressed—a lingering, tender kiss of a breeze—and I had the strongest feeling that we were being protected and cushioned from the world; somehow blessed. Then, as quickly as it had arrived, it departed, though the feeling remained.

As I allowed myself dare believe in this unexpected, yet longed for, turn of events, I looked deep into Nick's eyes and recognised fragments of Nat's older soul watching me in wonder.

Holding me close and in a voice thick with emotion, he whispered, "My love, my life . . ."

At last I had truly found my way home.

About the Author

Kate Ryder is a freelance writer who has had several articles and short stories published. *The Forgotten Promise* is her first novel, and a second novel is nearing completion.

She also runs a web-based business specialising in complementary health products and natural remedies for horses, people and other animals. www.equihealth.co.uk

Kate lives in Cornwall with her husband and a collection of animals.

www.kateryder.me

Lightning Source UK Ltd.
Milton Keynes UK
UKOW05f0823120114

224384UK00001B/22/P

9 781491 884577